Praise for *Still Alice*:

'I finished *Still Alice* on my [illegible] to my grandmother's house in South Woodford. I found it to be [illegible] involving, and as the characters gained more flesh I foun[illegible] hard to put down. It made me so aware of h[illegible] always see those catastrophes that [illegible] at the morning with my gran[illegible] hood, fragments of poems sh[illegible] of *Still Alice;* it just suddenly se[illegible] be done' David, Essex

'Quite unexpectedly the best read – very poignant [illegible] amusing. Wow' Pippa, Gloucestershire

'An incredibly moving and humbling book. There were times when I had to turn away from the page to count my own blessings. Lisa Genova's cool, unsentimental style makes Alice's descent into oblivion all the more heartbreaking' Louise, London

'There are few page-turners in this field of literature but this is one of them' *Alzheimer's Society*

'This remarkable first novel about a 50-year-old woman's descent into early onset Alzheimer's is frightening to read, especially for those who have experienced the odd "senior moment" . . . With 700,000 people suffering from dementia in the UK, this illuminating view inside the mind of an Alzheimer's patient is highly relevant today' *Daily Mail*

'Reads like a gripping memoir of a woman in her prime watching the life she once knew fade away . . . A poignant portrait of Alzheimer's, *Still Alice* is not a book you'll forget' *USA Today*

'Genova reveals a story of extraordinary bravery, endurance and love. *Still Alice* is a tremendous affirmation of the powers of fiction' Stefan Merrill Block, author of *The Story of Forgetting*

'After I read *Still Alice*, I wanted to stand up and tell a train full of strangers, "You have to get this book"' Beverly Beckham, *Boston Globe*

'This is the clearest and most truthful piece of fiction I have read depicting living with Alzheimer's. You accurately describe the feelings and actions of both persons, together, entangled in this dance with Alzheimer's Disease. Thank you for writing this story' Chuck Jackson, diagnosed with Alzheimer's age 50

'A wonderful, moving journey with relationships that inspire, sadden, charm, convince and terrify' Rachel, Edinburgh

'The most accurate account of what it feels like to be inside the mind of an Alzheimer's patient I've ever read. Beautifully written and very illuminating' Rosie Boycott

'Utterly brilliant' Chrissy Iley

'A poignant account' *Bella*

'I totally loved this book, I read it on holiday and it totally consumed me for about three days – I insisted on telling everyone about it. It's currently doing the rounds with all my friends as well. Sad and informative yet so well-written and moving' Ailsa, Kent

'Immensely readable and thought-provoking' Liz, London

'Unlike most people with Alzheimer's, Alice knows exactly what's happening to her and believes she can still make her own decisions about her life. Whether this knowledge is a curse or a blessing is for the reader to decide as Alice's condition unfolds. The most moving book ever written about this devastating condition, *Still Alice* tops this summer's must-read list' Meg, Chepstow

'Heartbreakingly real . . . so real, in fact, that it kept me from sleeping for several nights. I couldn't put it down . . . *Still Alice* is a story that must be told' Brunonia Barry, *New York Times* bestselling author of *The Lace Reader*

Still Alice

A NOVEL

lisa genova

POCKET
BOOKS

LONDON • SYDNEY • NEW YORK • TORONTO

First published in Great Britain by Simon & Schuster UK Ltd, 2009
First published by Pocket Books, 2010
An imprint of Simon & Schuster UK Ltd
A CBS COMPANY

1 3 5 7 9 10 8 6 4 2

Information from the Activities of Daily Living Questionnaire
was taken with permission from "The Record of Independent Living"
by Sandra Weintraub, Ph.D., in the *American Journal of Alzheimer's Disease
and Other Dementia*, Vol.1, No. 2, 35–39 (1986), a SAGE publication.

Designed by Mary Austin Speaker

Simon & Schuster UK Ltd
1st Floor
222 Gray's Inn Road
London WC1X 8HB

www.simonandschuster.co.uk

Simon & Schuster Australia
Sydney

A CIP catalogue record for this book is available
from the British Library

ISBN: 978-1-47110-050-5
Australian edition ISBN: 978-1-92147-027-1

Printed by CPI Group (UK) Ltd, Croydon, CR0 4YY

In Memory of Angie

For Alena

Acknowledgments

I'm deeply grateful to the many people I've come to know through the Dementia Advocacy and Support Network International and DementiaUSA, especially Peter Ashley, Alan Benson, Christine Bryden, Bill Carey, Lynne Culipher, Morris Friedell, Shirley Garnett, Candy Harrison, Chuck Jackson, Lynn Jackson, Sylvia Johnston, Jenny Knauss, Jaye Lander, Jeanne Lee, Mary Lockhart, Mary McKinlay, Tracey Mobley, Don Moyer, Carole Mulliken, Jean Opalka, Charley Schneider, James Smith, Jay Smith, Ben Stevens, Richard Taylor, Diane Thornton, and John Willis. Your intelligence, courage, humor, empathy, and willingness to share what was individually vulnerable, scary, hopeful, and informative have taught me so much. My portrayal of Alice is richer and more human because of your stories.

I'd especially like to thank James and Jay, who have given me so much beyond the boundaries of Alzheimer's and this book. I am truly blessed to know you.

I'd also like to thank the following medical professionals, who generously shared their time, knowledge, and imaginations, helping me to gain a true and specific sense for how events might unfold as Alice's dementia is discovered and progresses:

Dr. Rudy Tanzi and Dr. Dennis Selkoe for an in-depth understanding of the molecular biology of this disease

Dr. Alireza Atri for allowing me to shadow him for two days in the Memory Disorders Unit at Massachusetts General Hospital, for showing me your brilliance and compassion

Dr. Doug Cole and Dr. Martin Samuels for additional understanding of the diagnosis and treatment of Alzheimer's

Sara Smith for allowing me to sit in on neuropsychological testing

Barbara Hawley Maxam for explaining the role of the social worker and Mass General's Caregivers' Support Group

Erin Linnenbringer for being Alice's genetic counselor

Dr. Joe Maloney and Dr. Jessica Wieselquist for role-playing as Alice's general practice physician

Thank you to Dr. Steven Pinker for giving me a look inside life as a Harvard psychology professor and to Dr. Ned Sahin and Dr. Elizabeth Chua for similar views from the student's seat.

Thank you to Dr. Steve Hyman, Dr. John Kelsey, and Dr. Todd Kahan for answering questions about Harvard and life as a professor.

Thank you to Doug Coupe for sharing some specifics about acting and Los Angeles.

Thank you to Martha Brown, Anne Carey, Laurel Daly,

Kim Howland, Mary MacGregor, and Chris O'Connor for reading each chapter, for your comments, encouragement, and wild enthusiasm.

Thank you to Diane Bartoli, Lyralen Kaye, Rose O'Donnell, and Richard Pepp for editorial feedback.

Thank you to Jocelyn Kelley at Kelley & Hall for being a phenomenal publicist.

An enormous thank-you to Beverly Beckham, who wrote the best review any self-published author could dream of. And you pointed the way to Julia Fox Garrison.

Julia, I cannot thank you enough. Your generosity has changed my life.

Thank you to Vicky Bijur for representing me and for insisting that I change the ending. You're brilliant.

Thank you to Louise Burke, John Hardy, Kathy Sagan, and Anthony Ziccardi for believing in this story.

I need to thank the very large and loud Genova family for shamelessly telling everyone you know to buy your daughter's/niece's/cousin's/sister's book. You're the best guerrilla marketers in the world!

I also need to thank the not as large but arguably just as loud Seufert family for spreading the word.

Last, I'd like to thank Christopher Seufert for technical and web support, for the original cover design, for helping me make the abstract tangible, and so much more, but mostly, for giving me butterflies.

Even then, more than a year earlier, there were neurons in her head, not far from her ears, that were being strangled to death, too quietly for her to hear them. Some would argue that things were going so insidiously wrong that the neurons themselves initiated events that would lead to their own destruction. Whether it was molecular murder or cellular suicide, they were unable to warn her of what was happening before they died.

SEPTEMBER 2003

Alice sat at her desk in their bedroom distracted by the sounds of John racing through each of the rooms on the first floor. She needed to finish her peer review of a paper submitted to the *Journal of Cognitive Psychology* before her flight, and she'd just read the same sentence three times without comprehending it. It was 7:30 according to their alarm clock, which she guessed was about ten minutes fast. She knew from the approximate time and the escalating volume of his racing that he was trying to leave, but he'd forgotten something and couldn't find it. She tapped her red pen on her bottom lip as she watched the digital numbers on the clock and listened for what she knew was coming.

"Ali?"

She tossed her pen onto the desk and sighed. Downstairs, she found him in the living room on his knees, feeling under the couch cushions.

"Keys?" she asked.

"Glasses. Please don't lecture me, I'm late."

She followed his frantic glance to the fireplace mantel, where the antique Waltham clock, valued for its precision, declared 8:00. He should have known better than to trust it. The clocks in their home rarely knew the real time of day. Alice had been duped too often in the past by their seemingly honest faces and had learned long ago to rely on her watch. Sure enough, she lapsed back in time as she entered the kitchen, where the microwave insisted that it was only 6:52.

She looked across the smooth, uncluttered surface of the granite countertop, and there they were, next to the mushroom bowl heaping with unopened mail. Not under something, not behind something, not obstructed in any way from plain view. How could he, someone so smart, a scientist, not see what was right in front of him?

Of course, many of her own things had taken to hiding in mischievous little places as well. But she didn't admit this to him, and she didn't involve him in the hunt. Just the other day, John blissfully unaware, she'd spent a crazed morning looking first all over the house and then in her office for her BlackBerry charger. Stumped, she'd surrendered, gone to the store, and bought a new one, only to discover the old one later that night plugged in the socket next to her side of the bed, where she should have known to look. She could probably chalk it all up for both of them to excessive multitasking and being way too busy. And to getting older.

He stood in the doorway, looking at the glasses in her hand but not at her.

"Next time, try pretending you're a woman while you look," said Alice, smiling.

"I'll wear one of your skirts. Ali, please, I'm really late."

"The microwave says you have tons of time," she said, handing them to him.

"Thanks."

He grabbed them like a relay runner taking a baton in a race and headed for the front door.

"Will you be here when I get home on Saturday?" she asked his back as she followed him down the hallway.

"I don't know, I've got a huge day in lab on Saturday."

He collected his briefcase, phone, and keys from the hall table.

"Have a good trip, give Lydia a hug and kiss for me. And try not to battle with her," said John.

She caught their reflection in the hallway mirror—a distinguished-looking, tall man with white-flecked brown hair and glasses; a petite, curly-haired woman, her arms crossed over her chest, each readying to leap into that same, bottomless argument. She gritted her teeth and swallowed, choosing not to jump.

"We haven't seen each other in a while. Please try to be home?" she asked.

"I know, I'll try."

He kissed her, and although desperate to leave, he lingered in that kiss for an almost imperceptible moment. If she didn't know him better, she might've romanticized his kiss. She might've stood there, hopeful, thinking it said, *I love you, I'll miss you.* But as she watched him hustle down the street alone, she felt pretty certain he'd just told her, *I love you, but please don't be pissed when I'm not home on Saturday.*

They used to walk together over to Harvard Yard every

morning. Of the many things she loved about working within a mile from home and at the same school, their shared commute was the thing she loved most. They always stopped at Jerri's—a black coffee for him, a tea with lemon for her, iced or hot, depending on the season—and continued on to Harvard Yard, chatting about their research and classes, issues in their respective departments, their children, or plans for that evening. When they were first married, they even held hands. She savored the relaxed intimacy of these morning walks with him, before the daily demands of their jobs and ambitions rendered them each stressed and exhausted.

But for some time now, they'd been walking over to Harvard separately. Alice had been living out of her suitcase all summer, attending psychology conferences in Rome, New Orleans, and Miami, and serving on an exam committee for a thesis defense at Princeton. Back in the spring, John's cell cultures had needed some sort of rinsing attention at an obscene hour each morning, but he didn't trust any of his students to show up consistently. So he did. She couldn't remember the reasons that predated spring, but she knew that each time they'd seemed reasonable and only temporary.

She returned to the paper at her desk, still distracted, now by a craving for that fight she hadn't had with John about their younger daughter, Lydia. Would it kill him to stand behind her for once? She gave the rest of the paper a cursory effort, not her typical standard of excellence, but it would have to do, given her fragmented state of mind and lack of time. Her comments and suggestions for revision finished, she packaged and sealed the envelope, guiltily aware that she might've missed an error in the study's design or interpretation, cursing John for compromising the integrity of her work.

She repacked her suitcase, not even emptied yet from her

last trip. She looked forward to traveling less in the coming months. There were only a handful of invited lectures penciled in her fall semester calendar, and she'd scheduled most of those on Fridays, a day she didn't teach. Like tomorrow. Tomorrow she would be the guest speaker to kick off Stanford's cognitive psychology fall colloquium series. And afterward, she'd see Lydia. She'd try not to battle with her, but she wasn't making any promises.

Alice found her way easily to Stanford's Cordura Hall on the corner of Campus Drive West and Panama Drive. Its white stucco exterior, terra-cotta roof, and lush landscaping looked to her East Coast eyes more like a Caribbean beach resort than an academic building. She arrived quite early but ventured inside anyway, figuring she could use the extra time to sit in the quiet auditorium and look over her talk.

Much to her surprise, she walked into an already packed room. A zealous crowd surrounded and circled a buffet table, aggressively diving in for food like seagulls at a city beach. Before she could sneak in unnoticed, she noticed Josh, a former Harvard classmate and respected egomaniac, standing in her path, his legs planted firmly and a little too wide, as if he was ready to dive at her.

"All this, for me?" asked Alice, smiling playfully.

"What, we eat like this every day. It's for one of our developmental psychologists, he was tenured yesterday. So how's Harvard treating you?"

"Good."

"I can't believe you're still there after all these years. You ever get too bored over there, you should consider coming here."

"I'll let you know. How are things with you?"

"Fantastic. You should come by my office after the talk, see our latest modeling data. It'll really knock your socks off."

"Sorry, I can't, I have to catch a flight to L.A. right after this," she said, grateful to have a ready excuse.

"Oh, too bad. Last time I saw you I think was last year at the psychonomic conference. I unfortunately missed your presentation."

"Well, you'll get to hear a good portion of it today."

"Recycling your talks these days, huh?"

Before she could answer, Gordon Miller, head of the department and her new superhero, swooped in and saved her by asking Josh to help pass out the champagne. As at Harvard, a champagne toast was a tradition in the psychology department at Stanford for all faculty who reached the coveted career milestone of tenure. There weren't many trumpets that heralded the advancement from point to point in the career of a professor, but tenure was a big one, loud and clear.

When everyone was holding a cup, Gordon stood at the podium and tapped the microphone. "Can I have everyone's attention for a moment?"

Josh's excessively loud, punctuated laugh reverberated alone through the auditorium just before Gordon continued.

"Today, we congratulate Mark on receiving tenure. I'm sure he's thrilled to have this particular accomplishment behind him. Here's to the many exciting accomplishments still ahead. To Mark!"

"To Mark!"

Alice tapped her cup with her neighbors', and everyone quickly resumed the business of drinking, eating, and discussing. When all of the food had been claimed from the serving trays and the last drops of champagne emptied from the last bottle, Gordon took the floor once again.

"If everyone would take a seat, we can begin today's talk."

He waited a few moments for the crowd of about seventy-five to settle and quiet down.

"Today, I have the honor of introducing you to our first colloquium speaker of the year. Dr. Alice Howland is the eminent William James Professor of Psychology at Harvard University. Over the last twenty-five years, her distinguished career has produced many of the flagship touchstones in psycholinguistics. She pioneered and continues to lead an interdisciplinary and integrated approach to the study of the mechanisms of language. We are privileged to have her here today to talk to us about the conceptual and neural organization of language."

Alice switched places with Gordon and looked out at her audience looking at her. As she waited for the applause to subside, she thought of the statistic that said people feared public speaking more than they feared death. She loved it. She enjoyed all of the concatenated moments of presenting in front of a listening audience—teaching, performing, telling a story, teeing up a heated debate. She also loved the adrenaline rush. The bigger the stakes, the more sophisticated or hostile the audience, the more the whole experience thrilled her. John was an excellent teacher, but public speaking often pained and terrified him, and he marveled at Alice's verve for it. He probably didn't prefer death, but spiders and snakes, sure.

"Thank you, Gordon. Today, I'm going to talk about some of the mental processes that underlie the acquisition, organization, and use of language."

Alice had given the guts of this particular talk innumerable times, but she wouldn't call it recycling. The crux of the talk did focus on the main tenets of linguistics, many of which she'd discovered, and she'd been using a number of the same slides for years. But she felt proud, and not ashamed or lazy, that this part of her talk, these discoveries of hers, continued to hold true, withstanding the test of time. Her contributions mattered and propelled future discovery. Plus, she certainly included those future discoveries.

She talked without needing to look down at her notes, relaxed and animated, the words effortless. Then, about forty minutes into the fifty-minute presentation, she became suddenly stuck.

"The data reveal that irregular verbs require access to the mental . . ."

She simply couldn't find the word. She had a loose sense for what she wanted to say, but the word itself eluded her. Gone. She didn't know the first letter or what the word sounded like or how many syllables it had. It wasn't on the tip of her tongue.

Maybe it was the champagne. She normally didn't drink any alcohol before speaking. Even if she knew the talk cold, even in the most casual setting, she always wanted to be as mentally sharp as possible, especially for the question-and-answer session at the end, which could be confrontational and full of rich, unscripted debate. But she hadn't wanted to offend anyone, and she'd drunk a little more than she probably should have when she became trapped again in passive-aggressive conversation with Josh.

Maybe it was jet lag. As her mind scoured its corners for the word and a rational reason for why she'd lost it, her heart pounded and her face grew hot. She'd never lost a word in front of an audience before. But she'd never panicked in front of an audience either, and she'd stood before many far larger and more intimidating than this. She told herself to breathe, forget about it, and move on.

She replaced the still blocked word with a vague and inappropriate "thing," abandoned whatever point she'd been in the middle of making, and continued on to the next slide. The pause had seemed like an obvious and awkward eternity to her, but as she checked the faces in the audience to see if anyone had noticed her mental hiccup, no one appeared alarmed, embarrassed, or ruffled in any way. Then, she saw Josh whispering to the woman next to him, his eyebrows furrowed and a slight smile on his face.

She was on the plane, descending into LAX, when it finally came to her.

Lexicon.

LYDIA HAD BEEN LIVING IN Los Angeles for three years now. If she'd gone to college right after high school, she would've graduated this past spring. Alice would've been so proud. Lydia was probably smarter than both of her older siblings, and they had gone to college. And law school. And medical school.

Instead of college, Lydia first went to Europe. Alice had hoped she'd come home with a clearer sense of what she wanted to study and what kind of school she wanted to go to. Instead, upon her return, she'd told her parents that she'd done a little acting while in Dublin and had fallen in love. She was moving to Los Angeles immediately.

Alice nearly lost her mind. Much to her maddening frustration, she recognized her own contribution to this problem. Because Lydia was the youngest of three, the daughter of parents who worked a lot and traveled regularly, and had always been a good student, Alice and John had ignored her to a large extent. They'd granted her a lot of room to run in her world, free to think for herself and free from the kind of micromanagement placed on a lot of children her age. Her parents' professional lives served as shining examples of what could be gained from setting lofty and individually unique goals and pursuing them with passion and hard work. Lydia understood her mother's advice about the importance of getting a college education, but she had the confidence and audacity to reject it.

Plus, she didn't stand entirely alone. The most explosive fight Alice had ever had with John had followed his two cents on the subject: *I think it's wonderful, she can always go to college later, if she decides she even wants to.*

Alice checked her BlackBerry for the address, rang the doorbell to apartment number seven, and waited. She was just about to press it again when Lydia opened the door.

"Mom, you're early," said Lydia.

Alice checked her watch.

"I'm right on time."

"You said your flight was coming in at eight."

"I said five."

"I have eight o'clock written down in my book."

"Lydia, it's five forty-five, I'm here."

Lydia looked indecisive and panicky, like a squirrel caught facing an oncoming car in the road.

"Sorry, come in."

They each hesitated before they hugged, as if they were about to practice a newly learned dance and weren't quite confident of the first step or who should lead. Or it was an old dance, but they hadn't performed it together in so long that each felt unsure of the choreography.

Alice could feel the contours of Lydia's spine and ribs through her shirt. She looked too skinny, a good ten pounds lighter than Alice remembered. She hoped it was more a result of being busy than of conscious dieting. Blond and five foot six, three inches taller than Alice, Lydia stood out among the predominance of short Italian and Asian women in Cambridge, but in Los Angeles, the waiting rooms at every audition were apparently full of women who looked just like her.

"I made reservations for nine. Wait here, I'll be right back."

Craning her neck, Alice inspected the kitchen and living room from the hallway. The furnishings, most likely yard sale finds and parent hand-me-downs, looked rather hip together—an orange sectional couch, retro-inspired coffee table, Brady Bunch–style kitchen table and chairs. The white walls were bare except for a poster of Marlon Brando taped above the couch. The air smelled strongly of Windex, as if Lydia had taken last-second measures to clean the place before Alice's arrival.

In fact, it was a little too clean. No DVDs or CDs lying around, no books or magazines thrown on the coffee table, no pictures on the refrigerator, no hint of Lydia's interests or aesthetic anywhere. Anyone could be living here. Then, Alice noticed the pile of men's shoes on the floor to the left of the door behind her.

"Tell me about your roommates," she said as Lydia returned from her room, cell phone in hand.

"They're at work."

"What kind of work?"

"One's bartending and the other delivers food."

"I thought they were both actors."

"They are."

"I see. What are their names again?"

"Doug and Malcolm."

It flashed only for a moment, but Alice saw it and Lydia saw her see it. Lydia's face flushed when she said Malcolm's name, and her eyes darted nervously away from her mother's.

"Why don't we get going? They said they can take us early," said Lydia.

"Okay, I just need to use the bathroom first."

As Alice washed her hands, she looked over the products sitting on the table next to the sink—Neutrogena facial cleanser and moisturizer, Tom's of Maine mint toothpaste, men's deodorant, a box of Playtex tampons. She thought for a moment. She hadn't had her period all summer. Did she have it in May? She'd be turning fifty next month, so she wasn't alarmed. She hadn't yet experienced any hot flashes or night sweats, but not all menopausal women did. That would be just fine with her.

As she dried her hands, she noticed the box of Trojan condoms behind Lydia's hairstyling products. She was going to have to find out more about these roommates. Malcolm, in particular.

They sat at a table outside on the patio at Ivy, a trendy restaurant in downtown Los Angeles, and ordered two drinks, an espresso martini for Lydia and a merlot for Alice.

"So how's Dad's *Science* paper coming?" asked Lydia.

She must've talked recently with her father. Alice hadn't heard from her since a phone call on Mother's Day.

"It's done. He's very proud of it."

"How's Anna and Tom?"

"Good, busy, working hard. So how did you meet Doug and Malcolm?"

"They came into Starbucks one night while I was working."

The waiter appeared, and each of them ordered dinner and another drink. Alice hoped the alcohol would dilute the tension between them, which felt heavy and thick and just beneath the tracing-paper-thin conversation.

"So how did you meet Doug and Malcolm?" she asked.

"I just told you. Why don't you ever listen to anything I say? They came into Starbucks one night talking about looking for a roommate while I was working."

"I thought you were waitressing at a restaurant."

"I am. I work at Starbucks during the week and waitress on Saturday nights."

"Doesn't sound like that leaves a lot of time for acting."

"I'm not cast in anything right now, but I'm taking workshop classes, and I'm auditioning a lot."

"What kind of classes?"

"Meisner technique."

"And what've you been auditioning for?"

"Television and print."

Alice swirled her wine, drank the last, big gulp, and licked her lips. "Lydia, what exactly is your plan here?"

"I'm not planning on stopping, if that's what you're asking."

The drinks were taking effect, but not in the direction Alice had hoped for. Instead, they served as the fuel that burned that little piece of tracing paper, leaving the tension between them fully exposed and at the helm of a dangerously familiar conversation.

"You can't live like this forever. Are you still going to work at Starbucks when you're thirty?"

"That's eight years away! Do you know what you'll be doing in eight years?"

"Yes, I do. At some point, you need to be responsible, you need to be able to afford things like health insurance, a mortgage, savings for retirement—"

"I have health insurance. And I might make it as an actor. There are people who do, you know. And they make a hell of a lot more money than you and Dad combined."

"This isn't just about money."

"Then what? That I didn't become you?"

"Lower your voice."

"Don't tell me what to do."

"I don't want you to become me, Lydia. I just don't want you to limit your choices."

"You want to make my choices."

"No."

"This is who I am, this is what I want to do."

"What, serving up Venti lattes? You should be in college. You should be spending this time in your life learning something."

"I *am* learning something! I'm just not sitting in a Harvard classroom killing myself trying to get an A in political science. I'm in a serious acting class for fifteen hours a week. How many hours of class a week do your students take, twelve?"

"It's not the same thing."

"Well, Dad thinks it is. He's paying for it."

Alice clenched the sides of her skirt and pressed her lips together. What she wanted to say next wasn't meant for Lydia.

"You've never even seen me act."

John had. He'd flown out alone last winter to see her perform in a play. Swamped with too many urgent things at the time, Alice couldn't free up to go. As she looked at Lydia's pained eyes, she couldn't remember now what those urgent things had been. She didn't have anything against an acting career itself, but she believed her daughter's singular pursuit of it, without an education, bordered on reckless. If she didn't go to college now, acquire a knowledge base or formal training in some field, if she didn't get a degree, what would she do if acting didn't pan out?

Alice thought about those condoms in the bathroom. What if Lydia got pregnant? Alice worried that Lydia might someday find herself trapped in a life that was unfulfilled, full of regret. She looked at her daughter and saw so much wasted potential, so much wasted time.

"You're not getting any younger, Lydia. Life goes by too fast."

"I agree."

The food came, but neither of them picked up a fork. Lydia dabbed her eyes with her hand-embroidered linen napkin. They always fell into the same battle, and it felt to Alice like trying to knock down a concrete wall with their heads. It was never going to be productive and only resulted in hurting them, causing lasting damage. She wished Lydia could see the love and wisdom in what she wanted for her. She wished she could just reach across the table and hug her daughter, but there were too many dishes, glasses, and years of distance between them.

A sudden flurry of activity a few tables away pulled their attention from themselves. Several camera flashes popped, and a small crowd of patrons and waitstaff gathered, all focused on a woman who looked a bit like Lydia.

"Who's that?" asked Alice.

"Mom," said Lydia in a tone both embarrassed and superior, perfected at the age of thirteen. "That's Jennifer Aniston."

They ate their dinner and talked only of safe things, like the food and the weather. Alice wanted to discover more about Lydia's relationship with Malcolm, but the embers of Lydia's emotions still glowed hot, and Alice feared igniting another fight. She paid the bill and they left the restaurant, full but dissatisfied.

"Excuse me, ma'am!"

Their waiter caught up to them on the sidewalk.

"You left this."

Alice paused, trying to comprehend how their waiter might come to possess her BlackBerry. She hadn't checked her email or calendar in the restaurant. She felt inside her bag. No BlackBerry. She must've removed it when she fished her wallet out to pay.

"Thank you."

Lydia looked at her quizzically, as if she wanted to say something about something other than food or weather, but then didn't. They walked back to her apartment in silence.

"JOHN?"

Alice waited, suspended in the front hallway, holding the handle of her suitcase. *Harvard Magazine* lay on the top of a pile of unclaimed mail strewn on the floor in front of her. The clock in the living room ticked and the refrigerator hummed. A warm, sunny late afternoon at her back, the air inside felt chilly, dim, and stale. Uninhabited.

She picked up the mail and walked into the kitchen, her

suitcase on wheels accompanying her like a loyal pet. Her flight had been delayed, and she was late getting in, even according to the microwave. He'd had a whole day, a whole Saturday, to work.

The red voice-mail light on their answering machine stared her down, unblinking. She checked the refrigerator. No note on the door. Nothing.

Still clutching the handle of her suitcase, she stood in the dark kitchen and watched several minutes advance on the microwave. The disappointed but forgiving voice in her head faded to a whisper as the volume of a more primal one began to build and spread out. She thought about calling him, but the expanding voice rejected the suggestion outright and refused all excuses. She thought about deciding not to care, but the voice, now seeping down into her body, echoing in her belly, vibrating in each of her fingertips, was too powerful and pervasive to ignore.

Why did it bother her so much? He was in the middle of an experiment and couldn't leave it to come home. She'd certainly been in his shoes innumerable times. This was what they did. This was who they were. The voice called her a stupid fool.

She spotted her running shoes on the floor next to the back door. A run would make her feel better. That was what she needed.

Ideally, she ran every day. For many years now, she'd treated running like eating or sleeping, as a vital daily necessity, and she'd been known to squeeze in a jog at midnight or in the middle of a blinding snowstorm. But she'd neglected this basic need over the last several months. She'd been so busy. As she laced her shoes, she told herself she hadn't bothered bringing them with her to California because she'd known she wouldn't have the time. In truth, she'd simply forgotten to pack them.

When starting from her house on Poplar Street, she invariably followed the same route—down Massachusetts Avenue, through Harvard Square to Memorial Drive, along the Charles River to the Harvard Bridge over by MIT, and back—a little over five miles, a forty-five-minute round trip. She had long been attracted to the idea of running in the Boston Marathon but each year decided that she realistically didn't have the time to train for that kind of distance. Maybe someday she would. In excellent physical condition for a woman her age, she imagined running strong well into her sixties.

Clustered pedestrian traffic on the sidewalks and intermittent negotiations with car traffic in street intersections littered the first part of her run through Harvard Square. It was crowded and ripe with anticipation at that time of day on a Saturday, with crowds forming and milling around on street corners waiting for walk signals, outside restaurants waiting for tables, in movie theater lines waiting for tickets, and in double-parked cars waiting for an unlikely opening in a metered space. The first ten minutes of her run required a good deal of conscious external concentration to navigate through it all, but once she crossed Memorial Drive to the Charles River, she was free to run in full stride and completely in the zone.

A comfortable and cloudless evening invited a lot of activity along the Charles, yet the grassy area beside the river felt less congested than the streets of Cambridge. Despite a steady stream of joggers, dogs and their owners, walkers, Rollerbladers, cyclists, and women pushing babies in jogger strollers, like an experienced driver on a regularly traveled stretch of road, Alice retained only a vague sense for what went on around her now. As she ran along the river, she became mindful of nothing but the sounds of her Nikes hitting the pavement in syncopated rhythm with the pace of her breath. She didn't replay her argument with Lydia. She didn't acknowledge her growling stomach. She didn't think about John. She just ran.

As was her routine, she stopped running once she made it back to the John Fitzgerald Kennedy Park, a pocket of manicured lawns abutting Memorial Drive. Her head cleared, her body relaxed and rejuvenated, she began walking home. The JFK Park funneled into Harvard Square through a pleasant, bench-lined corridor between the Charles Hotel and the Kennedy School of Government.

At the other end of the corridor, she stood at the intersection of Eliot Street and Brattle, ready to cross, when a woman grabbed her forearm with startling force and said, "Have you thought about heaven today?"

The woman fixed Alice with a penetrating, unwavering stare. She had long hair the color and texture of a teased Brillo pad and wore a handmade placard hung over her chest that read AMERICA REPENT, TURN TO JESUS FROM SIN. There was always someone selling God in Harvard Square, but Alice had never been singled out so directly and intimately before.

"Sorry," she said and, noticing a break in the flow of traffic, escaped to the other side of the street.

She wanted to continue walking but stood frozen instead. She didn't know where she was. She looked back across the street. The Brillo-haired woman pursued another sinner down the corridor. The corridor, the hotel, the stores, the illogically meandering streets. She knew she was in Harvard Square, but she didn't know which way was home.

She tried again, more specifically. The Harvard Square Hotel, Eastern Mountain Sports, Dickson Bros. Hardware, Mount Auburn Street. She knew all of these places—this square had been her stomping ground for over twenty-five years—but they somehow didn't fit into a mental map that told her where she lived relative to them. A black-and-white circular "T" sign directly in front of her marked an entrance to the Red Line trains and buses underground, but there were three such entrances in Harvard Square, and she couldn't piece together which one of the three this was.

Her heart began to race. She started sweating. She told herself that an accelerated heart rate and perspiration were part of an orchestrated and appropriate response to running. But as she stood on the sidewalk, it felt like panic.

She willed herself to walk another block and then another, her rubbery legs feeling like they might give way with each bewildered step. The Coop, Cardullo's, the magazines on the corner, the Cambridge visitors' center across the street, and Harvard Yard beyond that. She told herself she could still read and recognize. None of it helped. It all lacked a context.

People, cars, buses, and all kinds of unbearable noise rushed and wove around and past her. She closed her eyes. She listened to her own blood whoosh and pulse behind her ears.

"Please stop this," she whispered.

She opened her eyes. Just as suddenly as it had left her, the landscape snapped snugly back into place. The Coop, Cardullo's, Nini's Corner, Harvard Yard. She automatically understood that she should turn left at the corner and head west on Mass Ave. She began to breathe easier, no longer bizarrely lost within a mile of home. But she'd just been bizarrely lost within a mile of home. She walked as fast as she could without running.

She turned onto her street, a quiet, tree-lined, residential road a couple of blocks removed from Mass Ave. With both feet on her road and her house in sight, she felt much safer, but not yet safe. She kept her eyes on her front door and her legs moving and promised herself that the sea of anxiety swelling furiously inside her would drain when she walked in the front hallway and saw John. If he was home.

"John?"

He appeared in the threshold of the kitchen, unshaven, his glasses sitting on top of his mad-scientist hair, sucking on a red Popsicle and sporting his lucky gray T-shirt. He'd been up all night. As she'd promised herself, her anxiety began to drain. But her energy and bravery seemed to leak out with it, leaving her fragile and wanting to collapse into his arms.

"Hey, I was wondering where you were, just about to leave you a note on the fridge. How'd it go?" he asked.

"What?"

"Stanford."

"Oh, good."

"And how's Lydia?"

The betrayal and hurt over Lydia, over him not being home when she got there, exorcised by the run and displaced by her terror at being inexplicably lost, reclaimed its priority in the pecking order.

"You tell me," she said.

"You guys fought."

"You're paying for her acting classes?" she accused.

"Oh," he said, sucking the last of the Popsicle into his red-stained mouth. "Look, can we talk about this later? I don't have time to get into it right now."

"Make the time, John. You're keeping her afloat out there without telling me, and you're not here when I get home, and—"

"And you weren't here when I got home. How was your run?"

She heard the simple reasoning in his veiled question. If she had waited for him, if she had called, if she hadn't done exactly what she'd wanted and gone for a run, she could've spent the last hour with him. She had to agree.

"Fine."

"I'm sorry, I waited as long as I could, but I've really got to get back to the lab. I've had an incredible day so far, gorgeous results, but we're not done, and I've got to analyze the numbers before we get started again in the morning. I only came home to see you."

"I need to talk about this with you now."

"This really isn't new information, Ali. We disagree about Lydia. Can't it wait until I get back?"

"No."

"You want to walk over with me, talk about it on the way?"

"I'm not going to the office, I need to be home."

"You need to talk now, you need to be home, you're awfully needy all of a sudden. Is something else going on?"

The word *needy* smacked a vulnerable nerve. *Needy* equaled weak, dependent, pathological. Her father. She'd made a lifelong point of never being like that, like him.

"I'm just exhausted."

"You look it, you need to slow down."

"That's not what I need."

He waited for her to elaborate, but she took too long.

"Look, the sooner I go, the sooner I'll be back. Get some rest, I'll be home later tonight."

He kissed her sweat-drenched head and walked out the door.

Standing in the hallway where he'd left her, with no one to confess to or confide in, she felt the full emotional impact of what she'd just experienced in Harvard Square flood over her. She sat down on the floor and leaned against the cool wall, watching her hands shake in her lap as if they couldn't be hers. She tried to focus on steadying her breath as she did when she ran.

After minutes of breathing in and breathing out, she was finally calm enough to attempt to assemble some sense out of what had just happened. She thought about the missing word during her talk at Stanford and her missing period. She got up, turned on her laptop, and Googled "menopause symptoms."

An appalling list filled the screen—hot flashes, night sweats, insomnia, crashing fatigue, anxiety, dizziness, irregular heartbeat, depression, irritability, mood swings, disorientation, mental confusion, memory lapses.

Disorientation, mental confusion, memory lapses. Check, check, and check. She leaned back in her chair and raked her fingers through her curly black hair. She looked over at the pictures displayed on the shelves of the floor-to-ceiling bookcase—her Harvard graduation day, she and John dancing on their wedding day, family portraits from when the kids were little, a family portrait from Anna's wedding. She returned to the list on her computer screen. This was just the natural, next phase in her life as a woman. Millions of women coped with it every day. Nothing life-threatening. Nothing abnormal.

She wrote herself a note to make an appointment with her doctor for a checkup. Maybe she should go on estrogen replacement therapy. She read through the list of symptoms one last time. Irritability. Mood swings. Her recent shrinking fuse with John. It all added up. Satisfied, she shut down her computer.

She sat in the darkening study awhile longer, listening to her quiet house and the sounds of neighborhood barbecues. She inhaled the smell of hamburger grilling. For some reason, she wasn't hungry anymore. She took a multivitamin with water, unpacked, read several articles from *The Journal of Cognition,* and went to bed.

Sometime after midnight, John finally came home. His weight in their bed woke her, but only slightly. She remained still and pretended to stay asleep. He had to be exhausted from being up all night and working all day. They could talk about Lydia in the morning. And she'd apologize for being so sensitive and moody lately. His warm hand on her hip brought her into the curve of his body. With his breath on her neck, she fell into a deep sleep, convinced that she was safe.

OCTOBER 2003

"That was a lot to digest," said Alice, opening the door to her office.

"Yah, those enchiladas were huge," said Dan, grinning behind her.

Alice smacked him lightly on the arm with her notepad. They'd just sat through an hour-long lunch seminar. A fourth-year graduate student, Dan had an overall J. Crew appearance—muscular and lean with clean-cut, short blond hair, and a toothy, cocky smile. Physically, he looked nothing like John, but he possessed a confidence and sense of humor that often reminded Alice of John when he was that age.

After several false starts, Dan's thesis research had finally taken off, and he was experiencing an intoxication that Alice fondly recognized and hoped would develop into a sustainable passion. Anyone could be seduced by research when the results poured in. The trick was to love it when the results weren't forthcoming, and the reasons why were elusive.

"When do you leave for Atlanta?" she asked as she rifled through the papers on her desk, looking for the draft of his research paper that she'd edited.

"Next week."

"You can probably have it submitted by then; it's in good shape."

"I can't believe I'm getting married. God, I'm old."

She found it and handed it to him. "Please, you're hardly old. You're at the beginning of it all."

He sat down and flipped through the pages, furrowing his brows at the red scrawls in the margins. The introduction and discussion sections were the areas where Alice, with her deep and ready knowledge, contributed the most to rounding out Dan's work, filling in the holes in his narrative, creating a more contiguous picture of where and how this new piece fit into the historical and current linguistics puzzle as a whole.

"What does this say?" asked Dan, showing her a specific set of red scribbles with his finger.

"Differential effects of narrow versus distributed attention."

"What's the reference for that?" he asked.

"Oh, oh, what is it?" she asked herself, squeezing her eyes shut, waiting for the name of the first author and the year of the work to bubble to the surface. "See, this is what happens when you're old."

"Please, you're hardly old either. Don't worry, I can look it up."

One of the big memory burdens for anyone with a serious career in the sciences was knowing the years of the published studies, the details of the experiments, and who did them. Alice frequently awed her students and postdocs by offhandedly rattling off the seven studies relevant to a certain phenomenon, along with their respective authors and years of publication. Most of the senior faculty in her department had this skill at their fingertips. In fact, there existed an unspoken competition among them to see who possessed the most complete, readily accessible mental catalog of their discipline's library. Alice wore the imaginary blue ribbon more than anyone.

"Nye, MBB, 2000!" she exclaimed.

"It always amazes me that you can do that. Seriously, how do you hold all that information in your head?"

She smiled, accepting his admiration. "You'll see, like I said, you're just at the beginning."

He browsed through the rest of the pages, his eyebrows relaxed. "Okay, I'm psyched, this looks good. Thanks so much. I'll get it back to you tomorrow!"

And he bounded out of her office. That task completed, Alice referred to her to-do list, written on a yellow Post-it note stuck to the hanging cabinet just above her desktop screen.

Cognition class ✓
Lunch seminar ✓
Dan's paper
Eric
Birthday dinner

She placed a satisfying check mark next to "Dan's paper."

Eric? What does that mean?

Eric Wellman was the head of the psychology department at Harvard. Did she intend to tell him something, show him something, ask him something? Did she have a meeting with him? She consulted her calendar. October eleventh, her birthday. Nothing about Eric. *Eric.* It was too cryptic. She opened her inbox. Nothing from Eric. She hoped it wasn't time-sensitive. Irritated, but confident that she'd recover whatever it was about Eric eventually, she threw the reminder list, her fourth one that day, in the trash and pulled off a new Post-it.

Eric?
Call doctor

Memory disturbances like these were rearing their ugly little heads with a frequency that ruffled her. She'd been putting off calling her primary-care physician because she assumed that these kinds of forgetting episodes would simply resolve with time. She hoped she might learn something reassuring about the natural transience of this phase casually from someone she knew, possibly avoiding a visit to the doctor entirely. This was unlikely ever to happen, however, as all of her friends and Harvard colleagues of menopausal age were men. She admitted it was probably time that she sought some real medical advice.

ALICE AND JOHN WALKED TOGETHER from campus to Epulae in Inman Square. Inside, Alice spotted their older daughter, Anna, already sitting at the copper bar with her husband, Charlie. They both wore impressive blue suits, his accessorized with a solid gold tie and hers with a single strand of pearls. They'd been working for a couple of years at the third biggest corporate law firm in Massachusetts, Anna practicing in the area of intellectual property and Charlie working in litigation.

From the martini glass in her hand and the unchanged B-cup size of her chest, Alice knew that Anna wasn't pregnant. She'd been trying without success or secrecy to conceive for six months now. Like everything with Anna, the harder it was to obtain, the more she wanted it. Alice had advised her to wait, not to be in such a rush to check off this next major milestone in her life's to-do list. Anna was only twenty-seven, she'd just married Charlie last year, and she worked eighty to ninety hours a week. But Anna countered with the point that every professional woman considering children realized eventually: There's never going to be a good time to do this.

Alice worried about how having a family would affect Anna's career. It had been an arduous journey to tenured full professorship for Alice, not because the responsibilities became too daunting or because she didn't produce an outstanding body of work in linguistics along the way, but essentially because she was a woman who had children. The vomiting, anemia, and preeclampsia she'd experienced during the two and a half cumulative years of pregnancy had certainly distracted her and slowed her down. And the demands of the three little human beings born out of those pregnancies were more constant and time-consuming than those of any hard-ass department head or type A student she'd ever come across.

Time and again she'd watched with dread as the most promising careers of her reproductively active female colleagues slowed to a crawl or simply jumped the track entirely. Watching John, her male counterpart and intellectual equal, accelerate past her had been tough. She often wondered whether his career would have survived three episiotomies, breast-feeding, potty training, mind-numbingly endless days of singing "The wheels on the bus go round and round," and even more nights of getting only two to three hours of uninterrupted sleep. She seriously doubted it.

As they all exchanged hugs, kisses, pleasantries, and birthday greetings, a woman with severely bleached hair and dressed entirely in black approached them at the bar.

"Is everyone in your party here now?" she asked, smiling pleasantly, but a little too long to be sincere.

"No. We're still waiting for one," said Anna.

"I'm here!" said Tom, entering behind them. "Happy birthday, Mom."

Alice hugged and kissed him and then realized that he'd come in alone.

"Do we need to wait for . . . ?"

"Jill? No, Mom, we broke up last month."

"You go through so many girlfriends, we're having a hard time keeping track of their names," said Anna. "Is there a new one we should be saving a seat for?"

"Not yet," said Tom to Anna, and "We're all here," to the woman in black.

The period of time that Tom was between girlfriends came with a regular frequency of about six to nine months but never lasted long. He was smart, intense, the spitting image of his father, in his third year at Harvard Medical School, and planning on a career as a cardiothoracic surgeon. He looked like he could use a good meal. He admitted, with irony, that every medical student and surgeon he knew ate like shit and on the fly—donuts, bags of chips, vending machine and hospital cafeteria food. None of them had the time to exercise, unless they counted taking the stairs instead of the elevator. He joked that at least they'd be qualified to treat each other for heart disease in a few years.

Once they were all settled in a semicircular booth with drinks and appetizers, the topic of conversation turned to the missing family member.

"When was the last time Lydia came to one of the birthday dinners?" asked Anna.

"She was here for my twenty-first," said Tom.

"That was almost five years ago! Was that the last one?" Anna asked.

"No, it couldn't be," said John, without offering anything more specific.

"I'm pretty sure it was," Tom insisted.

"It wasn't. She was here for your father's fiftieth on the Cape, three years ago," said Alice.

"How's she doing, Mom?" asked Anna.

Anna took transparent pleasure in the fact that Lydia didn't go to college; Lydia's abbreviated education somehow secured Anna's position as the smartest, most successful Howland daughter. The oldest, Anna had been the first to demonstrate her intelligence to her delighted parents, the first to hold the status of being their brilliant daughter. Although Tom was also very bright, Anna had never paid much attention to him, maybe because he was a boy. Then, Lydia came along. Both girls were smart, but Anna suffered to get straight A's, whereas Lydia's unblemished report cards came with little noticeable effort. Anna paid attention to that. They were both competitive and fiercely independent, but Anna wasn't a risk taker. She tended to pursue goals that were safe and conventional, and that were sure to be accompanied by tangible accolades.

"She's good," said Alice.

"I can't believe she's still out there. Has she been in anything yet?" Anna asked.

"She was fantastic in that play last year," said John.

"She's taking classes," said Alice.

Only as the words left her mouth did she remember that John had been bankrolling Lydia's nondegree curriculum behind her back. How could she have forgotten to talk to him about that? She shot him an outraged look. It landed squarely on his face, and he felt the impact. He shook his head subtly and rubbed her back. Now wasn't the time or place. She'd get into it with him later. If she could remember.

"Well, at least she's doing something," said Anna, seemingly satisfied that everyone was aware of the current Howland daughter standing.

"So Dad, how'd that tagging experiment go?" asked Tom.

John leaned in and launched into the specifics of his latest study. Alice watched her husband and son, both biologists, absorbed in analytical conversation, each trying to impress the other with what he knew. The branches of laugh lines growing out from the corners of John's eyes, visible even when he was in the most serious of moods, became deep and lively when he talked about his research, and his hands joined in like puppets on a stage.

She loved to watch him like this. He didn't talk to her about his research with such detail and enthusiasm. He used to. She still always knew enough about what he was working on to give a decent cocktail party summary, but nothing beyond the barest skeleton. She recognized these meaty conversations he used to have with her when they spent time with Tom or John's colleagues. He used to tell her everything, and she used to listen in rapt attention. She wondered when that had changed and who'd lost interest first, he in the telling or she in the listening.

The calamari, the Maine crab–crusted oysters, the arugula salad, and the pumpkin ravioli were all impeccable. After dinner, everyone sang "Happy Birthday" loudly and off-key, attracting generous and amused applause from patrons at other tables. Alice blew out the single candle in her slice of warm chocolate cake. As everyone held their flutes of Veuve Clicquot, John raised his a bit higher.

"Happy birthday to my beautiful and brilliant wife. To your next fifty years!"

They all clinked glasses and drank.

In the ladies' room, Alice studied her image in the mirror. The reflected older woman's face didn't quite match the picture that she had of herself in her mind's eye. Her golden brown eyes appeared tired even though she was fully rested, and the texture of her skin appeared duller, looser. She was clearly older than forty, but she wouldn't say she looked old. She didn't feel old, although she knew that she was aging. Her recent entry into an older demographic announced itself regularly with the unwelcome intrusion of menopausal forgetting. Otherwise, she felt young, strong, and healthy.

She thought about her mother. They looked alike. Her memory of her mother's face, serious and intent, freckles sprinkled on her nose and cheekbones, didn't contain a single sag or wrinkle. She hadn't lived long enough to earn them. Alice's mother had died when she was forty-one. Alice's sister, Anne, would've been forty-eight now. Alice tried to visualize what Anne might look like, sitting in the booth with them tonight, with her own husband and children, but couldn't imagine her.

As she sat to pee, she saw the blood. Her period. Of course, she understood that menstruation at the beginning of menopause was often irregular, that it didn't always disappear all at once. But the possibility that she wasn't actually in menopause snuck in, grabbed on tight, and wouldn't let go.

Her resolve, softened by the champagne and blood, caved in on her completely. She started crying, hard. She was having trouble taking in enough air. She was fifty years old, and she felt like she might be losing her mind.

Someone knocked on the door.

"Mom?" asked Anna. "Are you okay?"

NOVEMBER 2003

Dr. Tamara Moyer's office was located on the third floor of a five-story professional office building a few blocks west of Harvard Square, not far from where Alice had momentarily lost herself. The waiting and examining rooms, still decorated with framed Ansel Adams prints and pharmaceutical advertisement posters on the high-school-locker-gray walls, held no negative associations for her. In the twenty-two years that Dr. Moyer had been Alice's physician, she'd only ever been to see her for preventative checkups—physical exams, immunization boosters, and more recently, mammograms.

"What brings you here today, Alice?" asked Dr. Moyer.

"I'm having a lot of memory problems lately that I've been

attributing to symptoms of menopause. I stopped getting my period about six months ago, but it came back last month, so maybe I'm not in menopause, and then, well, I thought I should come in and see you."

"What are the specific kinds of things that you're forgetting?" Dr. Moyer asked while writing and without looking up.

"Names, words in conversation, where I put my BlackBerry, why something is on my to-do list."

"Okay."

Alice watched her doctor closely. Her confession didn't seem to grab her in any way. Dr. Moyer received the information like a priest listening to a teenage boy's admission of impure thoughts about a girl. She probably heard this type of complaint from perfectly healthy people countless times a day. Alice almost apologized for being so alarmist, silly even, for wasting her doctor's time. Everyone forgot these sorts of things, especially as they got older. Add menopause and that she was always doing three things at once and thinking of twelve, and these kinds of memory lapses suddenly seemed small, ordinary, harmless, and even reasonably expected. Everyone's stressed. Everyone's tired. *Everyone forgets things.*

"I also became disoriented in Harvard Square. I didn't know where I was for at least a couple of minutes before it all came back to me."

Dr. Moyer ceased documenting symptoms on her evaluation sheet and looked directly at Alice. That grabbed her.

"Did you have any tightness in your chest?"

"No."

"Did you have any numbness or tingling?"

"No."

"Did you have a headache or were you dizzy?"

"No."

"Did you notice any heart palpitations?"

"My heart was pounding, but that was after I became confused, more like an adrenaline response to being scared. I remember feeling great, actually, just before it happened."

"Did anything else unusual happen that day?"

"No, I'd just come home from Los Angeles."

"Are you having any hot flashes?"

"No. Well, I felt what could've been one while I was disoriented, but again, I think I was just scared."

"Okay. How are you sleeping?"

"Fine."

"How many hours are you getting each night?"

"Five to six."

"Is this a change from what it's been in the past?"

"No."

"Any difficulty falling asleep?"

"No."

"How many times do you typically wake up during the night?"

"I don't think I do."

"Do you go to bed at the same time every night?"

"Usually. Except when I travel, which has been a lot lately."

"Where have you traveled?"

"In the last few months, California, Italy, New Orleans, Florida, New Jersey."

"Were you sick after any of these trips? Any fevers?"

"No."

"Are you taking any medications, anything for allergies,

supplements, anything that you might not normally think of as a medicine?"

"Just a multivitamin."

"Any heartburn?"

"No."

"Any weight changes?"

"No."

"Any bleeding in your urine or bowel movements?"

"No."

She asked each question rapidly on the heels of each answer, and the topics jumped from one to the next before Alice had time to follow the reasoning behind them. As if she were riding a roller coaster with her eyes shut, she couldn't predict which way she was being turned next.

"Are you feeling more anxious or stressed than typical?"

"Just about not being able to remember things. Otherwise, no."

"How are things with your husband?"

"Fine."

"Do you think your mood is pretty good?"

"Yes."

"Do you think you could be depressed?"

"No."

Alice knew depression. Following the deaths of her mother and sister when she was eighteen, she'd lost her appetite, she'd been unable to sleep for more than a couple of hours at a time despite being endlessly tired, and she'd lost an interest in enjoying anything. It had lasted a little over a year, and she'd never experienced anything like it since. This was entirely different. This wasn't a job for Prozac.

"Do you drink alcohol?"

"Just socially."

"How much?"

"One or two glasses of wine with dinner, maybe a little more on a special occasion."

"Any drug use?"

"No."

Dr. Moyer looked at her, thinking. She tapped her pen on her notes as she read them. Alice suspected the answer wasn't anywhere on that piece of paper.

"So am I in menopause?" she asked as she gripped her parchment-papered seat with both hands.

"Yes. We can run an FSH, but everything you tell me is completely consistent with menopause. The average age of onset is forty-eight to fifty-two, so you're right in there. You may continue to get a couple of periods a year for a while. That's perfectly normal."

"Can estrogen replacement help with the memory problems?"

"We don't put women on estrogen replacement anymore, unless they're having sleep disturbances, really awful hot flashes, or they're already osteoporotic. I don't think your memory problems are due to menopause."

The blood rushed from Alice's head. Precisely the words she'd dreaded and only recently dared to consider. With that one, professionally uttered opinion, her tidy and safe explanation shattered. Something was wrong with her, and she wasn't sure that she was ready to hear what it was. She fought the impulses growing louder inside her, begging her to either lie down or get the hell out of that examining room immediately.

"Why not?"

"The symptoms of memory disturbances and disorientation listed for menopause are secondary to poor sleep hygiene.

Those women aren't coping well cognitively because they aren't sleeping. It's possible that you're not sleeping as well as you think you are. Perhaps your schedule and jet lag are taking a toll, perhaps you're worrying about things throughout the night."

Alice thought about the times she'd suffered from fuzzy thinking caused by bouts of sleep deprivation. She certainly hadn't played at the top of her mental game during the last weeks of each pregnancy, following the birth of each child, and at times, when she was up against a grant deadline. In none of those circumstances, however, did she get lost in Harvard Square.

"Maybe. Could I suddenly need more sleep because I'm older or because I'm in menopause?"

"No. I don't usually see that."

"If it's not lack of sleep, what are you thinking?" she asked, the clarity and confidence now completely absent from her voice.

"Well, I'm concerned about the disorientation in particular. I don't think it was a vascular event. I think we should do some tests. I'm going to send you for blood work, a mammogram, and bone density because it's time, and a brain MRI."

A brain tumor. She hadn't even considered that. A new predator loomed in her imagination, and she felt the ingredients of panic once again brewing in her gut.

"If you don't think it was a stroke, what are you looking for in the MRI?"

"It's always good to definitively rule these things out. Make the appointment for the MRI and then one to see me right after, and we'll go over everything."

Dr. Moyer had avoided answering the question directly, but Alice didn't push her to reveal her suspicions. And Alice didn't share her tumor theory. They would both just have to wait and see.

William James Hall housed the departments of psychology, sociology, and social anthropology and was located just beyond the gates of Harvard Yard on Kirkland Street, a region referred to by students as Siberia. Geography, however, was not the most prominent factor that alienated it from the main campus. William James Hall could never be mistaken for any of the stately, classically collegiate structures that adorned the prestigious Yard and housed the freshman dormitories and classes in mathematics, history, and English. It could, however, be mistaken for a parking garage. It possessed no Doric or Corinthian columns, no red brick, no Tiffany stained glass, no spires, no grand atrium, no physical detail whatsoever that might obviously or subtly affiliate it with its parent institution. It was a 210-foot, unimaginative beige block, quite possibly the inspiration for B. F. Skinner's box. Not surprisingly, it had never been featured in the student walking tour or the Harvard calendar, spring, summer, winter, or fall.

Although the view of William James Hall was inarguably abysmal, the view from it, in particular from many of the offices and conference rooms on the upper floors, was nothing short of splendid. As Alice drank her tea at her desk in her office on the tenth floor, she relaxed in the beauty of the Charles River and Boston's Back Bay framed before her by the enormous southeast-facing window. It captured a scene that many artists and photographers have reproduced in oil, watercolor, and film, and that could be found matted and framed on the walls of office buildings all over the Boston area.

Alice appreciated the glorious advantages available to those fortunate enough to regularly observe the live version of this landscape. With the changes in the time of day or year, the quality and movement within the picture in her window altered in tirelessly interesting ways. On this sunny morning in November, Alice's *View of Boston from WJH: Fall* displayed the sunlight sparkling like champagne fizz off the pale blue glass of the John Hancock building and several sculls steadily sliding along a smooth and silvery Charles toward the Museum of Science as if being pulled by a string in a motion experiment.

The view also provided her with a healthy awareness of life outside Harvard. A glimpse of the red-and-white neon CITGO sign flashing against a darkening sky over Fenway Park fired her nervous system like the sudden ring of an alarm clock, awakening her from the daily trance of her ambitions and obligations and triggering thoughts of heading home. Years ago, before she was tenured, her office had been in a small, windowless room within the interior of William James Hall. Lacking visual access to the world beyond its solid beige walls, Alice had regularly worked late into the night without even realizing it. On more than one occasion, she'd been stunned at the end of the day to discover that a nor'easter had buried Cambridge in more than a foot of snow and that the less focused and/or window-owning faculty had all wisely abandoned William James Hall in search of bread, milk, toilet paper, and home.

But now she needed to stop staring out the window. She was leaving later that afternoon for the annual Psychonomic Society meeting in Chicago, and she had a ton to accomplish before then. She looked over her to-do list.

Review Nature Neuroscience paper ✓
Department meeting ✓
Meet with TA's ✓
Cognition class
Finalize conference poster and itinerary
Run
Airport

She drank the last watery sip of her iced tea and began to study her lecture notes. Today's lecture focused on semantics, the meaning of language, the third of six classes on linguistics, her favorite series of classes for this course. Even after twenty-five years of teaching, Alice still set aside an hour before class to prepare. Of course, at this point in her career, she could meticulously deliver 75 percent of any given lecture without consciously thinking about it. The other 25 percent, however, contained insights, innovative techniques, or points for discussion from current findings in the field, and she used the time immediately before class to refine the organization and presentation of this newer material. The inclusion of this constantly evolving information kept her passionate about her course subjects and mentally present in each class.

Emphasis for the faculty at Harvard tipped heavily toward research performance, and so a lot of less than optimal teaching was tolerated, by both the students and the administration. The emphasis Alice placed on teaching was in part motivated by the belief that she had both a duty and the opportunity to inspire the next generation in the field, or at the very least not to be the reason that the next would-be great thought leader in cognition abandoned psychology to major in political science instead. Plus, she simply loved teaching.

Ready for class, she checked her email.

Alice,

We're still waiting on you for 3 slides to be included in Michael's talk: 1 word retrieval graph, 1 model of language cartoon, and 1 text slide. His talk isn't until Thursday at 1:00, but it would be a good idea for him to drop your slides into the presentation as soon as possible, make sure he's comfortable with it all, and that it still falls within the allotted time. You can email them to either me or Michael.

We're staying at the Hyatt. See you in Chicago.

Kind regards,

Eric Greenberg

A cold and dusty lightbulb flickered on inside Alice's head. That was what the mysterious "Eric" had meant on one of her to-do lists last month. It didn't refer to Eric Wellman at all. It was meant to remind her to email those slides to Eric Greenberg, a former colleague at Harvard, now a professor in the psychology department at Princeton. Alice and Dan had put together three slides describing a quick and dirty experiment Dan had run as part of a collaboration with Eric's postdoc Michael, to be included in Michael's talk at the psychonomic meeting. Before doing anything else that might distract her, Alice emailed the slides, along with sincerest apologies, to Eric. Fortunately, he'd get them in plenty of time. No harm done.

As with most everything at Harvard, the lecture auditorium used for Alice's cognition course was grander than necessary. The blue upholstered chairs arranged in stadium seating numbered several hundred more than the students enrolled in the class. An impressive, state-of-the-art audiovisual center stood at the back of the room, and a projection screen as big as those in any movie cinema hung at the front. While three men busily hooked up various cables to Alice's computer and checked the lighting and sound, students wandered in, and Alice opened her "Linguistics Classes" folder on her laptop.

It contained six files: "Acquisition," "Syntax," "Semantics," "Comprehension," "Modeling," and "Pathologies." Alice read the titles again. She couldn't remember which lecture she was supposed to give today. She'd just spent the last hour looking over one of these subjects but couldn't remember which one. Was it "Syntax"? They all looked familiar to her, but none more salient than the others.

Ever since her visit with Dr. Moyer, each time Alice forgot something, her foreboding intensified. This wasn't like forgetting where she left her BlackBerry charger or where John left his glasses. This wasn't normal. She'd begun telling herself, in a tortured and paranoid voice, that she probably had a brain tumor. She also told herself not to freak out or worry John until she heard the more informed voice of Dr. Moyer, which unfortunately wouldn't be until next week, after the psychonomic conference.

Determined to get through the next hour, she took a deep, frustrated breath. Although she didn't remember the topic of today's lecture, she did remember who her audience was.

"Can someone please tell me what it says on your syllabus for today?" Alice asked the class.

Several students called out in a staggered, collective voice, "Semantics."

She had gambled correctly that at least a few of her students would pounce on the opportunity to be visibly helpful and knowledgeable. She didn't worry for a second that any of them would think it grievous or strange that she didn't know the subject of today's class. There existed a great metaphysical distance in age, knowledge, and power between undergraduate students and professors.

Plus, over the course of the semester, they'd witnessed specific demonstrations of her competence in class and had been wowed by her dominant presence in the course literature. If any of them gave it any consideration whatsoever, they probably assumed that she was so distracted with other obligations more important than Psychology 256 that she didn't have time even to glance at the syllabus before class. Little did they know that she'd just spent the last hour concentrating almost exclusively on semantics.

THE SUNNY DAY HAD TURNED cloudy and raw by evening, the first real flirtation with winter. A hard rain the night before had knocked most of the remaining leaves off their branches, leaving the trees nearly naked, underdressed for the coming weather. Comfortably warm in her fleece, Alice took her time walking home, enjoying the cold autumn air smell and the crunchy swishing sound her feet made as they strolled through the piles of grounded leaves.

The lights were on inside her house, and John's bag and shoes rested next to the table by the door.

"Hello? I'm home," said Alice.

John walked out from the study and stared at her, looking confused and at a loss for words. Alice stared back and waited, nervously sensing that something was dreadfully wrong. Her mind raced straight to her children. She stood frozen in the doorway, braced for horrible news.

"Aren't you supposed to be in Chicago?"

"WELL, ALICE, ALL OF YOUR blood work came back normal, and your MRI is clean," said Dr. Moyer. "We can do one of two things. We can wait, see how things go, see how you're sleeping and how you're doing in three months, or—"

"I want to see a neurologist."

DECEMBER 2003

On the night of Eric Wellman's holiday party, the sky felt low and thick, like it was going to snow. Alice hoped it would. Like most New Englanders, she'd never outgrown a childlike anticipation of the season's first snow. Of course, also like most New Englanders, what she wished for in December she'd come to loathe by February, cursing her shovel and boots, desperate to replace the frigid, monochromatic tedium of winter with the milder pinks and yellow-greens of spring. But for tonight, snow would be lovely.

Each year, Eric and his wife, Marjorie, hosted a holiday party at their home for the entire psychology department. Nothing extraordinary ever happened at this event, but there were always small moments that Alice wouldn't dream of missing—Eric sitting comfortably on the floor in a living room full of students and junior faculty on couches and chairs, Kevin and Glen wrestling for ownership of a Yankee-swapped Grinch doll, the race to get a slice of Marty's legendary cheesecake.

Her colleagues were all brilliant and odd, quick to help and argue, ambitious and humble. They were family. Maybe she felt this way because she didn't have living siblings or parents. Maybe the time of year made her sentimental, searching for meaning and belonging. Maybe that was part of it, but it was also much more.

They were more than colleagues. Triumphs of discovery, promotion, and publication were celebrated, but so were weddings and births and the accomplishments of their children and grandchildren. They traveled together to conferences all over the world, and many meetings were piggybacked with family vacations. And like in any family, it wasn't always good times and yummy cheesecake. They supported one another through slumps of negative data and grant rejection, through waves of crippling self-doubt, through illness and divorce.

But most of all, they shared a passionate quest to understand the mind, to know the mechanisms driving human behavior and language, emotion and appetite. While the holy grail of this quest carried individual power and prestige, at its core it was a collaborative effort to know something valuable and give it to the world. It was socialism powered by capitalism. It was a strange, competitive, cerebral, and privileged life. And they were in it together.

The cheesecake gone, Alice snatched the last hot-fudge-drenched cream puff and looked for John. She found him in the living room in conversation with Eric and Marjorie just as Dan arrived.

Dan introduced them to his new wife, Beth, and they offered hearty congratulations and exchanged handshakes. Marjorie took their coats. Dan had on a suit and tie, and Beth wore a floor-length red dress. Late and much too formal for this party, they'd probably gone to another one first. Eric offered to get them drinks.

"I'll have another one, too," said Alice, the glass of wine in her hand still half full.

John asked Beth how she liked married life so far. Although they'd never met, Alice knew a little about her from Dan. She and Dan had been living together in Atlanta when Dan was accepted at Harvard. She'd stayed in Atlanta, originally content with a long-distance relationship and the promise of marriage after he graduated. Three years later, Dan had carelessly mentioned that it could easily take five to six, maybe even seven years for him to finish. They had married last month.

Alice excused herself to use the ladies' room. On the way, she lingered in the long hallway that connected the newer front of the house to the older back, finishing her wine and cream puff as she admired the happy faces of Eric's grandchildren pictured on the walls. After she found and used the bathroom, she wandered into the kitchen, poured herself another glass of wine, and fell captive to a boisterous conversation among several of the faculty wives.

The wives touched elbows and shoulders as they moved about the kitchen, they knew the characters in each other's stories, they praised and teased each other, they laughed easily. These women all shopped and lunched and attended book clubs together. These women were close. Alice was close with their husbands, and it set her apart. She mostly listened and drank her wine, nodding and smiling as she followed along, her interest not truly engaged, like running on a treadmill instead of on an actual road.

She filled her wineglass again, slipped unnoticed out of the kitchen, and found John in the living room in conversation with Eric, Dan, and a young woman in a red dress. Alice stood next to Eric's grand piano and strummed the top of it with her fingers while she listened to them talk. Each year, Alice hoped that someonc would offer to play it, but no one ever did. She and Anne had taken lessons for several years as children, but now she could remember only "Baby Elephant Walk" and "Turkey in the Straw" without sheet music, and only the right hand. Maybe this woman in the fancy red dress knew how to play.

At a pause in the conversation, Alice and the woman in red made eye contact.

"I'm sorry, I'm Alice Howland. I don't believe we've met."

The woman looked nervously at Dan before she answered. "I'm Beth."

She seemed young enough to be a graduate student, but by December, Alice would have at least recognized even a first-year student. She remembered Marty mentioning that he'd hired a new postdoctoral fellow, a woman.

"Are you Marty's new postdoc?" asked Alice.

The woman checked with Dan again. "I'm Dan's wife."

"Oh, so nice to finally meet you, congratulations!"

No one spoke. Eric's gaze bounced from John's eyes to Alice's wineglass and back to John, carrying a silent secret. Alice wasn't in on it.

"What?" asked Alice.

"You know what? It's getting late, and I've got to get up early. You mind if we get going?" asked John.

Once they were outside, she meant to ask John what that awkward saccade was about, but she became distracted by the gentle beauty of the cotton-candy snow that had begun to fall while they were inside, and she forgot.

THREE DAYS BEFORE CHRISTMAS, ALICE sat in the waiting room of the Memory Disorders Unit at Massachusetts General Hospital in Boston pretending to read *Health* magazine. Instead, she observed the others who waited. They were all in pairs. A woman who looked twenty years older than Alice sat next to a woman who looked at least twenty years older than her—most likely her mother. A woman with big, unnaturally black hair and big gold jewelry talked loudly and slowly in a thick Boston accent to her father, who sat in a wheelchair and never looked up from his perfectly white shoes. A bony, silver-haired woman flipped pages of a magazine too quickly to be reading anything next to an overweight man with matching hair and a resting tremor in his right hand. Probably husband and wife.

The wait to hear her name took forever and seemed longer. Dr. Davis had a young, hairless face. He wore black-rimmed glasses and a white lab coat, unbuttoned. He looked like he used to be thin, but his lower torso slumped a bit beyond the outline of his open coat, reminding Alice of Tom's comments about the poor health habits of physicians. He sat in a chair behind his desk and invited her to have a seat across from him.

"So Alice, tell me what's been going on."

"I've been having lots of problems remembering, and it doesn't feel normal. I'm forgetting words in lectures and conversation, I need to put 'cognition class' on my to-do list or I might forget to go teach it, I completely forgot to go to the airport for a conference in Chicago and missed my flight. I also didn't know where I was for a couple of minutes once in Harvard Square, and I'm a professor at Harvard, I'm there every day."

"How long have these things been going on?"

"Since September, maybe this summer."

"Alice, did anyone come here with you?"

"No."

"Okay. In the future, you're going to have to bring a family member or someone who sees you regularly in with you. You're complaining about a problem with your memory; you may not be the most reliable source of what's been going on."

She felt embarrassed, like a child. And his words "in the future" harassed her every thought, commanding obsessive attention, like water dripping from a faucet.

"Okay," she said.

"Are you taking any kind of medicine?"

"No, just a multivitamin."

"Any sleeping pills, diet pills, drugs of any kind?"

"No."

"How much do you drink?"

"Not a lot. One or two glasses of wine with dinner."

"Are you a vegan?"

"No."

"Have you had any sort of past injury to your head?"

"No."

"Have you had any surgeries?"

"No."

"How are you sleeping?"

"Perfectly fine."

"Have you ever been depressed?"

"Not since I was a teenager."

"How's your stress level?"

"The usual, I thrive under stress."

"Tell me about your parents. How's their health?"

"My mother and sister died in a car accident when I was eighteen. My father died of liver failure last year."

"Hepatitis?"

"Cirrhosis. He was an alcoholic."

"How old was he?"

"Seventy-one."

"Did he have any other problems with his health?"

"Not that I know of. I didn't really see much of him over the last several years."

And when she did, he was incoherent, drunk.

"What about other family?"

She relayed her limited knowledge of her extended family's medical history.

"Okay, I'm going to tell you a name and address, and you're going to repeat it back to me. Then, we're going to do some other things, and I'm going to ask you to repeat the same name and address again later. Ready, here it is—John Black, 42 West Street, Brighton. Can you repeat that for me?"

She did.

"How old are you?"

"Fifty."

"What is today's date?"

"December twenty-second, 2003."

"What season is it?"

"Winter."

"Where are we right now?"

"Eighth floor, MGH."

"Can you name some of the streets near here?"

"Cambridge, Fruit, Storrow Drive."

"Okay, what time of day is it?"

"Late morning."

"Name the months backward from December."

She did.

"Count backward from one hundred by six."

He stopped her at seventy-six.

"Name these objects."

He showed her a series of six cards with pencil drawings on them.

"Hammock, feather, key, chair, cactus, glove."

"Okay, before pointing to the window, touch your right cheek with your left hand."

She did.

"Can you write a sentence about today's weather on this piece of paper?"

She wrote, "It is a sunny but cold winter morning."

"Now, draw a clock and show the time as twenty minutes to four."

She did.

"And copy this design."

He showed her a picture of two intersecting pentagons. She copied them.

"Okay, Alice, hop up on the table. We're going to do a neurological exam."

She followed his penlight with her eyes, she tapped her thumbs and pointer fingers together rapidly, she walked heel to toe in a straight line across the room. She did everything easily and quickly.

"Okay, what was that name and address I told you earlier?"

"John Black . . ."

She stopped and searched Dr. Davis's face. She couldn't remember the address. What did that mean? Maybe she just hadn't paid close enough attention.

"It's Brighton, but I can't remember the street address."

"Okay, is it twenty-four, twenty-eight, forty-two, or forty-eight?"

She didn't know.

"Take a guess."

"Forty-eight."

"Was it North Street, South Street, East Street, or West Street?"

"South Street?"

His face and body language didn't expose whether she'd guessed right, but if she had to guess again, that wasn't it.

"Okay, Alice, we have your recent blood work and MRI. I want you to go for some additional blood work and a lumbar puncture. You're going to come back in four to five weeks, and you'll have an appointment for neuropsychological testing on that same day, before you see me."

"What do you think is going on? Is this just normal forgetting?"

"I don't think it is, Alice, but we need to investigate it further."

She looked him directly in the eye. A colleague of hers had once told her that eye contact with another person for more than six seconds without looking away or blinking revealed a desire for either sex or murder. She reflexively hadn't believed this, but it had intrigued her enough to test it out on various friends and strangers. To her surprise, with the exception of John, one of them always looked away before the six seconds was up.

Dr. Davis looked down at his desk after four seconds. Arguably, this meant only that he wanted neither to kill her nor tear her clothes off, but she worried that it meant more. She would get prodded and assayed, scanned and tested, but she guessed that he didn't need to investigate anything further. She'd told him her story, and she couldn't remember John Black's address. He already knew exactly what was wrong with her.

ALICE SPENT THE EARLIEST PART of Christmas Eve morning on the couch, sipping tea and browsing through photo albums. Over the years, she had transferred any newly developed pictures to the next available slots beneath the clear plastic sleeves. Her diligence had preserved their chronology, but she'd labeled nothing. It didn't matter. She still knew it all cold.

Lydia, age two; Tom, age six; and Anna, seven, at Hardings Beach in June of their first summer at the Cape house. Anna at a youth soccer game on Pequossette Field. She and John on Seven Mile Beach on Grand Cayman Island.

Not only could she place the ages and setting in each snapshot but she could also elaborate in great detail on most of them. Each print prompted other, unphotographed memories from that day, of who else had been there, and of the larger context of her life at the time that the image was captured.

Lydia in her itchy, powder blue costume at her first dance recital. That was pretenure, Anna was in junior high and in braces, Tom was lovesick over a girl on his baseball team, and John lived in Bethesda, on sabbatical for the year.

The only ones she had any real trouble with were the baby pictures of Anna and Lydia, their flawless, pudgy faces often indistinguishable. She could usually find clues, however, that revealed their identities. John's muttonchop sideburns placed him solidly in the 1970s. The baby in his lap had to be Anna.

"John, who's this?" she asked, holding up a picture of a baby.

He looked up from the journal he'd been reading, slid his glasses down his nose, and squinted.

"Is that Tom?"

"Honey, she's in a pink onesie. It's Lydia."

She checked the Kodak-printed date on the back to be sure. May 29, 1982. Lydia.

"Oh."

He pushed his glasses back up onto the bridge of his nose and resumed reading.

"John, I've been meaning to talk to you about Lydia's acting classes."

He looked up, dog-eared the page, set the journal on the table, folded his glasses, and settled back in the chair. He knew this wouldn't be quick.

"All right."

"I don't think we should be supporting her out there in any way, and I certainly don't think you should be paying for her classes behind my back."

"I'm sorry, you're right, I meant to tell you, but then I got busy and forgot, you know how it gets. But I disagree with you on this, you know I do. We supported the other two."

"That's different."

"It's not. You just don't like what she picked."

"It's not the acting. It's the not going to college. The window of time she's likely to ever go is rapidly closing, John, and you're making it easier for her to stay out."

"She doesn't want to go to college."

"I think she's just rebelling against who we are."

"I don't think it has anything to do with what we want or don't want or who we are."

"I want more for her."

"She's working hard, she's excited and serious about what she's doing, she's happy. That's what we want for her."

"It's our job to pass on our wisdom about life to our kids. I'm really afraid she's missing out on something essential. The exposure to different subjects, different ways of thinking, the challenges, opportunities, the people you meet. We met in college."

"She's getting all that."

"It's not the same."

"So it's different. I think paying for her classes is more than fair. I'm sorry I didn't tell you, but you're hard to talk to about this. You don't ever budge."

"Neither do you."

He glanced at the clock on the fireplace mantel, reached for his glasses, and placed them on top of his head.

"I've got to go to lab for about an hour, then I'll pick her up at the airport. You need anything while I'm out?" he asked as he stood to leave.

"No."

They locked eyes.

"She's going to be fine, Ali, don't worry."

She raised her eyebrows but didn't say anything. What else could she say? They'd played this scene out together before, and this was how it ended. John argued the logical path of least resistance, always maintaining his status as the favorite parent, never convincing Alice to switch over to the popular side. And nothing she said swayed him.

John left the house. Relaxed in his absence, she returned to the pictures in her lap. Her adorable children as babies, toddlers, teenagers. Where did the time go? She held the baby picture of Lydia that John had guessed was Tom. She felt a renewed and reassuring confidence in the strength of her memory. But of course, these pictures only opened the doors to histories housed in long-term memories.

John Black's address would have lived in recent memory. Attention, rehearsal, elaboration, or emotional significance was needed if perceived information was to be pushed beyond the recent memory space into longer-term storage, else it would be quickly and naturally discarded with the passage of time. Focusing on Dr. Davis's questions and instructions had divided her attention and prevented her from rehearsing or elaborating on the address. And although his name elicited a bit of fear and anger now, the fictitious John Black had meant nothing to her in Dr. Davis's examining room. Under these circumstances, the average brain would be quite susceptible to forgetting. Then again, she didn't have an average brain.

She heard the mail drop through the slot in the front door and had an idea. She looked at each item once—a baby wearing a Santa hat pictured on a holiday greeting card from a former graduate student, an advertisement for a fitness club, the phone bill, the gas bill, yet another L.L.Bean catalog. She returned to the couch, drank her tea, stacked the photo albums back on the shelf, and then sat very still. The ticking clock and brief eruptions of steam from various radiators made the only sounds in the house. She stared at the clock. Five minutes passed. Long enough.

Without looking at the mail, she said aloud, "Baby in Santa hat card, gym membership offering, phone bill, gas bill, another L.L.Bean catalog."

Piece of cake. But to be fair, the time between being presented with John Black's address and being asked to recall it had been much longer than five minutes. She needed an extended delay interval.

She grabbed the dictionary off the shelf and devised two rules for picking a word. It had to be low frequency, one she didn't use every day, and it had to be a word that she already knew. She was testing her recent memory, not learning acquisition. She opened the dictionary to an arbitrary page and put her finger down on the word "berserk." She wrote it on a piece of paper, folded it, put it in her pants pocket, and set the timer on the microwave for fifteen minutes.

One of Lydia's favorite books when she was a toddler was *Hippos Go Berserk!* Alice went about the business of readying for Christmas Eve dinner. The timer beeped.

"Berserk," without hesitation or needing to consult the piece of paper.

She continued playing this game throughout the day, increasing the number of words to remember to three and the delay period to forty-five minutes. Despite this added degree of difficulty and the added likelihood of interference from the distraction of dinner preparation, she remained error-free. *Stethoscope, millennium, hedgehog.* She made the ricotta raviolis and the red sauce. *Cathode, pomegranate, trellis.* She tossed the salad and marinated the vegetables. *Snapdragon, documentary, vanish.* She put the roast in the oven and set the dining room table.

Anna, Charlie, Tom, and John sat in the living room. Alice could hear Anna and John arguing. She couldn't make out the topic from the kitchen, but she could tell it was an argument by the emphasis and volume of the back-and-forth. Probably politics. Charlie and Tom were staying out of it.

Lydia stirred the hot mulled cider on the stove and talked about her acting classes. Between concentrating on making dinner, the words she needed to remember, and Lydia, Alice didn't have the mental reserve to protest or disapprove. Uninterrupted, Lydia spoke in a free and passionate monologue about her craft, and despite Alice's strong bias against it, she found she couldn't resist being interested.

"After the imagery, you layer on the Elijah question, 'Why this night rather than any other?' " said Lydia.

The timer beeped. Lydia stepped aside without being asked, and Alice peeked in the oven. She waited for an explanation from the undercooked roast long enough for her face to become uncomfortably hot. *Oh.* It was time to recall the three words in her pocket. *Tambourine, serpent. . .*

"You're never playing everyday life as usual, the stakes are always life and death," said Lydia.

"Mom, where's the wine opener?" Anna hollered from the living room.

Alice struggled to ignore her daughters' voices, the ones her mind had been trained to hear above all other sounds on the planet, and to concentrate on her own inner voice, the one repeating the same two words like a mantra.

Tambourine, serpent, tambourine, serpent, tambourine, serpent.

"Mom?" asked Anna.

"I don't know where it is, Anna! I'm busy, look for it yourself."

Tambourine, serpent, tambourine, serpent, tambourine, serpent.

"It's always about survival when you boil it down. What does my character need to survive and what will happen to me if I don't get it?" said Lydia.

"Lydia, please, I don't want to hear about this right now," Alice snapped, holding her sweaty temples.

"Fine," said Lydia. She turned herself squarely toward the stove and stirred vigorously, obviously hurt.

Tambourine, serpent.

"I still can't find it!" yelled Anna.

"I'll go help her," said Lydia.

Compass! Tambourine, serpent, compass.

Relieved, Alice took out the ingredients for the white-chocolate bread pudding and placed them on the counter—vanilla extract, a pint of heavy cream, milk, sugar, white chocolate, a loaf of challah bread, and two half-dozen cartons of eggs. *A dozen eggs?* If the piece of notebook paper with her mother's recipe on it still existed, Alice didn't know where it was. She hadn't needed to refer to it in years. It was a simple recipe, arguably better than Marty's cheesecake, and she'd made it every Christmas Eve since she was a young girl. How many eggs? It had to be more than six, or she would've taken out only one carton. Was it seven, eight, nine?

She tried skipping over the eggs for a moment, but the other ingredients looked just as foreign. Was she supposed to use all of the cream or measure out only some of it? How much sugar? Was she supposed to combine everything all at once or in a particular sequence? What pan did she use? At what temperature did she bake it and for how long? No possibility rang true. The information just wasn't there.

What the hell is wrong with me?

She revisited the eggs. Still nothing. She hated those fucking eggs. She held one in her hand and threw it as hard as she could into the sink. One by one, she destroyed them all. It was marginally satisfying, but not enough. She needed to break something else, something that required more muscle, something that would exhaust her. She scanned the kitchen. Her eyes were furious and wild when they met Lydia's in the doorway.

"Mom, what are you doing?"

The massacre had not been confined to the sink. Empty shards of shell and yolk were splattered all over the wall and counter, and the faces of the cabinets were streaked with tears of albumen.

"The eggs were past the expiration date. There's no pudding this year."

"Aw, we have to have the pudding, it's Christmas Eve."

"Well, there aren't any more eggs, and I'm tired of being in this hot kitchen."

"I'll go to the store. Go into the living room and relax, I'll make the pudding."

Alice walked into the living room, shaking but no longer riding that powerful wave of anger, not sure whether she was feeling deprived or thankful. John, Tom, Anna, and Charlie were all seated and in conversation, holding glasses of red wine. Apparently, someone had found the opener. With her coat and hat on, Lydia poked her head into the room.

"Mom, how many eggs do I need?"

JANUARY 2004

She had good reasons to cancel her appointments on the morning of January nineteenth with the neuropsychologist and Dr. Davis. Harvard's exam week for the fall semester fell in January, after the students returned from Winter Break, and the final exam for Alice's cognition class was scheduled for that morning. Her attendance wasn't crucial, but she liked the sense of closure that being there provided, of seeing her students through the course from start to finish. With some reluctance, she arranged for a teaching fellow to proctor the exam. The bigger good reason was that her mother and sister had died on January nineteenth, thirty-two years ago. She didn't consider herself superstitious like John, but she'd never received good news on that day. She'd asked the receptionist for another date, but it was either then or four weeks from then. So she took it, and she didn't cancel. The idea of waiting another month was that unappealing.

She imagined her students back at Harvard, nervous about what questions they would be asked, hurrying a semester's worth of knowledge onto the pages of their blue exam books, hoping their heavily crammed short-term memories wouldn't fail them. She understood exactly how they felt. Most of the neuropsychological tests administered to her that morning—Stroop, Raven's Colored Progressive Matrices, Luria Mental Rotation, Boston Naming, WAIS-R Picture Arrangement, Benton Visual Retention, NYU Story Recall—were familiar to her. They were designed to tease out any subtle weakness in the integrity of language fluency, recent memory, and reasoning processes. She had, in fact, taken many of them before, serving as a negative control in the cognition studies of various graduate students. But today, she wasn't a control. She was the subject being tested.

The copying, recalling, arranging, and naming took almost two hours to complete. Like the students she imagined, she felt relieved to be done and fairly confident in her performance. Escorted by the neuropsychologist, Alice entered Dr. Davis's office and sat in one of the two chairs arranged side by side, facing him. He acknowledged the empty chair next to her with a disappointed sigh. Even before he spoke, she knew she was in trouble.

"Alice, didn't we talk about you coming here with someone last time?"

"We did."

"Okay, it's a requirement of this unit that every patient comes in with someone who knows them. I won't be able to treat you properly unless I have an accurate picture of what's going on, and I can't be sure I have that information without this person present. Next time, Alice, no excuses. Do you agree to this?"

"Yes."

Next time. Any solid relief and confidence generated from her self-evaluated competence in the neuropsychological exams evaporated.

"I have the results of all of your tests now, so we can go over everything. I don't see anything abnormal in your MRI. No cerebral vascular disease, no evidence of any small, silent strokes, no hydrocephalus or masses. Everything there looks fine. And your blood work and lumbar puncture all came back negative as well. I was as aggressive here as we can be and looked for every condition that could sensibly account for the kinds of symptoms you're experiencing. So we know you don't have HIV, cancer, a vitamin deficiency, mitochondrial disease, or a number of other rare conditions."

His speech was well constructed, obviously not his first delivery of its kind. The "what she did have" would come at the end. She nodded, letting him know that she followed him and that he should continue.

"You scored in the ninety-ninth percentile in your ability to attend, in things like abstract reasoning, spatial skills, and language fluency. But unfortunately, here's what I do see. You have a recent memory impairment that is out of proportion to your age and is a significant decline in your previous level of functioning. I know this from your own account of the problems you've been having and from your description of the degree to which they've been interfering with your professional life. I also personally witnessed it when you couldn't retrieve the address I'd asked you to remember the last time you were here. And although you were perfect in most of the cognitive domains today, you showed a lot of variability in two of the tasks that were related to recent memory. In fact, you were down to the sixtieth percentile in one.

"When I put all of this information together, Alice, what it tells me is that you fit the criteria of having probable Alzheimer's disease."

Alzheimer's disease.

The words knocked the wind out of her. What exactly did he just tell her? She repeated his words in her head. *Probable.* It gave her the will to inhale, the ability to speak.

"So 'probable' means that I might not fit the criteria."

"No, we use the word 'probable' because the only definitive diagnosis for Alzheimer's right now is by examining the histology of the brain tissue, which requires either an autopsy or a biopsy, neither of which is a good option for you. It's a clinical diagnosis. There's no dementia protein in your blood that can tell us you have it, and we wouldn't expect to see any brain atrophy on an MRI until much later stages in the disease."

Brain atrophy.

"But this can't be possible, I'm only fifty."

"You have early-onset Alzheimer's. You're right, we typically think of Alzheimer's as a disease that affects the elderly, but ten percent of people with Alzheimer's have this early-onset form and are under the age of sixty-five."

"How is that different from the older form?"

"It's not, except that its cause usually has a strong genetic linkage, and it manifests much earlier."

Strong genetic linkage. Anna, Tom, Lydia.

"But if you only know for sure what I don't have, how can you say with any certainty that this is Alzheimer's?"

"After listening to you describe what's been happening

and to your medical history, after testing your orientation, registration, attention, language, and recall, I was ninety-five percent sure. With no other explanation turning up in your neurological exam, blood, cerebral spinal fluid, or MRI, the other five percent goes away. I'm sure, Alice."

Alice.

The sound of her name penetrated her every cell and seemed to scatter her molecules beyond the boundaries of her own skin. She watched herself from the far corner of the room.

"So what does this mean?" she heard herself ask.

"We have a couple of drugs for treating Alzheimer's now that I want to put you on. The first is Aricept. It boosts cholinergic functioning. The second is Namenda. It was just approved this fall and has shown a lot of promise. Neither of these is a cure, but they can slow the progression of symptoms, and we want to buy you as much time as possible."

Time. How much time?

"I also want you to take vitamin E twice a day and vitamin C, baby aspirin, and a statin once a day. You don't show any clear risk factors for cardiovascular disease, but anything that's good for the heart is going to be good for the brain, and we want to preserve every neuron and synapse we can."

He wrote this information down on a prescription pad.

"Alice, does anyone in your family know that you're here?"

"No," she heard herself say.

"Okay, you're going to have to tell someone. We can slow the rate of cognitive decline that you've been experiencing, but we can't stop it or reverse it. It's important to your safety that someone who sees you regularly knows what's going on. Will you tell your husband?"

She saw herself nod.

"Okay, good. Then fill these prescriptions, take everything as directed, call me if you have any problems with side effects, and make an appointment to come back in six months. Between now and then, you can call or email me if you have any questions, and I would also encourage you to contact Denise Daddario. She's the social worker here and can help you with resources and support. I'll see you and your husband together then in six months, and we'll look at how you're doing."

She searched his intelligent eyes for something else. She waited. She became strangely aware of her hands clenching the cold metal arms of the chair she sat in. *Her* hands. She hadn't become an ethereal collection of molecules hovering in the corner of the room. She, Alice Howland, was sitting on a cold, hard chair next to an empty chair in a neurologist's office in the Memory Disorders Unit on the eighth floor of Massachusetts General Hospital. And she'd just been diagnosed with Alzheimer's disease. She searched her doctor's eyes for something else, but could find only truth and regret.

January nineteenth. Nothing good ever happened on that day.

In her office with the door shut, she read through the Activities of Daily Living questionnaire that Dr. Davis had told her to give to John. **This should be filled out by an informant, NOT the patient** was typed in bold at the top of the first page. The word *informant,* the closed door, and her pounding heart all contributed to a feeling of conspicuous guilt, like she was hiding in some Eastern European city, in possession of illegal documents, and the police were on their way, sirens blaring.

The rating scale for each activity ranged from 0 (no problems, same as always) to 3 (severely impaired, totally dependent on others). She scanned down the descriptions next to the 3s and assumed they represented the end stages of this disease, the end of this straight and short road that she'd been suddenly forced onto in a car with no brakes and no steering.

Number 3 was a humiliating list: Must be fed most foods. Has no control over bowel or bladder. Must be given medication by others. Resists efforts of caretaker to clean or groom. No longer works. Home or hospital bound. No longer handles money. No longer goes out unaccompanied. Humiliating, but her analytical mind became instantly skeptical of the actual relevance of this list to her individual outcome. How much of this list was due to the progression of Alzheimer's disease and how much was confounded by the overwhelmingly elderly population it described? Were the eighty-year-olds incontinent because they had Alzheimer's or because they had eighty-year-old bladders? Perhaps these 3s wouldn't apply to someone like her, someone so young and physically fit.

The worst of it came under the heading "Communications." Speech is almost unintelligible. Does not understand what people are saying. Has given up reading. Never writes. *No more language.* Other than misdiagnosis, she couldn't formulate a hypothesis that would render her immune to this list of 3s. It could all apply to someone like her. Someone with Alzheimer's.

She looked at the rows of books and periodicals on her bookcase, the stack of final exams to be corrected on her desk, the emails in her inbox, the red, flashing voice-mail light on her phone. She thought about the books she'd always wanted to read, the ones adorning the top shelf in her bedroom, the ones she figured she'd have time for later. *Moby-Dick.* She had experiments to perform, papers to write, and lectures to give and attend. Everything she did and loved, everything she was, required language.

The last pages of the questionnaire asked the informant to rate the severity of the following symptoms experienced by the patient in the past month: delusions, hallucinations, agitation, depression, anxiety, euphoria, apathy, disinhibition, irritability, repetitive motor disturbances, sleep disruptions, changes in eating. She felt tempted to fill in the answers herself, to demonstrate that she was actually perfectly fine and that Dr. Davis must be wrong. Then she remembered his words: *You may not be the most reliable source of what's been going on.* Maybe, but then she still remembered he'd said that. She wondered when the time would come that she wouldn't.

Her knowledge of Alzheimer's disease admittedly swept the surface only lightly. She knew that the brains of Alzheimer's patients had reduced levels of acetylcholine, a neurotransmitter important in learning and memory. She also knew that the hippocampus, a sea-horse-shaped structure in the brain critical for the formation of new memories, became mired in plaques and tangles, although she didn't really understand what plaques and tangles were exactly. She knew that anomia, a pathological tip of the tongue, was another hallmark symptom. And she knew that someday, she'd look at her husband, her children, her colleagues, faces she'd known and loved forever, and she wouldn't recognize them.

And she knew there was more. There were layers of disturbing filth to uncover. She typed the words "Alzheimer's disease" into Google. Her middle finger was poised over the return key when two jolting knocks caused her to abort the mission with the speed of an involuntary reflex and hide the evidence. Without further warning or waiting for an answer, the door opened.

She feared her face read stunned, anxious, devious.

"Are you ready?" asked John.

No, she wasn't. If she confessed to John what Dr. Davis had told her, if she gave him the Activities of Daily Living questionnaire, it would all become real. John would become the informant, and Alice would become the dying, incompetent patient. She wasn't ready to turn herself in. Not yet.

"Come on, the gates close in an hour," said John.

"Okay," said Alice. "I'm ready."

FOUNDED IN 1831 AS AMERICA'S first nonsectarian garden cemetery, Mount Auburn was now a National Historic Landmark, a world-renowned arboretum and horticultural landscape, and the final resting place for Alice's sister, mother, and father.

This was the first time that her father would be present on the anniversary of that fateful car accident, dead or otherwise, and it irritated her. This had always been a private visit between her and her mother and sister. Now, he would be there, too. He didn't deserve to be.

They walked down Yew Avenue, an older section of the cemetery. Her eyes and pace lingered as they passed the familiar headstones of the Shelton family. Charles and Elizabeth had buried all three of their children—Susie, just a baby, maybe a stillbirth, in 1866; Walter, age two, in 1868; and Carolyn, age five, in 1874. Alice dared to imagine Elizabeth's grief by superimposing her own children's names on the gravestones. She could never hold the macabre images for long—Anna blue and silent at birth; Tom dead, probably following an illness, in his yellow feetie pajamas; and Lydia, rigid and lifeless after a day of coloring in kindergarten. The circuits of her imagination always rejected this sort of gruesome specificity, and all three of her children animated quickly back to the way they were.

Elizabeth was thirty-eight when her last child died. Alice wondered whether she tried to have more children but could no longer conceive, or whether she and Charles started sleeping in separate beds, too scarred to risk the purchase of another tiny headstone. She wondered whether Elizabeth, who lived twenty years longer than Charles, ever found comfort or peace in her life.

They continued in silence to her family's plot. Their gravestones were simple, like granite Brobdingnagian shoe boxes, and stood in a discrete row under the branches of a purple-leaf beech tree. Anne Lydia Daly, 1955–1972; Sarah Louise Daly, 1931–1972; Peter Lucas Daly, 1932–2003. The low-branched beech tree towered at least one hundred feet above them and wore beautiful, glossy deep purplish green leaves in the spring, summer, and fall. But now, in January, its leafless, black branches cast long, distorted shadows on her family's graves, and it looked perfectly creepy. Any horror movie director would love that tree in January.

John held her gloved hand as they stood under the tree. Neither of them spoke. In the warmer months, they'd hear the sounds of birds, sprinklers, grounds crew vehicles, and music from car radios. Today, the cemetery was silent but for the distant tide of traffic beyond the gates.

What did John think about while they stood there? She never asked him. He had never met her mother or sister, so he'd be hard-pressed to entertain thoughts of them for very long. Did he think about his own mortality or spirituality? About hers? Did he think about his parents and sisters, who were all still alive? Or was he in a different place entirely, going over the details of his research or classes or fantasizing about dinner?

How could she possibly have Alzheimer's disease? *Strong genetic linkage.* Would her mother have developed this if she had lived to be fifty? Or was it her father?

When he was younger, he drank obscene volumes of alcohol without ever appearing overtly drunk. He grew increasingly quiet and introverted but always retained enough communication skills to order the next whiskey or to insist that he was okay to drive. Like the night he drove the Buick off Route 93 and into a tree, killing his wife and younger daughter.

His drinking habits never changed, but his demeanor did, probably about fifteen years ago. The nonsensical, belligerent rants, a disgusting lack of hygiene, not knowing who she was—Alice had assumed it was the liquor, finally taking its toll on his pickled liver and marinated mind. Was it possible that he had been living with Alzheimer's disease and was never diagnosed? She didn't need an autopsy. It fit too precisely not to be true, and it provided her with the ideal target to throw her blame.

Well, Dad, are you happy? I've got your lousy DNA. You're going to get to kill us all. How does it feel to murder your entire family?

Her crying, explosive and anguished, would have seemed appropriate to any stranger observing the scene—her dead parents and sister buried in the ground, the darkening graveyard, the eerie beech tree. To John, it must've come completely unexpected. She hadn't shed a single tear over her father's death last February, and the sorrow and loss she felt for her mother and sister had long been tempered by time.

He held her without coaxing her to stop and without hint-ing that he'd do anything but hold her for as long as she cried. She realized the cemetery was closing any minute. She realized she was probably worrying John. She realized no amount of crying would cleanse her contaminated brain. She pressed her face harder into his wool peacoat and cried until she was exhausted.

He held her head in his hands and kissed the wet outside corner of each of her eyes.

"Ali, are you okay?"

I'm not okay, John. I have Alzheimer's disease.

She almost thought she'd said the words aloud, but she hadn't. They remained trapped in her head, but not because they were barricaded by plaques and tangles. She just couldn't say them aloud.

She pictured her own name on a matching headstone next to Anne's. She'd rather die than lose her mind. She looked up at John, his eyes patient, waiting for an answer. How could she tell him she had Alzheimer's disease? He loved her mind. How could he love her with this? She looked back at Anne's name carved in stone.

"I'm just having a really bad day."

She'd rather die than tell him.

SHE WANTED TO KILL HERSELF. Impulsive thoughts of suicide came at her with speed and brawn, outmaneuvering and muscling out all other ideas, trapping her in a dark and desperate corner for days. But they lacked stamina and withered into a flimsy flirtation. She didn't want to die yet. She was still a well-respected professor of psychology at Harvard University. She could still read and write and use the bathroom properly. She had time. And she had to tell John.

She sat on the couch with a gray blanket on her lap, hugging her knees, feeling like she might throw up. He sat on the edge of the wing chair opposite her, his body utterly still.

"Who told you this?" asked John.

"Dr. Davis, he's a neurologist at Mass General."

"A neurologist. When?"

"Ten days ago."

He turned his head and spun his wedding band while he seemed to examine the paint on the wall. She held her breath as she waited for him to look at her again. Maybe he'd never look at her the same way. Maybe she'd never breathe again. She hugged herself a little tighter.

"He's wrong, Ali."

"He's not."

"There's nothing wrong with you."

"Yes, there is. I've been forgetting things."

"Everyone forgets things. I can never remember where I put my glasses. Should this doctor diagnose me with Alzheimer's, too?"

"The kinds of problems I've been having aren't normal. It's not just misplacing glasses."

"All right, so you've been forgetting things, but you're menopausal, you're stressed, and your father's death probably brought back all sorts of feelings around losing your mom and Anne. You're probably depressed."

"I'm not depressed."

"How do you know? Are you a clinician? You should see your own doctor, not this neurologist."

"I did."

"Tell me exactly what she said."

"She didn't think it was depression or menopause. She didn't really have an explanation. She thought I might not be getting enough sleep. She wanted to wait and see me in a couple of months."

"See, you're just not taking care of yourself."

"She's not a neurologist, John. I get plenty of sleep. And that was in November. It's been a couple of months, and it's not getting any better. It's getting worse."

She was asking him to believe in a single conversation what she had denied for months. She started with an example he already knew.

"Remember I didn't go to Chicago?"

"That could happen to me or anyone we know. We have insane schedules."

"We've always had insane schedules, but I've never forgotten to get on a plane. It's not like I just missed my flight, I completely forgot about the conference altogether, and I'd been preparing for it all day."

He waited. There were giant secrets he didn't know about.

"I forget words. I completely forgot the topic of the lecture I was supposed to give in the time it took to walk from my office to class, I can't decipher the intention behind words I write in the morning on my to-do list by the middle of the afternoon."

She could read his unconvinced mind. Overtired, stress, anxiety. Normal, normal, normal.

"I didn't make the pudding on Christmas Eve because I couldn't. I couldn't remember a single step of the recipe. It was just gone, and I've made that dessert from memory every year since I was a kid."

She presented a surprisingly solid case against herself. A jury of her peers might've heard enough. But John loved her.

"I was standing in front of Nini's in Harvard Square and

had absolutely no idea how to get home. I couldn't figure out where I was."

"When was this?"

"September."

She broke his silence, but not his determination to defend the integrity of her mental health.

"That's only some of it. I'm terrified to think about what I'm forgetting that I'm not even aware of."

His expression shifted, as if he identified something potentially meaningful in the Rorschach-like smudges on one of his RNA films.

"Dan's wife." He said it more to himself than to her.

"What?" she asked.

Something cracked. She saw it. The possibility of it seeped in, diluting his conviction.

"I need to do some reading, and then I want to talk to your neurologist."

Without looking at her, he got up and went straight into the study, leaving her alone on the couch, hugging her knees, feeling like she needed to throw up.

FEBRUARY 2004

Friday:
Take your morning medications ✓
Department meeting, 9:00, room 545 ✓
Return emails ✓
Teach Motivation & Emotion Class, 1:00, Science Center, Auditorium B ("Homeostasis and Drives" lecture) ✓
Genetic counselor appointment (John has info)
Take your evening medications

Stephanie Aaron was the genetic counselor affiliated with Mass General Hospital's Memory Disorders Unit. She had shoulder-length black hair and arched eyebrows that suggested a curious openness. She greeted them with a warm smile.

"So, tell me why you're here today," Stephanie said.

"My wife was recently told she has Alzheimer's disease, and we want her screened for the APP, PS1, and PS2 mutations."

John had done his homework. He'd spent the last several weeks buried in literature on the molecular etiology of Alzheimer's. Errant proteins born from any of these three mutated genes were the known villains for the early-onset cases.

"Alice, tell me, what are you hoping to learn from the testing?" Stephanie asked.

"Well, it seems like a reasonable way to try to confirm my diagnosis. Certainly more so than a brain biopsy or an autopsy."

"Are you concerned that your diagnosis might be inaccurate?"

"We think it's a real possibility," said John.

"Okay, first, let's walk through what a positive versus a negative mutation screen would mean for you. These mutations are fully penetrant. If you're mutation positive for APP, PS1, or PS2, I would say that's a solid confirmation of your diagnosis. Things get a bit tricky, though, if your results come back negative. We can't really interpret with any certainty what that would mean. About fifty percent of people with early-onset Alzheimer's don't show a mutation in any of these three genes. This isn't to say that they don't actually have Alzheimer's or that their disease isn't genetically based, it's just that we don't yet know the gene in which their mutation resides."

"Isn't that number more like ten percent for someone her age?" asked John.

"The numbers are a bit more skewed for someone her age, that's true. But if Alice's screen comes back negative, we unfortunately can't say for sure that she doesn't have the disease. She may just happen to fall in the smaller percent of people that age with Alzheimer's who have a mutation in a gene not yet identified."

It was just as plausible, if not more so when coupled with Dr. Davis's medical opinion. Alice knew that John understood this, but his interpretation fit the null hypothesis of "Alice does not have Alzheimer's disease, our lives aren't ruined," whereas Stephanie's did not.

"Alice, does this all make sense to you?" Stephanie asked.

Although the context made the question legitimate, Alice resented it and glimpsed the subtext of conversations in her future. Was she competent enough to understand what was being said? Was she too brain-damaged and confused to consent to this? She'd always been addressed with great respect. If her mental prowess became increasingly replaced with mental illness, what would replace that great respect? Pity? Condescension? Embarrassment?

"Yes," said Alice.

"I also want to make it clear that if your screening comes back with a positive mutation, a genetic diagnosis isn't going to change anything about your treatment or prognosis."

"I understand."

"Good. Let's get some information on your family, then. Alice, are your parents living?"

"No. My mother died in a car accident when she was forty-one, and my father died last year at seventy-one of liver failure."

"How were their memories while they were alive? Did either of them show signs of dementia or personality changes?"

"My mother was perfectly fine. My father was a lifelong

alcoholic. He'd always been a calm man, but he got extremely volatile as he got older, and it became impossible to have a coherent conversation with him. I don't think he recognized me at all for the last several years."

"Was he ever brought in to see a neurologist?"

"No. I'd assumed it was the drinking."

"When would you say these changes began?"

"Around his early fifties."

"He was blind drunk, every day. He died of cirrhosis, not Alzheimer's," said John.

Alice and Stephanie paused and silently agreed to let him think what he wanted and move on.

"Do you have any brothers or sisters?"

"My only sister died in that car accident with my mother when she was sixteen. I don't have any brothers."

"How about aunts, uncles, cousins, grandparents?"

Alice relayed her incomplete knowledge of the health and death histories of her grandparents and other relatives.

"Okay, if you don't have any other questions, a nurse is going to come in and draw a sample of blood. We'll send it off to be sequenced and should have the results within a couple of weeks."

Alice stared out the window as they drove down Storrow Drive. It was frigid outside, already dark at 5:30, and she didn't see anyone braving the elements along the edges of the Charles. No signs of life. John had the stereo turned off. There was nothing to distract her from thoughts of damaged DNA and necrotic brain tissue.

"It's going to be negative, Ali."

"But that wouldn't change anything. It wouldn't mean I don't have it."

"Not technically, but it creates a whole lot more room for thinking this is something else."

"Like what? You talked to Dr. Davis. He already tested me for every cause of dementia you could come up with."

"Look, I think you jumped the gun going to see a neurologist. He looks at your set of symptoms and sees Alzheimer's, but that's what he's trained to see, it doesn't mean he's right. Remember when you hurt your knee last year? If you'd gone to see an orthopedic surgeon, he would've seen a torn ligament or worn cartilage, and he would've wanted to cut you open. He's a surgeon, so he sees surgery as the solution. But you just stopped running for a couple of weeks, you rested it, took ibuprofen, and you were fine.

"I think you're exhausted and stressed, I think the hormonal changes from menopause are wreaking havoc on your physiology, and I think you're depressed. We can handle all of these, Ali, we just have to address each one."

He sounded right. It wasn't likely that someone her age would have Alzheimer's disease. She was menopausal, and she was exhausted. And maybe she was depressed. That would explain why she didn't push back on her diagnosis harder, why she didn't fight to the teeth against even the suggestion of this doomed fate. It certainly wasn't characteristic of her. Maybe she was stressed, tired, menopausal, and depressed. Maybe she didn't have Alzheimer's disease.

Thursday:
7:00, Take your morning medications ✓
Complete Psychonomic review ✓
11:00, meeting with Dan, my office ✓
12:00, Lunch Seminar, room 700 ✓

3:00, Genetic counselor appointment (John has info)
8:00, Take your evening medications

Stephanie was sitting behind her desk when they came in, but this time, she didn't smile.

"Before we talk about your results, is there anything you'd like to review about any of the information we went over last time?" she asked.

"No," said Alice.

"Do you still want the results?"

"Yes."

"I'm sorry to tell you, Alice, you're positive for the PS1 mutation."

Well, there it was, absolute proof, served straight up, no sugar, no salt, no chaser. And it burned all the way down. She could go on a cocktail of estrogen replacement, Xanax, and Prozac and spend the next six months sleeping twelve hours a day at Canyon Ranch, and it wouldn't change a thing. She had Alzheimer's disease. She wanted to look at John, but she couldn't will herself to turn her head.

"As we talked about, this mutation is autosomal dominant; it's associated with certain development of Alzheimer's, so this result fits with the diagnosis you've already received."

"What's the lab's false positive rate? What's the name of the lab?" asked John.

"It's Athena Diagnostics, and they cite a greater than ninety-nine-percent accuracy level of detection for this mutation."

"John, it's positive," said Alice.

She looked at him now. His face, normally angular and determined, appeared slack and unfamiliar to her.

"I'm sorry, I know you were both searching for a way out of this diagnosis."

"What does this mean for our children?" asked Alice.

"Yes, there's a lot to think about there. How old are they?"

"They're all in their twenties."

"So we wouldn't expect any of them to be symptomatic yet. Each of your children has a fifty percent chance of inheriting this mutation, which has a one hundred percent chance of causing the disease. Presymptomatic genetic testing is possible, but there's a lot to consider. Is this something they'll want to live with knowing? How would it change their lives? What if one of them is positive and one is negative, how will that affect their relationship with each other? Alice, do they even know about your diagnosis?"

"No."

"You might want to think about telling them soon. I know it's a lot to unload all at once, especially since I know you're both still absorbing it yourselves. But with a progressive illness like this, you can lay out plans to tell them later, but then you may not be able to in the way you originally wanted. Or maybe this is something you're going to leave to John to do?"

"No, we'll tell them," said Alice.

"Do any of your children have children?"

Anna and Charlie.

"Not yet," said Alice.

"If they're planning to, this might be really important information for them to have. Here's some written information I gathered that you can give them if you want. Also, here's my card and the card of a therapist who's wonderful with talking to families who've gone through genetic screening and diagnosis. Are there any other questions that I can answer for you now?"

"No, none that I can think of."

"I'm sorry I couldn't give you the results you were hoping for."

"Me, too."

Neither of them spoke. They got in the car, John paid the garage attendant, and they made their way onto Storrow Drive in silence. For the second week in a row, temperatures were well below zero with the windchill. Runners were forced indoors to either jog on treadmills or simply wait for slightly more habitable weather. Alice hated treadmills. She sat in the passenger seat and waited for John to say something. But he didn't. He cried the whole way home.

MARCH 2004

Alice popped open the Monday lid of her plastic days-of-the-week pill dispenser and poured the seven little tablets into her cupped hand. John marched into the kitchen with purpose, but seeing what she held, he spun on his heels and left the room, as if he'd walked in on his mother naked. He refused to watch her take her medications. He could be midsentence, midconversation, but if she got out her plastic days-of-the-week pill dispenser, he left the room. Conversation over.

She swallowed the pills with three gulps of very hot tea and burned her throat. The experience wasn't exactly pleasant for her either. She sat down at the kitchen table, blew on her tea, and listened to John stomping through the bedroom above her.

"What are you looking for?" she yelled.

"Nothing," he hollered.

Probably his glasses. In the month since their visit to the genetic counselor, he'd stopped asking her for help finding his glasses and keys, even though she knew he still struggled to keep track of them.

He entered the kitchen with quick, impatient steps.

"Can I help?" she asked.

"No, I'm good."

She wondered about the source of this newfound stubborn independence. Was he trying to spare her the mental burden of tracking his own misplaced things? Was he practicing for his future without her? Was he just too embarrassed to ask for help from an Alzheimer's patient? She sipped her tea, engrossed in a painting of an apple and a pear that had been on the wall for at least a decade, and listened to him sift through the mail and papers on the counter behind her.

He walked past her into the front hallway. She heard the hall closet door open. She heard the hall closet door shut. She heard the drawers in the hall table open and close.

"You ready?" he called.

She finished her tea and met him in the hallway. He had his coat on, glasses perched on his ruffled hair, and his keys in his hand.

"Yes," said Alice, and she followed him outside.

The beginning of spring in Cambridge was an untrustworthy and ugly liar. There were no buds yet on the trees, no tulips brave or stupid enough to have emerged through the now month-old layer of crusted snow, and no spring peeper audio track playing in the background. The streets remained narrowed by blackened, polluted snowbanks. Any melting that occurred during the relative warmth of midday froze with the plummeting temperatures of late afternoon, turning the paths in Harvard Yard and the sidewalks of the city into treacherous lanes of black ice. The date on the calendar only made everyone feel offended or cheated, aware that it was already spring elsewhere, and there people wore short-sleeve shirts and awoke to the sounds of robins chirping. Here, the cold and misery showed no signs of relenting, and the only birds Alice heard as they walked to campus were crows.

John had agreed to walk with her to Harvard every morning. She'd told him she didn't want to risk getting lost. In truth, she simply wanted that time back with him, to rekindle their former morning tradition. Unfortunately, having deemed the risk of being run over by a car less than that of being injured from slipping on the icy sidewalks, they walked single file in the street, and they didn't talk.

Gravel kicked up into her right boot. She debated whether to stop in the road to empty it out or wait until they reached Jerri's. To empty it, she'd have to balance in the road on one foot while exposing the other to the frigid air. She decided to endure the discomfort for the remaining two blocks.

Located on Mass Ave about halfway between Porter and Harvard squares, Jerri's had become a Cambridge institution for the chronically caffeinated long before the invasion of Starbucks. The menu of coffee, tea, pastries, and sandwiches written in chalk capital lettering on the board behind the counter had remained unaltered since Alice's graduate student days. Only the prices next to the items showed signs of recent attention, outlined with chalk dust in the shape of a rectangular school eraser and printed in a penmanship belonging to someone other than the author of the offerings to their left. Alice studied the board, perplexed.

"Good morning, Jess, a coffee and a cinnamon scone, please," said John.

"I'll have the same," said Alice.

"You don't like coffee," said John.

"Yes, I do."

"No, you don't. She'll have a tea with lemon."

"I want a coffee and a scone."

Jess looked to John to see if there would be a return, but the volley was dead.

"Okay, two coffees and two scones," said Jess.

Outside, Alice took a sip. It tasted acrid and unpleasant and poorly reflected its delicious smell.

"So how's your coffee?" asked John.

"Wonderful."

As they walked to campus, Alice drank the coffee she hated to spite him. She couldn't wait to be alone in her office, where she could throw away what was left of the wretched beverage. Plus, she desperately wanted to empty the gravel out of her boot.

BOOTS OFF AND COFFEE IN the trash, she tackled her inbox first. She opened an email from Anna.

Hi Mom,

We'd love to go to dinner, but this week is kind of tough with Charlie's trial. How about next week? What days are good for you and Dad? We're free any night but Thursday and Friday.

Anna

She stared down the tauntingly ready, blinking cursor on her computer screen and tried to imagine the words she wanted to use in her reply. The conversion of her thoughts to voice, pen, or computer keys often required conscious effort and calm coaxing. And she held little confidence in the spelling of words she'd long ago been rewarded for her mastery of with gold stars and teachers' praise.

The phone rang.

"Hi, Mom."

"Oh good, I was just about to return your email."

"I didn't send you an email."

Unsure of herself, Alice reread the message on her screen.

"I just read it. Charlie has a trial this week—"

"Mom, this is Lydia."

"Oh, what are you doing up so early?"

"I'm always up now. I wanted to call you and Dad last night, but it was too late your time. I just got an incredible part in a play called *The Memory of Water.* It's with this phenomenal director, and it's going up for six shows in May. I think it's going to be really good, and with this director it should get a lot of attention. I was hoping maybe you and Dad could come out to see me in it?"

Cued by the hanging rise in her inflection and the silence that followed, Alice knew it was her turn to speak but was still catching up to all that Lydia had just said. Without the aid of the visual cues of the person she talked to, conversations on the phone often baffled her. Words sometimes ran together, abrupt changes in topic were difficult for her to anticipate and follow, and her comprehension suffered. Although writing presented its own set of problems, she could keep them hidden from discovery because she wasn't restricted to real-time responding.

"If you don't want to, you can just say it," said Lydia.

"No, I do, but—"

"Or you're too busy, whatever. I knew I should've called Dad."

"Lydia—"

"Never mind, I gotta go."

She hung up. Alice had been about to say that she needed to check with John, that if he could break away from the lab, she'd love to come. If he couldn't go, however, she wouldn't fly across the country without him, and she'd have to make up some excuse. Fearful of getting lost or confused far from home, she'd been avoiding travel. She'd declined an offer to speak at Duke University next month and thrown out the registration material for a language conference she'd attended every year since she was a graduate student. She wanted to see Lydia's play, but this time, her attendance would be at the mercy of John's availability.

She held the phone, thinking about trying to call Lydia back. She hung up, thinking better of it. She closed her unwritten reply to Anna and opened a new email to send to Lydia. She stared at the blinking cursor, her fingers frozen on the keyboard. The battery in her brain was running low today.

"Come on," she urged, wishing she could attach a couple of jumper cables to her head and give herself a good, strong zap.

She didn't have time for Alzheimer's today. She had emails to return, a grant proposal to write, a class to teach, and a seminar to attend. And at the end of the day, a run. Maybe a run would give her some clarity.

ALICE TUCKED A PIECE OF paper with her name, address, and phone number in her sock. Of course, if she became so confused that she didn't know her way home, she might not have the presence of mind to remember that she carried this piece of helpful information on her person. But it was a precaution she took anyway.

Running was becoming less and less effective at clearing her thoughts. In fact, these days, she felt more like she was physically chasing down the answers to an interminable stream of runaway questions. And no matter how hard she kicked, she could never catch them.

What should I be doing? She took her medications, slept for six to seven hours a night, and clung to the normalcy of day-to-day life at Harvard. She felt like a fraud, posing as a Harvard professor without a progressive neurodegenerative disease, working every day as if everything were just fine and would continue that way.

There weren't a lot of metrics for performance or day-to-day accountability in the life of a professor. She didn't have books to balance, a certain quota of widgets to make, or written reports to hand in. There was room for error, but how much? Ultimately, her functioning would deteriorate to a level that would be noticed and not tolerated. She wanted to leave Harvard before then, before the gossip and pity, but had no way of even guessing when that would be.

And although the thought of staying on too long terrified her, the thought of leaving Harvard terrified her much, much more. Who was she if she wasn't a Harvard psychology professor?

Should she try to spend as much time as possible with John and her children? What would that mean practically? Sit with Anna while she typed her briefs, shadow Tom on his rounds, observe Lydia in acting class? How was she supposed to tell them that they each had a 50 percent chance of going through this? What if they blamed and hated her like she blamed and hated her father?

It was too soon for John to retire. How much time could he realistically take off without killing his own career? How much time did she have? Two years? Twenty?

Although Alzheimer's tended to progress more quickly in the early-onset versus late-onset form, people with early-onset usually lived with the disease for many years longer, this disease of the mind residing in relatively young and healthy bodies. She could stick around all the way to the brutal end. She'd be unable to feed herself, unable to talk, unable to recognize John and her children. She'd be curled up in the fetal position, and because she'd forget how to swallow, she'd develop pneumonia. And John, Anna, Tom, and Lydia would agree not to treat it with a simple course of antibiotics, riddled with guilt over feeling grateful that something had finally come along that would kill her body.

She stopped running, bent over, and threw up the lasagna she'd eaten for lunch. It would be several more weeks before the snow melted enough to wash it away.

SHE KNEW EXACTLY WHERE SHE was. She was on her way home, in front of the All Saints' Episcopal Church, only a few blocks from her house. She knew exactly where she was but had never felt more lost in her life. The bells of the church began to chime to a tune that reminded her of her grandparents' clock. She turned the round, iron knob on the tomato red door and followed her impulse inside.

She was relieved to find no one there, because she hadn't

formulated a coherent story as to why she was. Her mother was Jewish, but her father had insisted that she and Anne be raised Catholic. So she went to mass every Sunday as a child, received communion, went to confession, and was confirmed, but because her mother never participated in any of this, Alice began questioning the validity of these beliefs at a young age. And without a satisfying answer from either her father or the Catholic Church, she never developed a true faith.

Light from the streetlamps outside streamed in through the Gothic stained-glass windows and provided almost enough illumination for her to see the entire church. In each of the stained-glass windows, Jesus, clad in robes of red and white, was pictured as a shepherd or a healer performing a miracle. A banner to the right of the altar read GOD IS OUR REFUGE AND STRENGTH, A VERY PRESENT HELP IN TROUBLE.

She couldn't be in more trouble and wanted so much to ask for help. But she felt like a trespasser, undeserving, unfaithful. Who was she to ask for help from a God she wasn't sure she believed in, in a church she knew nothing about?

She closed her eyes, listened to the calming, oceanlike waves of distant traffic, and tried to open her mind. She couldn't say how long she sat in the velvet-cushioned pew in that cold, darkened church, waiting for an answer. It didn't come. She stayed longer, hoping a priest or parishioner would wander in and ask her why she was there. Now, she had her explanation. But no one came.

She thought about the business cards she'd been given from Dr. Davis and Stephanie Aaron. Maybe she should talk to the social worker or a therapist. Maybe they could help her.

Then, with complete and simple lucidity, the answer came to her.

Talk to John.

SHE FOUND HERSELF UNARMED FOR the attack she faced when she walked through the front door.

"Where have you been?" asked John.

"I went for a run."

"You've been running, this whole time?"

"I also went to church."

"Church? I can't take this, Ali. Look, you don't drink coffee, and you don't go to church."

She smelled the booze on his breath.

"Well, I did today."

"We were supposed to have dinner with Bob and Sarah. I had to call and cancel, didn't you remember?"

Dinner with their friends Bob and Sarah. It was on her calendar.

"I forgot. I have Alzheimer's."

"I had absolutely no idea where you were, if you were lost. You have to start carrying your cell phone with you at all times."

"I can't bring it with me when I run, I don't have any pockets."

"Then duct tape it to your head, I don't care, I'm not going through this every time you forget you're supposed to show up somewhere."

She followed him into the living room. He sat down on the couch, held his drink in his hand, and wouldn't look up at her. The beads of sweat on his forehead matched those on his sweaty glass of scotch. She hesitated, then sat on his lap, hugged him hard around his shoulders with her hands touching her own elbows, her ear against his, and let it all out.

"I'm so sorry I have this. I can't stand the thought of how much worse this is going to get. I can't stand the thought of looking at you someday, this face I love, and not knowing who you are."

She traced the outline of his jaw and chin and the creases of his sorely out of practice laugh lines with her hands. She wiped the sweat from his forehead and the tears from his eyes.

"I can barely breathe when I think about it. But we have to think about it. I don't know how much longer I have to know you. We need to talk about what's going to happen."

He tipped his glass back, swallowed until there was nothing left, and then sucked a little more from the ice. Then he looked at her with a scared and profound sorrow in his eyes that she'd never seen there before.

"I don't know if I can."

APRIL 2004

As smart as they were, they couldn't cobble together a definitive, long-term plan. There were too many unknowns to simply solve for *x*, the most crucial of those being, How fast will this progress? They'd taken a year's sabbatical together six years ago to write *From Molecules to Mind,* and so they were each a year away from being eligible for taking another. Could she make it that long? So far, they'd decided that she'd finish out the semester, avoid travel whenever possible, and they'd spend the entire summer at the Cape. They could only imagine as far as August.

And they agreed to tell no one yet, except for their children. That unavoidable disclosure, the conversation they had agonized over the most, would unfold that very morning over bagels, fruit salad, Mexican frittata, mimosas, and chocolate eggs.

They hadn't all been together for Easter in a number of years. Anna sometimes spent that weekend with Charlie's family in Pennsylvania, Lydia had stayed in L.A. the last several years and was somewhere in Europe before that, and John had attended a conference in Boulder a few years back. It had taken some work to persuade Lydia to come home this year. In the middle of rehearsals for her play, she'd claimed she couldn't afford the interruption or the flight, but John had convinced her that she could spare two days and paid for her airfare.

Anna declined a mimosa and a Bloody Mary and instead washed down the caramel eggs she'd been eating like popcorn with a glass of iced water. But before anyone could harbor suspicions of pregnancy, she launched into the details of her impending intrauterine insemination procedure.

"We saw a fertility specialist over at the Brigham, and he can't figure it out. My eggs are healthy, and I'm ovulating each month, and Charlie's sperm are fine."

"Anna, really, I don't think they want to hear about my sperm," said Charlie.

"Well, it's true, and it's so frustrating. I even tried acupuncture, and nothing. Except my migraines are gone. So at least we know that I should be able to get pregnant. I start FSH injections on Tuesday, and next week I inject myself with something that will release my eggs, and then they'll inseminate me with Charlie's sperm."

"Anna," said Charlie.

"Well, they will, and so hopefully, I'll be pregnant next week!"

Alice forced a supportive smile, caging her dread behind her clenched teeth. The symptoms of Alzheimer's disease didn't manifest until after the reproductive years, after the deformed gene had unwittingly been passed on to the next generation. What if she'd known that she carried this gene, this fate, in every cell of her body? Would she have conceived these children or taken precautions to prevent them? Would she have been willing to risk the random roll of meiosis? Her amber eyes, John's aquiline nose, and her presenilin-1. Of course, now, she couldn't imagine her life without them. But before she had children, before the experience of that primal and previously inconceivable kind of love that came with them, would she have decided it would be better for everyone not to? Would Anna?

Tom walked in, with apologies for being late and without his new girlfriend. It was just as well. Today should be just the family. And Alice couldn't remember her name. He made a beeline for the dining room, likely worried that he'd missed out on the food, then returned to the living room with a grin on his face and a plate heaping with some of everything. He sat on the couch next to Lydia, who had her script in her hand and her eyes closed, silently mouthing her lines. They were all there. It was time.

"Your dad and I have something important we need to talk to you about, and we wanted to wait until we had all three of you together."

She looked to John. He nodded and squeezed her hand.

"I've been experiencing some difficulties with my memory for some time now, and in January, I was diagnosed with early-onset Alzheimer's disease."

The clock on the fireplace mantel ticked loudly, like someone had turned its volume up, the way it sounded when no one else was in the house. Tom sat frozen with a forkful of frittata midway between his plate and mouth. She should have waited until he'd finished eating his brunch.

"Are they sure it's Alzheimer's? Did you get a second opinion?" he asked.

"She had genetic screening. She has the presenilin-1 mutation," said John.

"Is it autosomal dominant?" asked Tom.

"Yes."

He said more to Tom, but only with his eyes.

"What does that mean? Dad, what did you just tell him?" Anna asked.

"It means we have a fifty percent chance of getting Alzheimer's disease," said Tom.

"What about my baby?"

"You're not even pregnant," said Lydia.

"Anna, if you have the mutation, it's the same for your children. Each child you have would have a fifty percent chance of inheriting it, too," said Alice.

"So what do we do? Do we go get tested?" asked Anna.

"You can," said Alice.

"Oh my god, what if I have it? And then my baby could have it," said Anna.

"There'll probably be a cure by the time any of our kids would need it," said Tom.

"But not in time for us, is that what you're saying? So my kids will be fine, but I'll be a mindless zombie?"

"Anna, that's enough!" John snapped.

His jaw clenched, and his face flushed. A decade ago, he would've sent Anna to her room. Instead, he gave Alice's hand a hard squeeze and jiggled his leg. In so many ways, he'd become powerless.

"Sorry," said Anna.

"It's very likely that there'll be a preventative treatment by the time you're my age. That's one of the reasons to know if you have the mutation. If you do, you might be able to go on a medication well before you're symptomatic and, hopefully, you never will be," said Alice.

"Mom, what kind of treatment do they have now, for you?" asked Lydia.

"Well, they have me on antioxidant vitamins and aspirin, a statin, and two neurotransmitter drugs."

"Are those going to keep the Alzheimer's from getting any worse?" asked Lydia.

"Maybe, for a little while, they don't really know for sure."

"What about what's in clinical trials?" asked Tom.

"I'm looking into that now," said John.

John had begun talking to clinicians and scientists in Boston who researched the molecular etiology of Alzheimer's, getting their perspectives on the relative promise of the therapies in the clinical pipeline. John was a cancer cell biologist, not a neuroscientist, but it wasn't a huge leap for him to understand the cast of molecular criminals run amok in another system. They all spoke the same language—receptor binding, phosphorylation, transcriptional regulation, clathrin-coated pits, secretases. Like owning a membership card to the most exclusive club, being from Harvard gave him instant credibility with and access to the most respected thought leaders in Boston's Alzheimer's research community. If a better treatment existed or might exist soon, John would find it for her.

"But Mom, you seem perfectly fine. You must've caught this really early on, I wouldn't even know anything was wrong," said Tom.

"I knew," said Lydia. "Not that she had Alzheimer's, but that something was wrong."

"How?" asked Anna.

"Like sometimes she doesn't make any sense on the phone, and she repeats herself a lot. Or she doesn't remember something I said five minutes ago. And she didn't remember how to make the pudding at Christmas."

"How long have you noticed this?" asked John.

"At least a year now."

Alice couldn't trace it quite that far back herself, but she believed her. And she sensed John's humiliation.

"I have to know if I have this. I want to get tested. Don't you guys want to get tested?" asked Anna.

"I think living with the anxiety of not knowing would be worse for me than knowing, even if I have it," said Tom.

Lydia closed her eyes. Everyone waited. Alice entertained the absurd idea that she had either resumed memorizing her lines or fallen asleep. After an uncomfortable silence, she opened her eyes and took her turn.

"I don't want to know."

Lydia always did things differently.

IT WAS ODDLY QUIET IN William James Hall. The usual chatter of students in the hallways—asking, arguing, joking, complaining, bragging, flirting—was missing. Spring Reading Period typically precipitated the sudden sequestering of students from the campus at large into dormitory rooms and library cubicles, but that didn't begin for another week. Many of the cognitive psychology students were scheduled to spend an entire day observing functional MRI studies in Charlestown. Maybe that was today.

Whatever the reason, Alice relished the opportunity to get a lot of work done without interruption. She had opted not to stop at Jerri's for tea on the way to her office and wished now that she had. She could use the caffeine. She read through the articles in the current *Linguistics Journal,* she put together this year's version of the final exam for her motivation and emotion class, and she answered all previously neglected emails. All without the phone ringing or a knock on the door.

She was home before she realized that she'd forgotten to go to Jerri's. She still wanted that tea. She walked into the kitchen and put the kettle on the stove. The microwave clock read 4:22 a.m.

She looked out the window. She saw darkness and her reflection in the glass. She was wearing her nightgown.

Hi Mom,

The IUI didn't work. I'm not pregnant. I'm not as upset as I thought I'd be (and Charlie seems almost relieved). Let's hope my other test comes back negative as well. Our appointment for that is tomorrow. Tom and I will come over after and let you and Dad know the results.

Love,

Anna

THE ODDS OF THEM BOTH being negative for the mutation descended from unlikely to remote when they still weren't home an hour after Alice had anticipated their arrival. If they were both negative, it would have been a quick appointment, a "you're both fine," "thank you very much," and out-the-door appointment. Maybe Stephanie was just running late today. Maybe Anna and Tom had sat in the waiting room much longer than Alice had allowed for in her mind.

The odds crashed from remote to infinitesimal when they finally walked through the front door. If they were both negative, they would have just blurted it out or it would have sprung, wild and jubilant, from their facial expressions. Instead, they muscled what they knew beneath the surface as they moved into the living room, stretching out the time of Life Before This Happened as long as possible, the time before they'd have to unleash the hideous information they so obviously held.

They sat side by side on the couch, Tom on the left and Anna on the right, like they had in the backseat of the car when they were kids. Tom was a lefty and liked the window, and Anna didn't mind the middle. They sat closer now than they ever did then, and when Tom reached over and held her hand, she didn't shriek, "Mommm, Tommy's touching me!"

"I don't have the mutation," said Tom.

"But I do," said Anna.

After Tom was born, Alice remembered feeling so blessed, that she had the ideal—one of each. It took twenty-six years for that blessing to deform into a curse. Alice's facade of stoic parental strength crumbled, and she started to cry.

"I'm sorry," she said.

"It's going to be okay, Mom. Like you said, they're going to find a preventative treatment," said Anna.

When Alice thought about it later, the irony was striking. Outwardly, at least, Anna appeared to be the strongest. She did most of the consoling. And yet, it didn't surprise her. Anna was the child who most mirrored their mother. She had Alice's hair, coloring, and temperament. And her mother's presenilin-1.

"I'm going to go ahead with the in vitro. I already talked with my doctor, and they're going to do a preimplantation genetic diagnosis on the embryos. They're going to test a single cell from each of the embryos for the mutation and only implant ones that are mutation-free. So we'll know for sure that my kids won't ever get this."

It was a solid piece of good news. But while everyone else continued to savor it, the taste turned slightly bitter for Alice. Despite her self-reproach, she envied Anna, that she could do what Alice couldn't—keep her children safe from harm. Anna would never have to sit opposite her daughter, her firstborn, and watch her struggle to comprehend the news that she would someday develop Alzheimer's. She wished that these kinds of advances in reproductive medicine had been available to her. But then the embryo that had developed into Anna would've been discarded.

According to Stephanie Aaron, Tom was okay, but he didn't look it. He looked pale, shaken, fragile. Alice had imagined that a negative result for any of them would be a relief, clean and simple. But they were a family, yoked by history and DNA and love. Anna was his older sister. She'd taught him how to snap and blow gum bubbles, and she always gave him her Halloween candy.

"Who's going to tell Lydia?" asked Tom.

"I will," said Anna.

MAY 2004

Alice first thought of peeking inside the week after she was diagnosed, but she didn't. Fortune cookies, horoscopes, tarot cards, and assisted living homes couldn't tempt her interest. Although closer to it every day, she was in no hurry to glimpse her future. Nothing in particular happened that morning to fuel her curiosity or the courage to go have a look inside the Mount Auburn Manor Nursing Center. But today, she did.

The lobby did nothing to intimidate her. An ocean scene watercolor hung on the wall, a faded Oriental carpet lay on the floor, and a woman with heavily made up eyes and short, licorice black hair sat behind a desk angled toward the front door. The lobby could almost be mistaken for that of a hotel, but the slight medicinal smell and the lack of luggage, concierge, and general coming and going weren't right. The people staying here were residents, not guests.

"Can I help you?" the woman asked.

"Um, yes. Do you care for Alzheimer's patients here?"

"Yes, we have a unit specifically dedicated to patients with Alzheimer's. Would you like to have a look at it?"

"Yes."

She followed the woman to the elevators.

"Are you looking for a parent?"

"I am," Alice lied.

They waited. Like most of the people they ferried, the elevators were old and slow to respond.

"That's a lovely necklace," said the woman.

"Thank you."

Alice placed her fingers on the top of her sternum and rubbed the blue paste stones on the wings of her mother's art nouveau butterfly necklace. Her mother used to wear it only on her anniversary and to weddings, and like her, Alice had reserved it exclusively for special occasions. But there weren't any formal affairs on her calendar, and she loved that necklace, so she'd tried it on one day last month while wearing a pair of jeans and a T-shirt. It had looked perfect.

Plus, she liked being reminded of butterflies. She remembered being six or seven and crying over the fates of the butterflies in her yard after learning that they lived for only a few days. Her mother had comforted her and told her not to be sad for the butterflies, that just because their lives were short didn't mean they were tragic. Watching them flying in the warm sun among the daisies in their garden, her mother had said to her, *See, they have a beautiful life.* Alice liked remembering that.

They exited onto the third floor and walked down a long, carpeted hallway through a set of unmarked double doors and stopped. The woman gestured back to the doors as they shut automatically behind them.

"The Alzheimer's Special Care Unit is locked, meaning you can't go beyond these doors without knowing the code."

Alice looked at the keypad on the wall next to the door. The numbers were arranged individually upside down and ordered backward from right to left.

"Why are the numbers like that?"

"Oh, that's to prevent the residents from learning and memorizing the code."

It seemed like an unnecessary precaution. *If they could remember the code, they wouldn't need to be here, would they?*

"I don't know if you've experienced this yet with your parent, but wandering and nighttime restlessness are very common behaviors with Alzheimer's. Our unit allows the residents to wander about at any time, but safely and without the risk of getting lost. We don't tranquilize them at night or restrict them to their rooms. We try to help them maintain as much freedom and independence as possible. It's something we know is important to them and to their families."

A small, white-haired woman in a pink and green floral housecoat confronted Alice.

"You're not my daughter."

"No, sorry, I'm not."

"Give me back my money!"

"She didn't take your money, Evelyn. Your money's in your room. Check your top dresser drawer, I think you put it there."

The woman eyed Alice with suspicion and disgust, but then followed the advice of authority and shuffled in her dirty white terry-cloth slippers back into her room.

"She has a twenty-dollar bill she keeps hiding because she's worried someone will steal it. Then, of course, she forgets where she put it and accuses everyone of taking it. We've tried to get her to spend it or put it in the bank, but she won't. At some point, she'll forget she owns it, and that'll be the end of it."

Safe from Evelyn's paranoid investigation, they proceeded unimpeded to a common room at the end of the hallway. The room was populated with elderly people eating lunch at round tables. Upon taking a closer look, Alice realized that the room was filled with elderly women.

"There are only three men?"

"Actually, only two out of the thirty-two residents are men. Harold comes every day to eat meals with his wife."

Perhaps reverting to the cootie rules of childhood, the two men with Alzheimer's disease sat together at their own table, apart from the women. Walkers crowded the spaces between the tables. Many of the women sat in wheelchairs. Most everyone had thinning white hair and sunken eyes magnified behind thick glasses, and they all ate in slow motion. There was no socializing, no conversation, not even between Harold and his wife. The only sounds other than the noises of eating came from a woman who sang while she ate, her internal needle skipping on the title line of "By the Light of the Silvery Moon" over and over. No one protested or applauded.

By the light of the silvery moon.

"As you might've guessed, this is our dining and activities room. Residents have breakfast, lunch, and dinner here at the same times every day. Predictable routines are important. Activities are here as well. There's bowling and beanbag toss, trivia, dancing and music, and crafts. They made these adorable birdhouses this morning. And we have someone read the newspaper to them every day to keep them up on current events."

By the light

"There's plenty of opportunity for our residents to keep their bodies and minds as engaged and enriched as possible."

of the silvery moon.

"And family members and friends are always welcome to come and participate in any of the activities and can join their loved one for any of the meals."

Aside from Harold, Alice saw no other loved ones. No other husbands, no wives, no children or grandchildren, no friends.

"We also have a highly trained medical staff should any of our residents require additional care."

By the light of the silvery moon.

"Do you have any residents here under the age of sixty?"

"Oh no, the youngest is I think seventy. The average age is about eighty-two, eighty-three. It's rare to see someone with Alzheimer's younger than sixty."

You're looking at one right now, lady.

By the light of the silvery moon.

"How much does all of this cost?"

"I can give you a packet of information on the way out, but

as of January, the Alzheimer's Special Care Unit rate runs at two hundred eighty-five dollars a day."

Alice did the rough math in her head. About a hundred thousand dollars a year. Multiply that by five, ten, twenty years.

"Can I answer anything else for you?"

By the light.

"No, thanks."

She followed her tour guide back to the locked double doors and watched her type in the code.

0791925

She didn't belong here.

IT WAS THE RAREST OF days in Cambridge, the kind of mythical day that New Englanders dreamed about but each year came to doubt the true existence of—a sunny, seventy-degree spring day. A Crayola blue sky, finally-don't-need-a-coat spring day. A day not to be wasted sitting in an office, especially if you had Alzheimer's.

She deviated a couple of blocks southeast of the Yard and walked into Ben & Jerry's with the giddy thrill of a teenager playing hooky.

"I'll have a triple-scoop Peanut Butter Cup in a cone, please."

Hell, I'm on Lipitor.

She beheld her giant, heavy cone as if it were an Oscar, paid with a five-dollar bill, dropped the change in the Tips for College jar, and continued on toward the Charles River.

She'd converted to frozen yogurt, a supposedly healthier alternative, many years ago and had forgotten how thick and creamy and purely enjoyable ice cream was. She thought about what she had just seen at the Mount Auburn Manor Nursing Center as she licked and walked. She needed a better plan, one that didn't include her playing beanbag toss with Evelyn in the Alzheimer's Special Care Unit. One that didn't cost John a fortune to keep alive and safe a woman who no longer recognized him and who, in the most important ways, he didn't recognize either. She didn't want to be here at that point, when the burdens, both emotional and financial, grossly outweighed any benefit of sticking around.

She was making mistakes and struggling to compensate for them, but she felt sure that her IQ still fell at least a standard deviation above the mean. And people with average IQs didn't kill themselves. Well, some did, but not for reasons having to do with IQ.

Despite the escalating erosion of her memory, her brain still served her well in countless ways. For example, at this very moment, she ate her ice cream without dripping any of it onto the cone or her hand by using a lick-and-turn technique that had become automatic to her as a child and was probably stored somewhere near the information for how to ride a bike and how to tie a shoe. Meanwhile, she stepped off the curb and crossed the street, her motor cortex and cerebellum solving the complex mathematical equations necessary to move her body to the other side without falling over or getting hit by a passing car. She recognized the sweet smell of narcissus and a brief waft of curry emanating from the Indian restaurant on the corner. With each lick, she savored the delicious tastes of chocolate and peanut butter, demonstrating the intact activation of her brain's pleasure pathways, the same ones required for enjoying sex or a good bottle of wine.

But at some point, she would forget how to eat an ice-cream cone, how to tie her shoe, and how to walk. At some point, her pleasure neurons would become corrupted by an onslaught of aggregating amyloid, and she'd no longer be capable of enjoying the things she loved. At some point, there would simply be no point.

She wished she had cancer instead. She'd trade Alzheimer's for cancer in a heartbeat. She felt ashamed for wishing this, and it was certainly a pointless bargaining, but she permitted the fantasy anyway. With cancer, she'd have something that she could fight. There was surgery, radiation, and chemotherapy. There was the chance that she could win. Her family and the community at Harvard would rally behind her battle and consider it noble. And even if defeated in the end, she'd be able to look them knowingly in the eye and say good-bye before she left.

Alzheimer's disease was an entirely different kind of beast. There were no weapons that could slay it. Taking Aricept and Namenda felt like aiming a couple of leaky squirt guns in the face of a blazing fire. John continued to probe into the drugs in clinical development, but she doubted that any of them were ready and capable of making a significant difference for her, else he would already have been on the phone with Dr. Davis, insisting on a way to get her on them. Right now, everyone with Alzheimer's faced the same outcome, whether they were eighty-two or fifty, resident of the Mount Auburn Manor or full professor of psychology at Harvard University. The blazing fire consumed all. No one got out alive.

And while a bald head and a looped ribbon were seen as

badges of courage and hope, her reluctant vocabulary and vanishing memories advertised mental instability and impending insanity. Those with cancer could expect to be supported by their community. Alice expected to be outcast. Even the well-intentioned and educated tended to keep a fearful distance from the mentally ill. She didn't want to become someone people avoided and feared.

Accepting the fact that she did indeed have Alzheimer's, that she could only bank on two unacceptably effective drugs available to treat it, and that she couldn't trade any of this in for some other, curable disease, what did she want? Assuming the in vitro procedure worked, she wanted to live to hold Anna's baby and know it was her grandchild. She wanted to see Lydia act in something she was proud of. She wanted to see Tom fall in love. She wanted one more sabbatical year with John. She wanted to read every book she could before she could no longer read.

She laughed a little, surprised at what she'd just revealed to herself. Nowhere in that list was there anything about linguistics, teaching, or Harvard. She ate her last bite of cone. She wanted more sunny, seventy-degree days and ice-cream cones.

And when the burden of her disease exceeded the pleasure of that ice cream, she wanted to die. But would she quite literally have the presence of mind to recognize it when those curves crossed? She worried that the future her would be incapable of remembering and executing this kind of plan. Asking John or any of her children to assist her with this in any way was not an option. She'd never put any of them in that position.

She needed a plan that committed the future her to a suicide she arranged for now. She needed to create a simple test, one that she could self-administer every day. She thought about the questions Dr. Davis and the neuropsychologist had asked her, the ones she already couldn't answer last December. She thought about what she still wanted. Intellectual brilliance wasn't required for any of them. She was willing to go on living with some serious holes in short-term memory.

She removed her BlackBerry from her baby blue Anna William bag, a birthday gift from Lydia. She wore it every day, slung over her left shoulder, resting on her right hip. It had become an indispensable accessory, like her platinum wedding ring and running watch. It looked great with her butterfly necklace. It contained her cell phone, her BlackBerry, and her keys. She took it off only to sleep.

She typed:

Alice, answer the following questions:

1. What month is it?
2. Where do you live?
3. Where is your office?
4. When is Anna's birthday?
5. How many children do you have?

If you have trouble answering any of these, go to the file named "Butterfly" on your computer and follow the instructions there immediately.

She set the alarm to vibrate and to appear as a recurring reminder every morning on her appointment calendar at 8:00, no end date. She realized that there were a lot of potential problems with this design, that it was by no means foolproof. She just hoped she opened "Butterfly" before she became that fool.

SHE PRACTICALLY RAN TO CLASS, worried that she was most certainly late, but nothing had started without her when she got there. She took an aisle seat, four rows back, left of center. A few students trickled in through the doors at the back of the room, but for the most part, the class was there, ready. She looked at her watch. 10:05. The clock on the wall agreed. This was most unusual. She kept herself busy. She looked over the syllabus and skimmed her notes from last class. She made a to-do list for the rest of the day:

Lab
Seminar
Run
Study for final

Time, 10:10. She tapped her pen to the tune of "My Sharona."

The students stirred, becoming restless. They checked notebooks and the clock on the wall, they flipped through textbooks and shut them, they booted up laptops and clicked and typed. They finished their coffees. They crinkled wrappers belonging to candy bars and chips and various other snacks and ate them. They chewed pen caps and fingernails. They twisted their torsos to search the back of the room, they leaned to consult friends in other rows, they raised eyebrows and shrugged shoulders. They whispered and giggled.

"Maybe it's a guest lecturer," said a girl who sat a couple of rows behind Alice.

Alice unfolded her motivation and emotion syllabus again. Tuesday, May 4: Stress, Helplessness and Control (chapters 12 and 14). Nothing about a guest lecturer. The energy in the room converted from expectant to awkward dissonance. They were like corn kernels on a hot stove. Once that first one popped, the rest would follow, but no one knew which one would be first or when. The formal rule at Harvard stated that students were required to wait twenty minutes for a tardy professor before the class was officially canceled. Unafraid of going first, Alice closed her notebook, capped her pen, and slid everything into her book bag. 10:21. Long enough.

As she turned to leave, she looked at the four girls who sat behind her. They all looked up at her and smiled, probably grateful to her for releasing the pressure and setting them free. She held up her wrist, displaying the time as her irrefutable data.

"I don't know about you guys, but I have better things to do."

She walked up the stairs, exited the auditorium through the back doors, and never looked back.

SHE SAT IN HER OFFICE and watched the shiny rush-hour traffic creep along Memorial Drive. Her hip vibrated. It was 8:00 a.m. She removed her BlackBerry from her baby blue bag.

Alice, answer the following questions:

1. What month is it?
2. Where do you live?
3. Where is your office?

4. When is Anna's birthday?
5. How many children do you have?

If you have trouble answering any of these, go to the file named "Butterfly" on your computer and follow the instructions there immediately.

May
34 Poplar Street, Cambridge, MA 02138
William James Hall, room 1002
September 14, 1976
Three

JUNE 2004

An unmistakably elderly woman with hot pink nails and lips tickled a little girl, about five years old, presumably the woman's granddaughter. Both looked to be having a grand old time. The advertisement read: "*THE #1 TUMMY TICKLER takes the #1 prescribed Alzheimer's drug.*" Alice had been flipping through *Boston* magazine but was unable to move past this page. A hatred of that woman and the ad filled her like a hot liquid. She studied the picture and the words, waiting for her thoughts to catch up to what her gut understood, but before she could figure out why she felt so personally antagonized, Dr. Moyer opened the door to the examining room.

"So Alice, I see you're having some difficulty sleeping. Tell me what's going on."

"It's taking me well over an hour to get to sleep, and then I usually wake up a couple of hours after that and go through the whole thing all over again."

"Are you experiencing any hot flashes or physical discomfort at bedtime?"

"No."

"What medications are you taking?"

"Aricept, Namenda, Lipitor, vitamins C and E, and aspirin."

"Well, unfortunately, insomnia can be a side effect of the Aricept."

"Right, but I'm not going off Aricept."

"Tell me what you do when you can't get to sleep."

"Mostly I lie there and worry. I know this is going to get a lot worse, but I don't know when, and I worry that I might go to sleep and wake up the next morning and not know where I am or who I am or what I do. I know it's irrational, but I have this idea that the Alzheimer's can only kill off my brain cells when I'm asleep, and that as long as I'm awake and sort of on watch, I'll stay the same.

"I know all this anxiety keeps me up, but I can't seem to help it. As soon as I can't fall asleep, I worry, and then I can't sleep because I'm worried. It's exhausting just telling you about it."

Only some of what she'd just said was true. She did worry. But she'd been sleeping like a baby.

"Are you overcome with this kind of anxiety at any other time of the day?" asked Dr. Moyer.

"No."

"I could prescribe you an SSRI."

"I don't want to go on an antidepressant. I'm not depressed."

The truth was, she might be a little depressed. She'd been diagnosed with a fatal, incurable illness. So had her daughter. She'd almost entirely stopped traveling, her once dynamic lectures had become unbearably boring, and even on the rare occasion when he was home with her, John seemed a million miles away. So yes, she was a little sad. But that seemed an appropriate response given the situation and not a reason to add yet another medication, with more side effects, to her daily intake. And it wasn't what she'd come here for.

"We could try you on Restoril, one each night at bedtime. It'll get you to sleep quickly and allow you to stay asleep for about six hours, and you shouldn't wake up groggy in the morning."

"I'd like something stronger."

There was a long pause.

"I think I'd like you to make an appointment to come back in with your husband, and we can talk about prescribing something stronger."

"This doesn't concern my husband. I'm not depressed, and I'm not desperate. I'm aware of what I'm asking for, Tamara."

Dr. Moyer studied her face carefully. Alice studied hers. They were both older than forty, younger than old, both married, highly educated professional women. Alice didn't know her doctor's politics. She'd see another doctor if she had to. Her dementia was going to get worse. She couldn't risk waiting any longer. She might forget.

She had rehearsed additional dialogue but didn't need to

use it. Dr. Moyer got out her prescription pad and began to write.

SHE WAS BACK IN THAT tiny testing room with Sarah Something, the neuropsychologist. She'd reintroduced herself to Alice just a moment ago, but Alice had promptly forgotten her last name. Not a good omen. The room, however, was as she remembered it from January—cramped, sterile, and impersonal. It contained one desk with an iMac computer on it, two cafeteria chairs, and a metal file cabinet. Nothing else. No windows, no plants, no pictures or calendar on the walls or desk. No distractions, no possible hints, no chance associations.

Sarah Something began with what felt almost like regular conversation.

"Alice, how old are you?"

"Fifty."

"When did you turn fifty?"

"October eleventh."

"And what time of year is this?"

"Spring, but it already feels like summer."

"I know, it's hot out there today. And where are we right now?"

"In the Memory Disorders Unit at Mass General Hospital, in Boston, Massachusetts."

"Can you name the four things shown in this picture?"

"A book, a phone, a horse, and a car."

"And what is this thing on my shirt?"

"A button."

"And this thing on my finger?"

"A ring."

"Can you spell 'water' backwards for me?"

"R-E-T-A-W."

"And repeat this after me: Who, what, when, where, why."

"Who, what, when, where, why."

"Can you lift your hand, close your eyes, and open your mouth?"

She did.

"Alice, what were those four objects in the picture you named before?"

"A horse, a car, a phone, and a book."

"Great, and write a sentence for me here."

I cannot believe that I won't be able to do this someday.

"Great, now name for me as many words as you can in a minute that begin with the letter *s*."

"Sarah, something, stupid, sound. Survive, sick. Sex. Serious. Something. Oops, I said that. Said. Scared."

"Now name as many words as you can that begin with the letter *f*."

"Forget. Forever. Fun. Fight, flight, fit. Fuck." She laughed, surprised at herself. "Sorry about that one."

Sorry begins with s.

"That's okay, I get that one a lot."

Alice wondered how many words she would've been able to rattle off a year ago. She wondered how many words per minute were considered normal.

"Now, name as many vegetables as you can."

"Asparagus, broccoli, cauliflower. Leeks, onion. Pepper. Pepper, I don't know, I can't think of any more."

"Last one, name as many animals with four legs as you can."

"Dogs, cats, lions, tigers, bears. Zebras, giraffes. Gazelle."

"Now read this sentence aloud for me."

Sarah Something handed her a sheet of paper.

"On Tuesday, July second, in Santa Ana, California, a wildfire shut down John Wayne Airport, stranding thirty travelers, including six children and two firemen," Alice read.

It was an NYU story, a test of declarative memory performance.

"Now, tell me as many details as you can about the story you just read."

"On Tuesday, July second, in Santa Ana, California, a fire stranded thirty people in an airport, including six children and two firemen."

"Great. Now, I'm going to show you a series of pictures on cards, and you're going to just tell me the names of them."

The Boston Naming Exam.

"Briefcase, pinwheel, telescope, igloo, hourglass, rhinoceros." *A four-legged animal.* "Racquet. Oh, wait, I know what it is, it's a ladder for plants, a lattice? No. A trellis! Accordion, pretzel, rattle. Oh, wait, again. We have one in our yard at the Cape. It's between the trees, you lie on it. It's not a hangar. It's a, halyard? No. Oh god, it begins with *h,* but I can't get it."

Sarah Something made a notation on her score sheet. Alice wanted to argue that her omission could just as easily have been a normal case of blocking as a symptom of Alzheimer's. Even perfectly healthy college students typically experienced one to two tips of the tongue per week.

"That's okay, let's keep going."

Alice named the rest of the pictures without further difficulties, but she still couldn't activate the neuron that encoded the missing name of the napping net. Theirs hung between the two spruce trees in their yard in Chatham. Alice remembered many late afternoon naps there with John, the pleasure of the breezy shade, the intersection of his chest and shoulder her pillow, the familiar scent of their fabric softener on his cotton shirt combined with the summer smells of his sunburned and ocean-salty skin intoxicating her every inhalation. She could remember all of that, but not the name of the damn h-thing they lay on.

She sailed through the WAIS-R Picture Arrangement test, Raven's Colored Progressive Matrices, the Luria Mental Rotation test, the Stroop test, and copying and remembering geometric figures. She checked her watch. She'd been in that little room for just over an hour.

"Okay, Alice, now I'd like you to think back to that short story you read earlier. What can you tell me about it?"

She swallowed her panic, and it lodged, heavy and hulking, right above her diaphragm, making it uncomfortable to breathe. Either her pathways to the details of the story were impassable or she lacked the electrochemical strength to knock loudly enough on the neurons housing them to be heard. Outside of this closet, she could look up lost information in her BlackBerry. She could reread her emails and write herself reminders on Post-it notes. She could rely on the default respect her Harvard position embodied. Outside of this little room, she could hide her impassable pathways and wimpy neural signals. And although she knew that these tests were designed to unveil what she couldn't access, she was caught unsuspecting and embarrassed.

"I don't really remember much."

There it was, her Alzheimer's, stripped and naked under the fluorescent lighting, on display for Sarah Something to scrutinize and judge.

"That's okay, tell me what you do remember, anything at all."

"Well, it was about an airport, I think."

"Did the story take place on a Sunday, Monday, Tuesday, or Wednesday?"

"I don't remember."

"Just take a guess then."

"Monday."

"Was there a hurricane, a flood, a wildfire, or an avalanche?"

"A wildfire."

"Did the story take place in April, May, June, or July?"

"July."

"Which airport was shut down: John Wayne, Dulles, or LAX?"

"LAX."

"How many travelers were stranded: thirty, forty, fifty, or sixty?"

"I don't know, sixty."

"How many children were stranded: two, four, six, or eight?"

"Eight."

"Who else became stranded: two firemen, two policemen, two businessmen, or two teachers?"

"Two firemen."

"Great, you're all done here. I'll walk you over to Dr. Davis."

Great? Was it possible that she remembered the story but didn't know she knew it?

SHE WALKED INTO DR. DAVIS'S office surprised to see John already there, sitting in the seat that had remained conspicuously empty on her previous two visits. They were all there now. Alice, John, and Dr. Davis. She couldn't believe that this was really happening, that this was her life, that she was a sick woman at her neurologist's appointment with her husband. She almost felt like a character in a play, this woman with Alzheimer's disease. The husband held his script in his lap. Only it wasn't a script, it was the Activities of Daily Living questionnaire. (Interior of Doctor's Office. The woman's neurologist sits across from the woman's husband. Enter the woman.)

"Alice, have a seat. I've just had a few minutes here with John."

John spun his wedding band and jiggled his right leg. Their chairs touched, so he was causing hers to vibrate. What had they been talking about? She wanted to talk to John in private before they began, to find out what had happened and to get their stories straight. And she wanted to ask him to stop shaking her.

"How are you?" asked Dr. Davis.

"I'm good."

He smiled at her. It was a kind smile, and it dulled the edges of her apprehension.

"Okay, how about your memory? Are there any additional concerns or changes since the last time you were here?"

"Well, I'd say I'm having a harder time keeping track of my schedule. I have to refer to my BlackBerry and to-do lists all day long. And I hate talking on the phone now. If I can't see the person I'm talking to, I have a really hard time understanding the entire conversation. I usually lose track of what the person is saying while I'm chasing down words in my head."

"How about disorientation, any more episodes of feeling lost or confused?"

"No. Well, sometimes I get confused as to what time of day it is, even looking at my watch, but I eventually figure it out. I did go to my office once thinking it was morning and didn't realize until I got back home that it was the middle of the night."

"You did?" asked John. "When was this?"

"I don't know, last month, I think."

"Where was I?"

"Asleep."

"Why am I just finding out about this now, Ali?"

"I don't know, I forgot to tell you?"

She smiled, but it didn't seem to change him. If anything, the edges of his apprehension got a little sharper.

"This type of confusion and night wandering is very common, and it's likely to happen again. You might want to consider attaching a jingle bell to the front door or something that would wake John up if it opened in the middle of the night. And you should probably register with the Alzheimer's Association's Safe Return program. I think it's something like forty dollars, and you wear an ID bracelet with a personal code on it."

"I have 'John' programmed into my cell phone, and I carry it with me in this bag at all times."

"Okay, that's good, but what if the battery goes dead or John's phone is off and you're lost?"

"How about a piece of paper in my bag that has my name, John's, our address and phone numbers?"

"That'll work, as long as you always have it on you. You

might forget to bring your bag. The bracelet, you wouldn't have to think about."

"It's a good idea," said John. "She'll get one."

"How are you doing with the medications, are you taking all of your doses?"

"Yes."

"Any problems with side effects, nausea, dizziness?"

"No."

"Aside from your night at the office, are you having any trouble sleeping?"

"No."

"Are you still getting regular exercise?"

"Yes, I'm still running, about five miles, usually every day."

"John, do you run?"

"No, I walk to work and home, that's about it for me."

"I think it'd be a good idea for you to take up running with her. There's convincing data in animal models that suggest exercise alone can slow the accumulation of amyloid-beta and cognitive decline."

"I've seen those studies," said Alice.

"Right, so keep up with the running. But I'd like it if you could pair up with a running partner; that way we don't have to worry about you getting lost or skipping your run because you forgot about it."

"I'll start running with her."

John hated running. He played squash and tennis and an occasional game of golf, but he never ran. He could certainly outpace her mentally now, but physically, she was still miles ahead of him. She loved the idea of running with him but doubted that he could commit to it.

"How's your mood been, are you feeling okay?"

"Generally good. I'm definitely frustrated a lot and exhausted from trying to keep up with everything. And I'm anxious about what lies ahead for us. But otherwise, I feel the same, better actually, in some ways, since telling John and the kids."

"Have you told anyone at Harvard?"

"No, not yet."

"Were you able to teach your classes and meet all your professional responsibilities this semester?"

"Yes, it took a lot more out of me than it did last semester, but yes."

"Have you been traveling alone to meetings and lectures?"

"I've pretty much stopped. I canceled two university lectures, and I skipped a big conference in April, and I'm missing the one in France this month. I normally travel a lot in the summer, we both do, but this year we're spending the whole summer at our house in Chatham. We're heading down there next month."

"Good, that sounds wonderful. Okay, it sounds like you'll be well taken care of for the summer. I do think you should come up with a plan for the fall that involves telling the people at Harvard, maybe coming up with a way of transitioning out of your job that makes sense, and I think traveling alone should be out of the question at that point."

She nodded. She dreaded September.

"There are some legal things to plan now as well, advance directives like power of attorney and a living will. Have you thought about whether or not you'd like to donate your brain to research?"

She had thought about it. She imagined her brain, bloodless, formalin-perfused, and Silly Putty–colored, sitting in the cupped hands of a medical student. The instructor would point to various sulci and gyri, indicating the locations of the somatosensory cortex, the auditory cortex, and the visual cortex. The smell of the ocean, the sounds of her children's voices, John's hands and face. Or she imagined it cut into thin, coronal slices, like a deli ham, and adhered to glass slides. In such a preparation, the enlarged ventricles would be striking. The empty spaces where she once resided.

"Yes, I'd like to."

John cringed.

"Okay, I'll have you fill out the paperwork before you leave. John, can I have that questionnaire you're holding?"

What did he say about me in there? They would never talk about it.

"When did Alice tell you about her diagnosis?"

"Just after you told her."

"Okay, how would you say she's been doing since then?"

"Very well, I think. It's true about the phone. She won't answer it at all anymore. Either I get it or she lets the machine pick it up. She's become glued to her BlackBerry, almost like a compulsion. She sometimes checks it every couple of minutes in the morning before she leaves the house. That's a little difficult to watch."

More and more, it seemed he couldn't bear to look at her. When he did, it was with a clinical eye, like she was one of his lab rats.

"Anything else, anything that Alice may not have mentioned?"

"Nothing I can think of."

"How's her mood and personality, any changes you've noticed there?"

"No, she's the same. A little defensive, maybe. And quieter, she doesn't initiate conversation as much."

"And how are you doing?"

"Me? I'm fine."

"I have some information for you to take with you about our caregivers' support group. Denise Daddario is the social worker here. You should make an appointment with her and just let her know what's going on."

"This is an appointment for me?"

"Yes."

"Really, I don't need one, I'm fine."

"Okay, well, these resources are here if you find you come to need them. Now, I have some questions for Alice."

"Actually, I want to talk about some additional therapies and clinical trials."

"Okay, let's do that, but first, let's finish up her exam. Alice, what day of the week is it?"

"Monday."

"And when were you born?"

"October eleventh, 1953."

"Who is the vice president of the United States?"

"Dick Cheney."

"Okay, now I'm going to tell you a name and address, and you're going to repeat it back to me. Then, I'm going to ask you to repeat it again later. Ready? John Black, 42 West Street, Brighton."

"The same as last time."

"Yes, it is, very good. Can you repeat it back to me now?"

"John Black, 42 West Street, Brighton."

John Black, 42 West Street, Brighton.

John never wears black, Lydia lives out west, Tom lives in Brighton, eight years ago I was forty-two.

John Black, 42 West Street, Brighton.

"Okay, can you count to twenty forwards and then backwards?"

She did.

"Now, I want you to raise the number of fingers on your left hand which corresponds to the place in the alphabet of the first letter of the city you're in."

She repeated what he said in her head and then made the peace sign with her left index and middle fingers.

"Good. Now, what is this thing called on my watch?"

"A clasp."

"Okay, now write a sentence about today's weather on this piece of paper."

It is hazy, hot, and humid.

"On the other side of that paper, draw a clock showing the time as forty-five minutes past three."

She drew a big circle and filled in the numbers starting at the top with twelve.

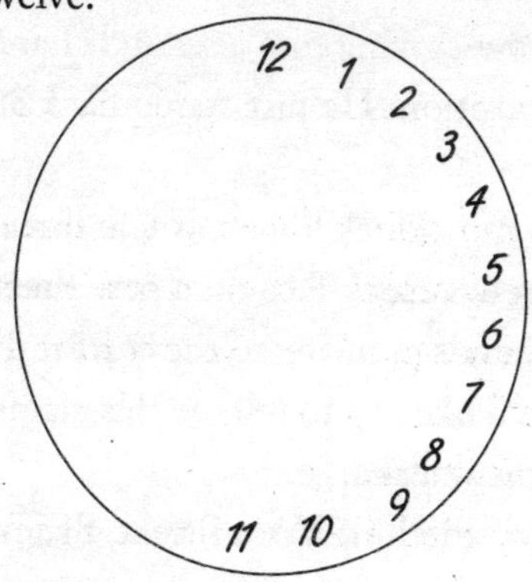

"Oops, I made the circle too big."

She scribbled it out.

3:45

"No, not digital. I'm looking for an analog clock," said Dr. Davis.

"Well, are you looking to see if I can draw or if I can still tell time? If you draw me a clock face, I can show you 3:45. I've never been any good at drawing."

When Anna was three, she'd loved horses and used to beg Alice to draw pictures of them for her. Alice's renditions had looked, at best, like postmodern dragon-dogs and always failed to satisfy even the wild and generously accepting imagination of her preschooler. *No, Mom, not that, draw me a horse.*

"I'm actually looking for both, Alice. Alzheimer's affects the parietal lobes pretty early on, and that's where we keep our internal representations of extrapersonal space. John, this is why I want you to go running with her."

John nodded. They were ganging up on her.

"John, you know I can't draw."

"Alice, it's a clock, not a horse."

Stunned that he didn't defend her, she glared at him and raised her eyebrows, giving him a second chance to verify her perfectly valid position. He just stared back at her and spun his ring.

"If you draw me a clock, I'll show you three forty-five."

Dr. Davis drew a clock face on a new sheet of paper, and Alice drew the hands pointing to the correct time.

"Okay, now I'd like you to tell me that name and address I asked you to remember earlier."

"John Black, something West Street, Brighton."

"Okay, was it forty-two, forty-four, forty-six, or forty-eight?"

"Forty-eight."

Dr. Davis wrote something lengthy on the piece of paper with the clock.

"John, please stop shaking my chair."

"Okay, now we can talk about clinical trial options. There

are several ongoing studies here and at the Brigham. The one I like the most for you starts enrolling patients this month. It's a phase three study, and it's a drug called Amylix. It appears to bind soluble amyloid-beta and prevent its aggregation, so unlike the drugs you're on now, there's the hope that this could prevent the disease from progressing further. The phase two study was very encouraging. It was well tolerated, and after a year on the medication, the patients' cognitive functioning seemed to have stopped declining or even improved."

"I assume it's placebo-controlled?" asked John.

"Yes, it's double-blind and randomized to placebo or one of two doses."

So I might get only sugar pills. She suspected that amyloid-beta didn't give a shit about placebo effects or the power of wishful thinking.

"What do you think of the secretase inhibitors?" asked John.

John liked these best. Secretases were the naturally occurring enzymes that released normal, unharmful levels of amyloid-beta. The mutation in Alice's presenilin-1 secretase rendered it insensitive to proper regulation, and it produced too much amyloid-beta. Too much was harmful. Like turning on a faucet that couldn't be turned off, her sink was rapidly overflowing.

"Right now, the secretase inhibitors are either too toxic for clinical use or—"

"What about Flurizan?"

Flurizan was an anti-inflammatory drug like Advil. Myriad Pharmaceuticals claimed it decreased the production of amyloid-beta 42. Less water into the sink.

"Yes, there's a lot of attention on that one. There's an ongoing phase two study, but only in Canada and the UK."

"How do you feel about Alice taking flurbiprofen?"

"We don't have the data yet to say whether or not it's effective for treating Alzheimer's. If she decides not to enroll in a clinical trial, I would say that it probably couldn't hurt. But if she wants to be in a study, flurbiprofen would be considered an investigational treatment for Alzheimer's, and taking it would exclude her from the study."

"All right, what about Elan's monoclonal antibody?" asked John.

"I like it, but it's only in phase one and enrollment is currently closed. Assuming it passes safety, they won't likely initiate phase two until spring of next year at the earliest, and I'd like to get Alice in a trial sooner if we can."

"Have you ever put anyone on IVIg therapy?" asked John.

John also liked the idea of this one. Derived from donated blood plasma, intravenous immunoglobulin was already approved safe and effective for treating primary immune deficiencies and a number of autoimmune neuromuscular disorders. It would be expensive and not reimbursable by their insurance company because of its off-label use but worth any price if it worked.

"I've never had a patient go on it. I'm not against it, but we don't know the proper dosing, and it's a very untargeted and crude method. I wouldn't expect its effects to be anything more than modest."

"We'll take modest," said John.

"Okay, but you need to understand what you'd be trading off. If you decide to go ahead with IVIg therapy, Alice wouldn't be eligible for any of these clinical trials with treatments that are potentially more specific and disease modifying."

"But she'd be guaranteed not to be in a placebo group."

"That's true. There are risks with either decision."

"Would I have to go off the Aricept and Namenda to participate in the clinical trial?"

"No, you'd keep taking them."

"Could I go on estrogen replacement therapy?"

"Yes. There's enough anecdotal evidence to suggest that it's at least to some degree protective, so I'd be willing to write you a prescription for CombiPatch. But again, it would be considered an investigational drug, and you wouldn't be able to participate in the Amylix trial."

"How long would I be in the trial for?"

"It's a fifteen-month study."

"What's your wife's name?" asked Alice.

"Lucy."

"What would you want Lucy to do if she had this?"

"I'd want her to enroll in the Amylix trial."

"So Amylix is the only option you can recommend?" asked John.

"Yes."

"I think we should do the IVIg along with flurbiprofen and the CombiPatch," said John.

The room became still and quiet. An enormous amount of information had just been passed back and forth. Alice pressed her fingers on her eyes and tried to think analytically about her treatment options. She did her best to set up columns and rows in her head to compare the drugs, but the imaginary chart didn't help, and she tossed it into the imaginary trash. She thought conceptually instead and arrived at a single, crisp image that made sense. A shotgun or a single bullet.

"You don't need to make a decision on this today. You can go home and think about it some more and get back to me."

No, she didn't need to think about it any further. She was a scientist. She knew how to risk everything with no guarantees in search of the unknown truth. As she'd done so many times over the years with her own research, she chose the bullet.

"I want to do the trial."

"Ali, I think you should trust me here," said John.

"I can still draw my own conclusions, John. I want to do the trial."

"Okay, I'll get you the forms to sign."

(Interior of Doctor's Office. The neurologist left the room. The husband spun his ring. The woman hoped for a cure.)

JULY 2004

"John? John? Are you home?"

She was sure that he wasn't, but being sure of anything these days was tattered with too many holes to contain the meaning that it used to. He had left to go somewhere, but she couldn't remember when he left or where he was going. Did he run to the store for milk or coffee? Did he go out to rent a movie? If either were the case, he'd be back any minute. Or did he drive back up to Cambridge, in which case he'd be gone for at least several hours and possibly the night? Or did he decide, at last, that he couldn't face what lay ahead for them, and he just plain left, never to return? No, he wouldn't do that. She was sure of it.

Their Chatham Cape, built in 1990, felt bigger, more

open, and less compartmentalized than their house in Cambridge. She walked into the kitchen. It was nothing like their kitchen at home. The bleached effect of the white painted walls and cabinets, white appliances, white barstools, and white tile floor was broken up only slightly by the soapstone countertops and splashes of cobalt blue in various white ceramic and clear glass containers. It looked like a coloring book page that had been only tentatively filled in with a single blue crayon.

The two plates and used paper napkins on the island counter displayed evidence of salad and a spaghetti and red sauce dinner. One of the glasses still held a gulp of white wine. With the detached curiosity of a forensic scientist, she picked up the glass and tested the temperature of the wine against her lips. It was still a little cold. She felt full. She looked at the time. It was just after nine o'clock.

They'd been in Chatham for a week now. In years past, after a week away from the day-to-day concerns at Harvard, she would have been fully committed to the relaxed lifestyle that the Cape insisted on and already deep into her third or fourth book. But this year, Harvard's day-to-day schedule itself, albeit packed and demanding, had provided a structure for her that was familiar and comforting. Meetings, symposia, class times, and appointments lay like bread crumbs that guided her through each day.

Here in Chatham, she had no schedule. She slept late, ate meals at varying times, and played everything by ear. She bookended each day with her medications, she took her butterfly test each morning, and she ran every day with John. But these didn't provide enough structure. She needed bigger bread crumbs and more of them.

She often didn't know the time of day or what day it was,

for that matter. On more than one occasion now when she sat down to eat, she didn't know which meal she was about to be presented with. When yesterday a waitress at the Sand Bar put a plate of fried clams in front of her, she would have just as readily and enthusiastically dug into a plate of pancakes.

The kitchen windows were open. She looked out into the driveway. No car. The outside air still held traces of the hot day and carried sounds of bullfrogs, a woman laughing, and the tide at Hardings Beach. She left a note for John next to the uncleared dishes:

Walk to beach. Love, A

She inhaled the clean night air. The midnight blue sky was punctured with backlit stars and a cartoon crescent moon. Not as dark as it would get that night, it was already darker than it ever got in Cambridge. Without streetlamps and tucked far enough in from Main Street, only lights from porches, rooms in houses, the occasional car high beams, and the moon illuminated their beach neighborhood. In Cambridge, that amount of darkness would have made her feel uneasy walking alone, but here, in this small seaside and vacationing community, she felt perfectly safe.

There were no cars parked in the lot and no one else on the beach. The town police discouraged activity there at night. At this hour, there were no screaming children or seagulls, no impossible-to-ignore cell phone conversations, no aggressive worries about needing to leave in time to get to the next thing, nothing to disrupt the peace.

She walked to the water's edge and let the ocean consume her feet. Warm waves licked her legs. Facing Nantucket Sound, Hardings Beach's protected waters were a good ten degrees milder than those of the nearby beaches that faced the cold Atlantic directly.

She removed her shirt and bra first, then slid off her skirt and underwear in one motion, and walked in. The water, free from the seaweed that normally tumbled in with the surf, lapped milky smooth against her skin. She began to breathe to the rhythm of the tide. As she treaded lightly, floating on her back, she marveled at the beads of phosphorescence that trailed her fingertips and heels like pixie dust.

Moonlight reflected off her right wrist. SAFE RETURN was engraved on the front of the flat, two-inch, stainless steel bracelet. A one-eight-hundred number, her identification, and the words *Memory Impaired* were etched on the reverse side. Her thoughts then rode a series of waves, traveling from unwanted jewelry to her mother's butterfly necklace, traversing from there to her plan for suicide, to the books she planned to read, and finally stranded themselves on the common fates of Virginia Woolf and Edna Pontellier. It would be so easy. She could swim straight out toward Nantucket until she was too tired to continue.

She looked out over the dark water. Her body, strong and healthy, held her buoyant, treading water, every instinct battling toward life. Yes, she didn't remember eating dinner with John tonight or where he'd said he was going. And she might very well not remember this night in the morning, but in this moment, she didn't feel desperate. She felt alive and happy.

She looked back toward the beach, the landscape dimly lit. A figure approached. She knew it was John before she could identify any of his features by the bounce and size of his walk. She didn't ask him where he'd been or how long he'd been gone. She didn't thank him for coming back. He didn't scold her for being out alone without her cell phone, and he didn't ask her to get out and come home. Without a word between them, he undressed and joined her in her ocean.

"JOHN?"

She found him painting the trim on the detached garage.

"I've been calling for you all over the house," said Alice.

"I was out here, I didn't hear you," said John.

"When do you leave for the conference?" she asked.

"Monday."

He was going to Philadelphia for a week to attend the ninth International Conference on Alzheimer's Disease.

"That's after Lydia gets here, right?"

"Yes, she'll be here on Sunday."

"Oh, right."

Following Lydia's written request, the Monomoy Theatre repertory company had invited her to join them as a guest artist for the summer.

"Are you ready to run?" asked John.

The early morning fog hadn't yet lifted, and the air felt cooler than she'd dressed for.

"I just need to grab another layer."

Inside the front door, she opened the coat closet. Dressing comfortably on the Cape in early summer posed a constant challenge, with temperatures on any given day beginning in the fifties, soaring up to eighty by afternoon and boomeranging back down into the fifties, often paired with a brisk ocean wind, by nightfall. It required a creative sense of fashion and a willingness to add and subtract articles of clothing many times a day. She touched the sleeves of each of the hanging coats. Although a number of them would be perfect now for sitting or walking on the beach, everything in there felt too heavy for running.

She ran up the stairs and into their bedroom. After searching through several drawers, she found a lightweight fleece and put it on. She noticed the book she'd been reading on her nightstand. She grabbed it and walked down the stairs and into the kitchen. She poured herself a glass of iced tea and walked out to the back porch. The early morning fog hadn't yet lifted, and it was cooler than she'd anticipated. She set her drink and book down on the table between the white Adirondack chairs and went back into the house to retrieve a blanket.

She returned, wrapped herself in the blanket, sat in one of the chairs, and opened her book to the dog-eared page. Reading was fast becoming a heartbreaking chore. She had to reread pages over and over to retain the continuity of the thesis or narrative, and if she put the book down for any length of time, she had to go back sometimes a full chapter to find the thread again. Plus, she felt anxious over deciding what to read. What if she didn't have time to read everything she'd always wanted to? Prioritizing hurt, a reminder that the clock was ticking, that some things would be left undone.

She'd just begun reading *King Lear*. She so loved Shakespeare's tragedies but had never read this one. Unfortunately, as was becoming routine, she found herself stuck after only a few minutes. She reread the previous page, tracing the imaginary line below the words with her index finger. She drank the entire glass of iced tea and watched the birds in the trees.

"There you are. What are you doing, aren't we going for a run?" John asked.

"Oh, yes, good. This book is making me crazy."

"Let's go then."

"Are you going to that conference today?"

"Monday."

"What's today?"

"Thursday."

"Oh. And when does Lydia get here?"

"Sunday."

"That's before you leave?"

"Yes. Ali, I just told you all this. You should put it in your BlackBerry, I think it'd make you feel better."

"Okay, sorry."

"Ready?"

"Yes. Wait, let me pee before we go."

"All right, I'll be out by the garage."

She placed her empty glass on the counter next to the sink and dropped the blanket and book on the slipcovered chair-and-a-half in the living room. She stood ready to move, but her legs needed further instruction. What did she come in here for? She retraced her steps—blanket and book, glass on counter, porch with John. He was leaving soon to attend the International Conference on Alzheimer's Disease. Sunday maybe? She'd have to ask him to be sure. They were about to go for a run. It was a little cool out. She came in for a fleece! No, that wasn't it. She was already wearing one. *To hell with it.*

Just as she reached the front door, an urgent pressure in her bladder announced itself, and she remembered that she really had to pee. She hastened back down the hall and opened the door to the bathroom. Only, to her utter disbelief, it wasn't the bathroom. A broom, mop, bucket, vacuum cleaner, stool, toolbox, lightbulbs, flashlights, bleach. The utility closet.

She looked farther down the hall. The kitchen to the left, the living room to the right, and that was it. There was a half bath on this floor, wasn't there? There had to be. It was right here. But it wasn't. She hurried to the kitchen but found only one door, and it led to the back porch. She raced over to the living room, but of course, there wasn't a bathroom off the living room. She rushed back to the hallway and held the doorknob.

"Please God, please God, please God."

She swung the door open like an illusionist revealing her most mystifying trick, but the bathroom didn't magically reappear.

How can I be lost in my own home?

She thought about bolting upstairs to the full bath, but she was strangely stuck and dumbfounded in the Twilight Zone–like, bathroomless dimension of the first floor. She was unable to hold it in any longer. She had an ethereal sense of observing herself, this poor, unfamiliar woman crying in the hallway. It didn't sound like the somewhat guarded cry of an adult woman. It was the scared, defeated, and unrestrained crying of a small child.

Her tears weren't all she wasn't able to contain any longer. John burst through the front door just in time to witness the urine streaming down her right leg, soaking her sweatpants, sock, and sneaker.

"Don't look at me!"

"Ali, don't cry, it's okay."

"I don't know where I am."

"It's okay, you're right here."

"I'm lost."

"You're not lost, Ali, you're with me."

He held her, and rocked her slightly side to side, soothing her as she'd seen him calm their children after innumerable physical injuries and social injustices.

"I couldn't find the bathroom."

"It's okay."

"I'm sorry."

"Don't be sorry, it's okay. Come on, let's get you changed. The day's already heating up, you need something lighter anyway."

BEFORE JOHN LEFT FOR THE conference, he gave Lydia detailed instructions concerning Alice's medications, her running routine, her cell phone, and the Safe Return program. He also gave her the neurologist's phone number, just in case. When Alice replayed his little speech in her head, it sounded very much like the ones they had delivered to their teenage babysitters before leaving the kids for weekends away in Maine or Vermont. Now she needed to be watched. By her own daughter.

After their first dinner alone together at the Squire, Alice and Lydia walked down Main Street without talking. The line of luxury cars and SUVs parked along the curb, outfitted with bike racks and kayaks bungeed on roofs, crammed with baby strollers, beach chairs, and umbrellas, and sporting license plates from Connecticut, New York, and New Jersey in addition to Massachusetts signaled the summer season officially in full swing. Families ambled along the sidewalk without regard for lanes of pedestrian traffic, unhurried and without specific destinations, stopping, backtracking, and window-shopping. Like they had all the time in the world.

An easy ten-minute stroll removed them from the congested downtown. They stopped in front of the Chatham Lighthouse and breathed in the panoramic view of the beach below before walking the thirty steps down to the sand. A modest line of sandals and flip-flops waited at the bottom, where they'd been kicked off earlier in the day. Alice and Lydia added their shoes to the end of the row and continued walking. The sign in front of them read:

> WARNING: STRONG CURRENT. Surf subject to unexpected life-threatening waves and currents. No lifeguard. Hazardous area for: swimming and wading, diving and waterskiing, sailboards and small boats, rafts and canoes.

Alice watched and listened to the relentless, breaking waves pounding the shore. If it weren't for the colossal seawall constructed at the edges of the properties of the million-dollar homes along Shore Road, the ocean would have taken each house in, devouring them all without sympathy or apology. She imagined her Alzheimer's like this ocean at Lighthouse Beach—unstoppable, ferocious, destructive. Only there were no seawalls in her brain to protect her memories and thoughts from the onslaught.

"I'm sorry I didn't get to go to your play," she said to Lydia.

"It's all right. I know it was because of Dad this time."

"I can't wait to see the one you're in this summer."

"Uh-huh."

The sun hung low and impossibly big in the pink and blue sky, ready to plunge into the Altantic. They walked by a man kneeling in the sand, aiming his camera at the horizon, trying to capture its fleeting beauty before it disappeared with the sun.

"This conference Dad's at is about Alzheimer's?"

"Yes."

"Is he trying to find a better treatment there?"

"He is."

"Do you think he'll find one?"

Alice watched the tide coming in, erasing footprints, demolishing an elaborate sand castle decorated with shells, filling in a hole dug earlier that day with plastic shovels, ridding the shore of its daily history. She envied the beautiful homes behind the seawall.

"No."

Alice picked up a shell. She rubbed the sand off, revealing its milky white shine and elegant ribbons of pink. She liked its smooth feel, but it was broken on one edge. She thought about tossing it into the water but decided to keep it.

"Well, I'm sure he wouldn't take the time to go if he didn't think he could find something," said Lydia.

Two girls wearing University of Massachusetts sweatshirts walked toward them, giggling. Alice smiled at them and said "Hello" as they passed.

"I wish you'd go to college," said Alice.

"Mom, please don't."

Not wanting to start their week together with a full-blown fight, Alice silently reminisced while they walked. The professors she'd loved and feared and made a fool of herself in front of, the boys she'd loved and feared and made an even bigger fool of herself in front of, the punchy all-nighters before exams, the classes, the parties, the friendships, meeting John—her memories of that time in her life were vivid, perfectly intact, and easily accessed. They were almost a little cocky the way they came to her, so full and ready, like they had no knowledge of the war going on just a few centimeters to their left.

Whenever she thought about college, her thoughts ultimately bumped into January of her freshman year. A little over three hours after her family had visited and left for home, Alice had heard a tentative knock on her dorm room door. She still remembered every detail of the dean standing in her doorway—the single, deep crease between his eyebrows, the boyish part in his grandfatherly gray hair, the woolly pills budding all over his forest green sweater, the low, careful cadence of his voice.

Her father had driven the car off Route 93 and into a tree. He might have fallen asleep. He might have had too much to drink at dinner. *He always had too much to drink at dinner.* He was in a hospital in Manchester. Her mother and her sister were dead.

"JOHN? IS THAT YOU?"

"No, it's just me bringing in the towels. It's about to pour," said Lydia.

The air was charged and heavy. They were due for some rain. The weather had cooperated all week with postcard sunny days and perfect sleeping temperatures each night. Her brain had cooperated all week, too. She'd come to recognize the difference between days that would be fraught with difficulties finding memories and words and bathrooms and days that her Alzheimer's would lie silent and not interfere. On those quiescent days, she was her normal self, the self she understood and had confidence in. On those days, she could almost convince herself that Dr. Davis and the genetic counselor had been wrong, or that the last six months had been a horrible dream, only a nightmare, the monster under her bed and clawing at her covers not real.

From the living room, Alice watched Lydia fold towels and stack them on one of the kitchen stools. She wore a light blue, spaghetti-strap tank top and a black skirt. She looked freshly showered. Alice still wore her bathing suit under a faded fish-print beach dress.

"Should I get changed?" she asked.

"If you want to."

Lydia returned clean mugs to a cabinet and checked her watch. Then she came into the living room, gathered the magazines and catalogs from the couch and floor, and piled them into a neat stack on the coffee table. She checked her watch. She took a copy of *Cape Cod Magazine* off the top of the pile, sat down on the couch, and began flipping through it. They seemed to be killing time, but Alice didn't understand why. Something wasn't right.

"Where's John?" asked Alice.

Lydia looked up from the magazine, either amused or embarrassed or maybe both. Alice couldn't tell.

"He should be home any minute."

"So we're waiting for him."

"Uh-huh."

"Where's Anne?"

"Anna's in Boston, with Charlie."

"No, Anne, my sister, where's Anne?"

Lydia stared at her without blinking, all lightness drained from her face.

"Mom, Anne's dead. She died in a car accident with your mother."

Lydia's eyes didn't move from Alice's. Alice stopped breathing, and her heart squeezed like a fist. Her head and fingers went numb, and the world around her became dark and narrow. She took in a huge breath of air. It filled her head and fingers with oxygen, and it filled her pounding heart with rage and grief. She began to shake and cry.

"No, Mom, this happened a long time ago, remember?"

Lydia was talking to her, but Alice couldn't hear what she was saying. She could only feel the rage and grief coursing through her every cell, her sick heart, and her hot tears, and she could only hear her own voice in her head screaming for Anne and her mother.

John stood over them, drenched.

"What happened?"

"She was asking for Anne. She thinks they just died."

He held her head in his hands. He was talking to her, trying to calm her down. *Why isn't he upset, too? He's known about this for a while, that's why, and he's been keeping it from me.* She couldn't trust him.

AUGUST 2004

Her mother and sister had died when she was a freshman in college. No pictures of her mother or Anne filled a single page in their family photo albums. There was no evidence of them at her graduations, her wedding, or with her, John, and the children on holidays, vacations, or birthdays. She couldn't picture her mother as an old woman, and she certainly would be now, and Anne hadn't aged beyond a teenager in her mind. Still, she'd been so sure that they were about to walk through the front door, not as ghosts from the past but alive and well, and that they were coming to stay at the house in Chatham with them for the summer. She was somewhat scared that she could become that confused, that, awake and sober, she could wholeheartedly expect a visit from her long-dead mother and sister. It was even scarier that this scared her only somewhat.

Alice, John, and Lydia sat at the patio table on the porch eating breakfast. Lydia was talking to them about the members of her summer ensemble and her rehearsals. But mostly, she was talking to John.

"I was so intimidated before I got here, you know? I mean, you should see all their bios. MFAs in theater from NYU and the Actors Studio and degrees from Yale, experience on Broadway."

"Wow, sounds like a very experienced group. What's the age range?" he asked.

"Oh, I'm easily the youngest. Most are probably in their thirties and forties, but there's a man and woman as old as you and Mom."

"That old, huh?"

"You know what I mean. Anyway, I didn't know if I'd be totally out of my league, but the training I've been piecing together and the work I've been getting has really given me the right tools. I totally know what I'm doing."

Alice remembered having the same insecurity and realization in her first months as a professor at Harvard.

"They all definitely have more experience than me, but none of them have studied Meisner. They all studied Stanislavsky, or the Method, but I really think Meisner is the most powerful approach for true spontaneity in acting. So even though I don't have as much onstage experience, I bring something unique to the group."

"That's great, honey. That's probably one of the reasons they cast you. What's 'spontaneity in acting' mean exactly?" John asked.

Alice had wondered the same thing, but her words, viscous in amyloid goo, lagged behind John's, as they so often seemed to now in real-time conversation. So she listened to her husband and daughter ramble effortlessly ahead of her and watched them as participants onstage from her seat in the audience.

She cut her sesame bagel in half and took a bite. She didn't like it plain. Several condiment options sat on the table—wild Maine blueberry jam, a jar of peanut butter, a stick of butter on a plate, and a tub of white butter. But it wasn't called white butter. What was it called? Not mayonnaise. No, it was too thick, like butter. What was its name? She pointed her butter knife at it.

"John, can you pass that to me?"

John handed her the tub of white butter. She spread a thick layer onto one of the bagel halves and stared at it. She knew exactly how it would taste, and that she liked it, but she couldn't bring herself to bite into it until she could tell herself its name. Lydia watched her mother studying her bagel.

"Cream cheese, Mom."

"Right. Cream cheese. Thank you, Lydia."

The phone rang, and John went inside the house to answer it. The first thought that jumped to the front of Alice's mind was that it was her mother, calling to let them know she was going to be late getting there. The thought, seemingly realistic and colored with immediacy, appeared as reasonable as expecting John to return to the patio table within the next few minutes. Alice corrected the impetuous thought, scolded it, and put it away. Her mother and sister had died when she was a freshman in college. It was maddening to have to keep reminding herself of this.

Alone with her daughter, at least for the moment, she took the opportunity to get a word in.

"Lydia, what about going to school for a degree in theater?"

"Mom, didn't you understand a word of what I was just saying? I don't need a degree."

"I heard every word of what you said, and I understood it all. I was thinking more big picture. I'm sure there are aspects of your craft that you haven't yet explored, things you could still learn, maybe even directing? The point is, a degree opens more doors should you ever need them."

"And what doors are those?"

"Well, for one, the degree would give you the credibility to teach if you ever wanted to."

"Mom, I want to be an actor, not a teacher. That's you, not me."

"I know that, Lydia, you've made that abundantly clear. I'm not necessarily thinking of a teacher at a university or college anyway, although you could. I was thinking that you could someday run workshops just like the ones you've been taking and love so much."

"Mom, I'm sorry, but I'm not going to spend any energy on thinking about what I might do if I'm not good enough to make it as an actor. I don't need to doubt myself like that."

"I'm not doubting that you can have a career as an actor. But what if you decide to have a family someday, and you'd like to slow down a bit but still stay in the business? Teaching workshops, even from your home, might be a nice flexibility to have. Plus, it's not always what you know, but who you know. The networking possibilities you'd have with classmates, professors, alumnae, I'm sure there's an inner circle you simply don't have access to without a degree or a body of work already proven in the business."

Alice paused, waiting for Lydia's "yeah, but," but she didn't say anything.

"Just consider it. Life only gets busier. It's a harder thing to fit in as you get older. Maybe talk to some of the people in your ensemble and get their perspectives on what's involved in continuing an acting career into your thirties and forties and older. Okay?"

"Okay."

Okay. That was the closest they'd ever come to agreement on the subject. Alice tried to think of something else to talk about but couldn't. For so long now, they had talked only about this. The silence between them grew.

"Mom, what does it feel like?"

"What does what feel like?"

"Having Alzheimer's. Can you feel that you have it right now?"

"Well, I know I'm not confused or repeating myself right now, but just a few minutes ago, I couldn't find 'cream cheese,' and I was having a hard time participating in the conversation with you and your dad. I know it's only a matter of time before those types of things happen again, and the times between when it happens are getting shorter. And the things that are happening are getting bigger. So even when I feel completely normal, I know I'm not. It's not over, it's just a rest. I don't trust myself."

As soon as she finished, she worried she'd admitted too much. She didn't want to scare her daughter. But Lydia didn't flinch and stayed interested, and Alice relaxed.

"So you know when it's happening?"

"Most of the time."

"Like what was happening when you couldn't think of the name for cream cheese?"

"I know what I'm looking for, my brain just can't get to it. It's like if you decided you wanted that glass of water, only your hand won't pick it up. You ask it nicely, you threaten it, but it just won't budge. You might finally get it to move, but then you grab the saltshaker instead, or you knock the glass and spill the water all over the table. Or by the time you get your hand to hold the glass and bring it to your lips, the itch in your throat has cleared, and you don't need a drink anymore. The moment of need has passed."

"That sounds like torture, Mom."

"It is."

"I'm so sorry you have this."

"Thanks."

Lydia reached out across the dishes and glasses and years of distance and held her mother's hand. Alice squeezed it and smiled. Finally, they'd found something else they could talk about.

ALICE WOKE UP ON THE couch. She'd been napping a lot lately, sometimes twice a day. While her attention and energy benefited greatly from the extra rest, reentry into the day was jarring. She looked at the clock on the wall. Four fifteen. She couldn't remember what time she'd dozed off. She remembered eating lunch. A sandwich, some kind of sandwich, with John. That was probably around noon. The corner of something hard pressed into her hip. The book she'd been reading. She must've fallen asleep while reading.

Four twenty. Lydia's rehearsal ran until seven. She sat up and listened. She could hear the seagulls squawking at Hardings and imagined their scavenger hunt, a mad race to find and devour every last crumb left behind by those careless, sunburned humans. She stood up and set out on her own hunt, less frenzied than the gulls', for John. She checked their bedroom and study. She looked out into the driveway. No car. Just about to curse him for not leaving a note, she found it under a magnet on the refrigerator door.

Ali—Went for a drive, be back soon, John

She sat back down on the couch and picked up her book, *Sense and Sensibility* by Jane Austen, but didn't open it. She didn't really want to be reading it now. She'd been about half-way through *Moby-Dick* and lost it. She and John had turned the house upside down without success. They'd even looked in every peculiar spot that only a demented person would place a book—the refrigerator and freezer, the pantry, their dresser drawers, the linen closet, the fireplace. But neither of them could find it. She'd probably left it at the beach. She hoped she'd left it at the beach. That was at least something she would've done before Alzheimer's.

John had offered to pick her up another copy. Maybe he'd gone to the bookstore. She hoped he had. If she waited much longer, she'd forget what she'd already read and have to start over. All that work. Just the thought of it made her tired again. In the meantime, she'd started Jane Austen, whom she'd always liked. But this one wasn't holding her attention.

She wandered upstairs to Lydia's bedroom. Of her three children, she knew Lydia the least. On the top of her dresser, turquoise and silver rings, a leather necklace, and a colorfully beaded one spilled over an open cardboard box. Next to the box sat a pile of hair clips and a tray for burning incense. Lydia was a bit of a hippie.

Her clothes lay all over the floor, some folded, most not.

There couldn't have been much of anything actually in her dresser drawers. She'd left her bed unmade. Lydia was a bit of a slob.

Books of poetry and plays lined the shelves of her bookcase—*'Night Mother, Dinner with Friends, Proof, A Delicate Balance, Spoon River Anthology, Agnes of God, Angels in America, Oleanna.* Lydia was an actress.

She picked up several of the plays and flipped through them. They were each only about eighty to ninety pages, and each of those pages was only sparsely filled with text. *Maybe it'd be easier and more satisfying to read plays. And I could talk about them with Lydia.* She held on to *Proof.*

Lydia's journal, iPod, *Sanford Meisner on Acting,* and a framed picture sat on her nightstand. Alice picked up the journal. She hesitated, but barely. She didn't have the luxury of time. Sitting on the bed, she read page after page of her daughter's dreams and confessions. She read about blocks and breakthroughs in acting classes, fears and hopes surrounding auditions, disappointments and joys over castings. She read about a young woman's passion and tenacity.

She read about Malcolm. While they were acting in a dramatic scene together in class, Lydia had fallen in love with him. She'd thought she might be pregnant once, but wasn't. She was relieved, not ready yet to get married or have children. She wanted to find her own way in the world first.

Alice studied the framed photograph of Lydia and a man, presumably Malcolm. Their smiling faces touched. They were happy, the man and woman in the picture. Lydia was a woman.

"Ali, are you here?" called John.

"I'm upstairs!"

She returned the journal and picture to the nightstand and stole downstairs.

"Where'd you go?" Alice asked.

"I went for a drive."

He held two white plastic bags, one in each hand.

"Did you buy me a new copy of *Moby-Dick*?"

"Sort of."

He handed Alice one of the bags. It was filled with DVDs—*Moby Dick* with Gregory Peck and Orson Welles, *King Lear* with Laurence Olivier, *Casablanca, One Flew over the Cuckoo's Nest,* and *The Sound of Music,* her all-time favorite.

"I was thinking these might be a lot easier for you. And we can do this together."

She smiled.

"What's in the other bag?"

She felt giddy, like a little kid on Christmas morning. He pulled out a package of microwave popcorn and a box of Milk Duds.

"Can we watch *The Sound of Music* first?" she asked.

"Sure."

"I love you, John."

She threw her arms around him.

"I love you, too, Ali."

With her hands high on his back, she pressed her face against his chest and breathed him in. She wanted to say more to him, about what he meant to her, but she couldn't find the words. He held her a little tighter. He knew. They stood still in the kitchen holding on to each other without uttering a word for a long time.

"Here, you nuke the popcorn, and I'll put the movie in and meet you on the couch," said John.

"Okay."

She walked over to the microwave, opened the door, and laughed. She had to laugh.

"I found *Moby-Dick*!"

ALICE HAD BEEN UP ALONE for a couple of hours. In that early morning solitude, she drank green tea, read a little, and practiced yoga outside on the lawn. Posed in downward dog, she filled her lungs with the delicious morning ocean air and luxuriated in the strange, almost painful pleasure of the stretch in her hamstrings and glutes. Out of the corner of her eye, she observed her left triceps engaged in holding her body in this position. Solid, sculpted, beautiful. Her whole body looked strong and beautiful.

She was in the best physical shape of her life. Good food plus daily exercise equaled the strength in her flexed triceps muscles, the flexibility in her hips, her strong calves, and easy breathing during a four-mile run. Then, of course, there was her mind. Unresponsive, disobedient, weakening.

She took Aricept, Namenda, the mystery Amylix trial pill, Lipitor, vitamins C and E, and baby aspirin. She consumed additional antioxidants in the form of blueberries, red wine, and dark chocolate. She drank green tea. She tried ginkgo biloba. She meditated and played Numero. She brushed her teeth with her left, nondominant hand. She slept when she was tired. Yet none of these efforts seemed to add up to visible, measurable results. Maybe her cognitive capabilities would noticeably worsen if she subtracted the exercise, the Aricept, or the blueberries. Maybe unopposed, her dementia would run amok. Maybe. But maybe all these things didn't affect anything. She couldn't know, unless she went off her meds, eliminated chocolate and wine, and sat on her ass for the next month. This was not an experiment she was willing to conduct.

She stepped into warrior pose. She exhaled and sank deeper into the lunge, accepting the discomfort and additional challenge to her concentration and stamina, determined to maintain the pose. Determined to remain a warrior.

John emerged from the kitchen, bed-headed and zombie-like but dressed to run.

"You want coffee first?" asked Alice.

"No, let's just go, I'll have it when we get back."

They ran two miles every morning along Main Street to the center of town and returned via the same route. John's body had grown noticeably leaner and defined, and he could run that distance easily now, but he didn't enjoy one second of it. He ran with her, resigned and uncomplaining, but with the same enthusiasm and zest he had for paying the bills or doing the laundry. And she loved him for it.

She ran behind him, letting him set the pace, watching and listening to him like he was a gorgeous musical instrument—the pendulum-like swinging back of his elbows, the rhythmic, airy puffs of his exhales, the percussion of his sneakers on the sandy pavement. Then he spit, and she laughed. He didn't ask why.

They were on their way back when she ran up beside him. On a compassionate whim, she was about to tell him that he didn't have to run with her anymore if he didn't want to, that she could handle this route alone. But then, following his turn, they ran right at a fork onto Mill Road toward home where she would've gone left. Alzheimer's did not like to be ignored.

Back home, she thanked him, kissed him on his sweaty

cheek, and then went straight and unshowered to Lydia, who was still in her pajamas and drinking coffee on the porch. Each morning, she and Lydia discussed whatever play Alice was reading over multigrain cereal with blueberries or a sesame bagel with *cream cheese* and coffee and tea. Alice's instinct had been right. She enjoyed reading plays infinitely more than reading novels or biographies, and talking over what she'd just read with Lydia, whether it was scene one, act one, or the entire play, proved a delightful and powerful way of reinforcing her memory of it. In analyzing scenes, character, and plot with Lydia, Alice saw the depth of her daughter's intellect, her rich understanding of human need and emotion and struggle. She saw Lydia. And she loved her.

Today, they discussed a scene from *Angels in America*. They passed eager questions and answers back and forth, their conversation two-way, equal, fun. And because Alice didn't have to compete with John to complete her thoughts, she could take her time and not get left behind.

"What was it like doing this scene with Malcolm?" Alice asked.

Lydia stared at her as if the question blew her mind.

"What?"

"Didn't you and Malcolm perform this scene together in your class?"

"You read my journal?"

Alice's stomach hollowed out. She thought Lydia had told her about Malcolm.

"Sweetie, I'm sorry—"

"I can't believe you did that! You have no right!"

Lydia shoved her chair back and stormed off, leaving Alice alone at the table, stunned and queasy. A few minutes later, Alice heard the front door slam.

"Don't worry, she'll calm down," said John.

All morning she tried to do something else. She tried to clean, to garden, to read, but all she could manage to do effectively was worry. She worried she'd done something unforgivable. She worried she'd just lost the respect, trust, and love of the daughter she'd only begun to know.

After lunch, Alice and John walked to Hardings Beach. Alice swam until her body felt too exhausted to feel anything else. The hollowed-out flip-flopping in her stomach gone, she returned to her beach chair, lay in the fully reclined position with her eyes closed and meditated.

She'd read that regular meditation could increase cortical thickness and slow age-related cortical thinning. Lydia was already meditating every day, and when Alice had expressed an interest, Lydia had taught her. Whether it helped to preserve her cortical thickness or not, Alice liked the time of quiet focus, how it so effectively hushed the cluttered noise and worry in her head. It literally gave her peace of mind.

After about twenty minutes, she returned to a more wakeful state, relaxed, energized, and hot. She waded back into the ocean, just for a quick dip this time, exchanging sweat and heat for salt and cool. Back in her chair, she overheard a woman on the blanket next to them talking about the wonderful play she'd just seen at the Monomoy Theatre. The hollowed-out flip-flopping surged back in.

That evening, John grilled cheeseburgers, and Alice made a salad. Lydia didn't come home for dinner.

"I'm sure rehearsal's just running a bit late," said John.

"She hates me now."

"She doesn't hate you."

After dinner, Alice drank two more glasses of red wine, and John drank three more glasses of scotch with ice. Still no

Lydia. After Alice added her evening dose of pills to her unsettled stomach, they sat on the couch together with a bowl of popcorn and a box of Milk Duds and watched *King Lear.*

John woke her on the couch. The television was off, and the house was dark. She must've fallen asleep before the movie ended. She didn't remember the ending anyway. He guided her up the stairs to their bedroom.

She stood at her side of the bed, her hand over her disbelieving mouth, tears in her eyes, the worry expelled from her stomach and mind. Lydia's journal lay on her pillow.

"SORRY I'M LATE," SAID TOM, walking in.

"Okay, everyone, now that Tom's here, Charlie and I have some news to share," said Anna. "I'm five weeks pregnant with twins!"

Hugs and kisses and congratulations were followed by excited questions and answers and interruptions and more questions and answers. As her ability to track what was said in complex conversations with many participants declined, Alice's sensitivity to what wasn't said, to body language and unspoken feelings, had heightened. She'd explained this phenomenon a couple of weeks ago to Lydia, who'd told her it was an enviable skill to have as an actor. She'd said that she and other actors had to focus extremely hard to divorce themselves from verbal language in an effort to be honestly affected by what the other actors were doing and feeling. Alice didn't quite understand the distinction, but she loved Lydia for seeing her handicap as an enviable skill.

John looked happy and excited, but Alice saw that he exposed only some of the happiness and excitement he actually felt, probably trying to respect Anna's caveat of "it's still early." Even without Anna's cautioning, he was superstitious, as most biologists were, and wouldn't be inclined to openly count these two little chickens before they hatched. But he already couldn't wait. He wanted grandchildren.

Just beneath Charlie's happiness and excitement, Alice saw a thick layer of nervousness covering a thicker layer of terror. Alice thought they were both obviously visible, but Anna seemed oblivious, and no one else commented. Was she simply seeing the typical worry of an expectant first-time father? Was he nervous about the responsibility of feeding two mouths at once and paying for two college tuitions simultaneously? That would explain only the first layer. Was he also terrified about the prospect of having two kids in college and, at the same time, a wife with dementia?

Lydia and Tom stood next to each other, talking to Anna. Her children were beautiful, her children who weren't children anymore. Lydia looked radiant; she was enjoying the good news on top of the fact that her entire family was here to see her act.

Tom's smile was genuine, but Alice saw a subtle uneasiness about him, his eyes and cheeks slightly sunken, his body bonier. Was it school? A girlfriend? He saw her studying him.

"Mom, how are you feeling?" he asked.

"Mostly good."

"Really?"

"Yes, honestly. I'm feeling great."

"You seem too quiet."

"There's too many of us talking at once and too quickly," said Lydia.

Tom's smile disappeared, and he looked like he might cry. Alice's BlackBerry in her baby blue bag vibrated against her hip, signaling the time for her evening dose of pills. She'd wait a few minutes. She didn't want to take them just now, in front of Tom.

"Lyd, what time is your performance tomorrow?" asked Alice, her BlackBerry in hand.

"Eight o'clock."

"Mom, you don't have to schedule it. We're all here. It's not like we're going to forget to bring you with us," said Tom.

"What's the name of the play we're going to see?" asked Anna.

"*Proof,*" said Lydia.

"Are you nervous?" asked Tom.

"A little, because it's opening night, and you're all going to be there. But I'll forget you exist once I'm onstage."

"Lydia, what time is your play?" asked Alice.

"Mom, you just asked that. Don't worry about it," said Tom.

"It's at eight o'clock, Mom," said Lydia. "Tom, you're not helping."

"No, you're not helping. Why should she have to worry about remembering something that she doesn't have to remember?"

"She won't worry about it if she puts it in her BlackBerry. Just let her do it," said Lydia.

"Well, she shouldn't be relying on that BlackBerry anyway. She should be exercising her memory whenever she can," said Anna.

"So which is it? Should she be memorizing my showtime or totally relying on us?" asked Lydia.

"You should be encouraging her to focus and really pay attention. She should try to recall the information on her own and not get lazy," said Anna.

"She's not lazy," said Lydia.

"You and that BlackBerry are enabling her. Look, Mom, what time is Lydia's show tomorrow?" asked Anna.

"I don't know. That's why I asked her," said Alice.

"She told you the answer twice, Mom. Can you try to remember what she said?"

"Anna, stop quizzing her," said Tom.

"I was going to enter it in my BlackBerry, but you interrupted me."

"I'm not asking you to look it up in your BlackBerry. I'm asking you to remember the time she said."

"Well, I didn't try to remember the time, because I was going to punch it in."

"Mom, just think for a second. What time is Lydia's show tomorrow?"

She didn't know the answer, but she knew that poor Anna needed to be put in her place.

"Lydia, what time is your show tomorrow?" asked Alice.

"Eight o'clock."

"It's at eight o'clock, Anna."

FIVE MINUTES BEFORE EIGHT O'CLOCK, they settled in their seats, second row center. The Monomoy Theatre was an intimate venue, with only a hundred seats and a stage floor just a few feet from the first row.

Alice couldn't wait for the lights to go down. She'd read this play and talked about it extensively with Lydia. She'd even helped her run lines. Lydia was playing Catherine, daughter of her mathematical genius-gone-mad father. Alice couldn't wait to see these characters come alive right in front of her.

From the very first scene, the acting was nuanced, honest, and multidimensional, and Alice became easily and completely absorbed in the imaginary world the actors created. Catherine claimed she'd written a groundbreaking proof, but neither her love interest nor her estranged sister believed her, and they both questioned her mental stability. She tortured herself with the fear that, like her genius father, she might be going crazy. Alice experienced her pain, betrayal, and fear right along with her. She was mesmerizing from beginning to end.

Afterward, the actors came out into the audience. Catherine beamed. John gave her flowers and a huge, emphatic hug.

"You were amazing, absolutely incredible!" said John.

"Thank you so much! Isn't it such a great play?"

The others hugged and kissed and praised her, too.

"You were brilliant, beautiful to watch," said Alice.

"Thank you."

"Will we get to see you in anything else this summer?" asked Alice.

She looked at Alice for an uncomfortably long time before she answered.

"No, this is my only role for the summer."

"Are you here for just the summer season?"

The question seemed to make her sad as she considered it. Her eyes welled with tears.

"Yes, I'm moving back to L.A. at the end of August, but I'll be back this way a lot to visit with my family."

"Mom, that's Lydia, your daughter," said Anna.

The well-being of a neuron depends on its ability to communicate with other neurons. Studies have shown that electrical and chemical stimulation from both a neuron's inputs and its targets support vital cellular processes. Neurons unable to connect effectively with other neurons atrophy. Useless, an abandoned neuron will die.

SEPTEMBER 2004

Although it was officially the beginning of fall semester at Harvard, the weather was steadfastly adhering to the rules according to the Roman calendar. It was a sticky eighty degrees that summer morning in September as Alice began her commute to Harvard Yard. In the days just before and following matriculation each year, it always amused her to see the first-year students who weren't from New England. Fall in Cambridge evoked images of vibrant leaves, apple picking, football games, and wool sweaters with scarves. While it wouldn't be unusual to wake up on a late September morning in Cambridge to find frost on the pumpkin, the days, especially in early September, were still filled with the sounds of window air conditioners tirelessly groaning and fevered, pathologically optimistic discussions about the Red Sox. Yet each year there they were, these newly transplanted students, moving with the uncertainty of unseasoned tourists along the sidewalks of Harvard Square, always burdened by too many layers of wool and fleece and an excess of shopping bags from the Harvard Coop packed with all the necessary desk gear and sweatshirts bearing the HARVARD brand. The poor sweaty things.

Even in her sleeveless white cotton T-shirt and ankle-length black rayon skirt, Alice felt uncomfortably damp by the time she reached Eric Wellman's office. Directly above hers, his was the same size, with the same furniture and the same view of the Charles River and Boston, but somehow his seemed more impressive and imposing. She always felt like a student whenever she was in his office, and that feeling hovered especially present today, as she'd been called in by him "to talk for a minute."

"How was your summer?" asked Eric.

"Very relaxing. How was yours?"

"Good, it went by too fast. We all missed seeing you at the conference in June."

"I know, I missed being there."

"Well, Alice, I wanted to talk with you about your course evaluations from last semester before classes begin."

"Oh, I haven't even had a chance to look at them yet."

An elastic-bound stack of evaluations from her motivation and emotion course sat somewhere in her office, unopened. Harvard's student evaluation responses were entirely anonymous and seen only by the instructor of the course and the chair of the department. In the past, she'd read them purely as a vanity check. She knew she was a great teacher, and her students' evaluations had always nodded in unwavering agreement. But Eric had never asked her to review them with him. She feared, for the very first time in her career, that she wouldn't like the image of herself she saw reflected in them.

"Here, take a few minutes and look them over now."

He handed her his copy of the stack with the summary page on top.

On a scale from one, disagree strongly, to five, agree strongly: The instructor held students to a high standard of performance.

All fours and fives.

Class meetings enhanced an understanding of the material.

Fours, threes, and twos.

The instructor helped me to understand difficult concepts and complex ideas.

Again, fours, threes, and twos.

The instructor encouraged questions and the consideration of differing viewpoints.

Two students gave her ones.

On a one-to-five scale from poor to excellent, give an overall evaluation of the instructor.

Mostly threes. If she remembered correctly, she'd never received lower than a four in this category.

The entire summary page was splattered with threes, twos, and ones. She didn't try to convince herself that it represented anything but the accurate and thoughtful judgment of her students, without malice. Her teaching performance had outwardly suffered more than she'd been aware of. Still, she'd be willing to bet anything that she was far from the worst-rated teacher in the department. She might be sinking fast, but she was nowhere near the bottom of the barrel.

She looked up at Eric, ready to face the music, maybe not her favorite tune but probably not wholly unpleasant.

"If I hadn't seen your name on that summary, I wouldn't have thought anything of it. It's decent, not what I've ever seen attached to you, but not horrible. It's the written comments that are particularly worrisome, and I thought we should talk."

Alice hadn't looked beyond the summary page. He referred to his notes and read aloud.

" 'She skips over huge sections of the outline, so you skip it, too, but then she expects us to know it for the exam.'

" 'She doesn't seem to know the information she's teaching.'

" 'Class was a waste of time. I could've just read the textbook.'

" 'I had a hard time following her lectures. Even she gets lost in them. This class was nowhere near as good as her intro course.'

" 'Once she came to class and didn't teach. She just sat down for a few minutes and left. Another time, she taught the exact same lecture she did the week before. I'd never dream of wasting Dr. Howland's time, but I don't think she should waste mine either.'"

That was tough to hear. It was much, much more than she'd been aware of.

"Alice, we've known each other a long time, right?"

"Yes."

"I'm going to risk being blunt and too personal here. Is everything okay at home?"

"Yes."

"How about you then, is it possible that you're overstressed or depressed?"

"No, that's not it."

"This is a little embarrassing to have to ask, but do you think you might have a drinking or substance problem?"

Now she'd heard enough. *I can't live with a reputation of being a depressed, stressed-out addict. Having dementia has to carry less of a stigma than that.*

"Eric, I have Alzheimer's disease."

His face went blank. He had been braced to hear about John's infidelity. He was ready with the name of a good psychiatrist. He was prepared to orchestrate an intervention or to have her admitted to McLean Hospital to dry out. He was not prepared for this.

"I was diagnosed in January. I had a hard time teaching last semester, but I didn't realize how much it showed."

"I'm sorry, Alice."

"Me, too."

"I wasn't expecting this."

"Neither was I."

"I was expecting something temporary, something you would get past. This isn't a temporary problem we're looking at."

"No, no, it's not."

Alice watched him think. He was like a father to everyone in the department, protective and generous, but also pragmatic and strict.

"Parents are paying forty grand a year now. This wouldn't go over well with them."

No, it certainly wouldn't. They weren't shelling out astronomical dollars to have their sons and daughters learn from someone with Alzheimer's. She could already hear the uproar, the scandalous sound bites on the evening news.

"Also, a couple of students from your class are contesting their grades. I'm afraid that would only escalate."

In twenty-five years of teaching, no one had ever contested a grade given by her. Not a single student.

"I think you probably shouldn't be teaching anymore, but I'd like to respect your time line. Do you have a plan?"

"I'd hoped to stay on for the year and then take my sabbatical, but I hadn't appreciated the extent to which my symptoms were showing and disrupting my lectures. I don't want to be a bad teacher, Eric. That's not who I am."

"I know it's not. How about a medical leave that would take you into your sabbatical year?"

He wanted her out now. She had an exemplary body of work and performance history, and most important, she had tenure. Legally, they couldn't fire her. But that was not how she wanted to handle this. As much as she didn't want to give up her career at Harvard, her fight was with Alzheimer's disease, not with Eric or Harvard University.

"I'm not ready to leave, but I agree with you, as much as it breaks my heart, I think I should stop teaching. I'd like to stay on as Dan's adviser, though, and I'd like to continue to attend seminars and meetings."

I am no longer a teacher.

"I think we can work that out. I'd like you to have a talk with Dan, explain to him what's going on and leave the decision up to him. I'd be happy to coadvise with you if that makes either of you more comfortable. Also, obviously, you shouldn't take on any new graduate students. Dan will be the last."

I am no longer a research scientist.

"You probably shouldn't be accepting invitations to speak at other universities or conferences. It probably wouldn't be a good idea for you to be representing Harvard in that kind of capacity. I have noticed that you've stopped traveling for the most part, so maybe you've already recognized this."

"Yes, I agree."

"How do you want to handle telling the administrative faculty and people in the department? Again, I'll respect your time line here, whatever you want to do."

She was going to stop teaching, researching, traveling, and lecturing. People were going to notice. They were going to speculate and whisper and gossip. They were going to think she was a depressed, stressed-out addict. Maybe some of them already did.

"I'll tell them. It should come from me."

September 17, 2004

Dear Friends and Colleagues,

Upon thoughtful consideration and with deep sorrow, I have decided to step down from my teaching, research, and traveling responsibilities at Harvard. In January of this year, I was diagnosed with early-onset Alzheimer's disease.

While I am likely still in the early to moderate stages of the disease, I've been experiencing unpredictable cognitive lapses that make it impossible for me to meet the demands of this position with the highest of standards that I've always held myself to and that are expected here.

While you'll no longer see me at the podium in the lecture auditoriums or busy writing new grant proposals, I will remain on as Dan Maloney's thesis adviser, and I'll still attend meetings and seminars, where it is my hope to continue to serve as an active and welcome participant.

With greatest affection and respect,
Alice Howland

THE FIRST WEEK OF THE fall semester, Marty took over Alice's teaching responsibilities. When she met with him to hand over the syllabus and lecture materials, he hugged her and said how very sorry he was. He asked her how she was feeling and if there was anything he could do. She thanked him and told him she was feeling fine. And as soon as he had everything he needed for the course, he left her office as fast as he could.

Pretty much the same drill followed with everyone in the department.

"I'm so sorry, Alice."

"I just can't believe it."

"I had no idea."

"Is there anything I can do?"

"Are you sure? You don't look any different."

"I'm so sorry."

"I'm so sorry."

Then they left her alone as quickly as possible. They were

politely kind to her when they ran into her, but they didn't run into her very often. This was largely because of their busy schedules and Alice's now rather empty one. But a not so insignificant reason was because they chose not to. Facing her meant facing her mental frailty and the unavoidable thought that, in the blink of an eye, it could happen to them. Facing her was scary. So for the most part, except for meetings and seminars, they didn't.

TODAY WAS THE FIRST PSYCHOLOGY Lunch Seminar of the semester. Leslie, one of Eric's graduate students, stood poised and ready at the head of the conference table with the title slide already projected onto the screen. "Searching for Answers: How Attention Affects the Ability to Identify What We See." Alice felt poised and ready as well, sitting in the first seat at the table, across from Eric. She began eating her lunch, an eggplant calzone and a garden salad, while Eric and Leslie talked, and the room filled in.

After a few minutes, Alice noticed that every seat at the table was occupied except for the one next to her, and people had begun taking up standing positions at the back of the room. Seats at the table were highly coveted, not only because the location made it easier to see the presentation but because sitting eliminated the awkward juggling of plate, utensils, drink, pen, and notebook. Apparently, that juggling was less awkward than sitting next to her. She looked at everyone not looking at her. About fifty people crowded into the room, people she'd known for many years, people she'd thought of as family.

Dan rushed in, his hair disheveled, his shirt untucked, wearing glasses instead of contact lenses. He paused for a moment, then went straight for the open seat next to Alice and declared it his by plopping his notebook down on the table.

"I was up all night writing. Gotta get some food, be right back."

Leslie's talk ran the full hour. It took an excessive amount of energy, but Alice followed her to the end. After Leslie advanced past the last slide and the screen went blank, she opened up the floor to discussion. Alice went first.

"Yes, Dr. Howland," said Leslie.

"I think you're missing a control group that measures the actual distractibility of your distracters. You could argue that some, for whatever reason, simply aren't noticed, and their mere presence isn't distracting. You could test the ability of the subjects to simultaneously notice and attend to the distracter, or you could run a series where you swap out the distracter for the target."

Many at the table nodded. Dan uh-huhed through a mouthful of calzone. Leslie grabbed her pen even before Alice finished her thought and took vigorous notes.

"Yes. Leslie, go back to the experimental design slide for a moment," said Eric.

Alice looked around the room. Everyone's eyes were glued to the screen. They listened intently as Eric elaborated on Alice's comment. Many continued nodding. She felt victorious and a little smug. The fact that she had Alzheimer's didn't mean that she was no longer capable of thinking analytically. The fact that she had Alzheimer's didn't mean that she didn't deserve to sit in that room among them. The fact that she had Alzheimer's didn't mean that she no longer deserved to be heard.

The questions and answers and follow-up questions and

answers continued for several minutes. Alice finished her calzone and her salad. Dan got up and came back with seconds. Leslie stumbled through an answer to an antagonistic question asked by Marty's new postdoc. Her experimental design slide was projected on the screen. Alice read it and raised her hand.

"Yes, Dr. Howland?" asked Leslie.

"I think you're missing a control group that measures the actual effectiveness of your distracters. It's possible that some of them simply aren't noticed. You could test their distractibility simultaneously, or you might swap out the distracter for the target."

It was a valid point. It was, in fact, the proper way to do the experiment, and her paper wouldn't be publishable without that possibility satisfied. Alice was sure of it. Yet no one else seemed to see it. She looked at everyone not looking at her. Their body language suggested embarrassment and dread. She reread the data on the screen. That experiment needed an additional control. The fact that she had Alzheimer's didn't mean that she couldn't think analytically. The fact that she had Alzheimer's didn't mean that she didn't know what she was talking about.

"Ah, okay, thanks," said Leslie.

But she didn't take any notes, and she didn't look Alice in the eye, and she didn't seem at all grateful.

SHE HAD NO CLASSES TO teach, no grants to write, no new research to conduct, no conferences to attend, and no invited lectures to give. Ever again. She felt like the biggest part of her self, the part she'd praised and polished regularly on its mighty pedestal, had died. And the other smaller, less admired parts of her self wailed with self-pitying grief, wondering how they would matter at all without it.

She looked out her enormous office window and watched the joggers as they traced the winding edges of the Charles.

"Will you have time for a run today?" she asked.

"Maybe," said John.

He looked out the window, too, as he drank his coffee. She wondered what he saw, if his eyes were drawn to the same joggers or if he saw something entirely different.

"I wish we'd spent more time together," she said.

"What do you mean? We just spent the whole summer together."

"No, not the summer, our whole lives. I've been thinking about it, and I wish we'd spent more time together."

"Ali, we live together, we work at the same place, we've spent our whole lives together."

In the beginning, they did. They lived their lives together, with each other. But over the years, it had changed. They had allowed it to change. She thought about the sabbaticals apart, the division of labor over the kids, the travel, their singular dedication to work. They'd been living next to each other for a long time.

"I think we left each other alone for too long."

"I don't feel left alone, Ali. I like our lives, I think it's been a good balance between an independence to pursue our own passions and a life together."

She thought about his pursuit of his passion, his research, always more extreme than hers. Even when the experiments failed him, when the data weren't consistent, when the hypotheses turned out to be wrong, his love for his passion never wavered. However flawed, even when it kept him up all night tearing his hair out, he loved it. The time, care, attention, and energy he gave to it had always inspired her to work harder at her own research. And she did.

"You're not left alone, Ali. I'm right here with you."

He looked at his watch, then downed the rest of his coffee.

"I've got to run to class."

He picked up his bag, tossed his cup in the trash, and went over to her. He bent down, held her head of curly black hair in his hands, and kissed her gently. She looked up at him and pressed her lips into a thin smile, holding back her tears just long enough for him to leave her office.

She wished she'd been his passion.

SHE SAT IN HER OFFICE while her cognition class met without her and watched the shiny traffic creep along Memorial Drive. She sipped her tea. She had the whole day in front of her with nothing to do. Her hip began to vibrate. It was 8:00 a.m. She removed her BlackBerry from her baby blue bag.

Alice, answer the following questions:

1. What month is it?
2. Where do you live?
3. Where is your office?
4. When is Anna's birthday?
5. How many children do you have?

If you have trouble answering any of these, go to the file named "Butterfly" on your computer and follow the instructions there immediately.

September
34 Poplar Street, Cambridge
William James Hall, room 1002
September 14
Three

She sipped her tea and watched the shiny traffic creep along Memorial Drive.

OCTOBER 2004

She sat up in bed and wondered what to do. It was dark, still middle of the night. She wasn't confused. She knew she should be sleeping. John lay on his back next to her, snoring. But she couldn't fall asleep. She'd been having a lot of trouble sleeping through the night lately, probably because she was napping a lot during the day. Or was she napping a lot during the day because she wasn't sleeping well at night? She was caught in a vicious cycle, a positive feedback loop, a dizzying ride that she didn't know how to step off. Maybe, if she fought through the urge to nap during the day, she'd sleep through the night and break the pattern. But every day, she felt so exhausted by late afternoon that she always succumbed to a rest on the couch. And the rest always seduced her to sleep.

She remembered facing a similar dilemma when her children were around two years old. Without an afternoon nap, they turned miserable and uncooperative by the evening. With a nap, they stayed wide awake hours past their usual bedtime. She couldn't remember the solution.

With all the pills I'm taking, you'd think at least one would have drowsiness as a side effect. Oh, wait. I have that sleeping pill prescription.

She got out of bed and walked downstairs. Although fairly confident it wasn't in there, she emptied her baby blue bag first. Wallet, BlackBerry, cell phone, keys. She opened her wallet. Credit card, bank card, license, Harvard ID, health insurance card, twenty dollars, a handful of change.

She rifled through the white mushroom bowl where they kept the mail. Light bill, gas bill, phone bill, mortgage statement, something from Harvard, receipts.

She opened and emptied the contents of the drawers to the desk and file cabinet in the study. She emptied the magazines and catalogs out of the baskets in the living room. She read a couple of pages from *The Week* magazine and dog-eared a page in the J.Jill catalog with a cute sweater. She liked it in sea-foam blue.

She opened the junk drawer. Batteries, a screwdriver, Scotch tape, blue tape, glue, keys, a number of chargers, matches, and so much more. This drawer probably hadn't been organized in years. She pulled the drawer completely off its tracks and dumped the entirety of its contents onto the kitchen table.

"Ali, what are you doing?" asked John.

Startled, she looked up at his bewildered hair and squinting eyes.

"I'm looking for . . ."

She looked down at the items jumbled before her on the table. Batteries, a sewing kit, glue, a tape measurer, several chargers, a screwdriver.

"I'm looking for something."

"Ali, it's after three. You're making a racket down here. Can you look for it in the morning?"

His voice sounded impatient. He didn't like having his sleep disrupted.

"Okay."

She lay in bed and tried to remember what she'd been looking for. It was dark, still middle of the night. She knew she should be sleeping. John had fallen back to sleep without ceremony and was already snoring. He was a fast sleeper. She used to be, too. But she couldn't fall asleep. She'd been having a lot of trouble sleeping through the night lately, probably because she was napping a lot during the day. Or was she napping a lot during the day because she wasn't sleeping well at night? She was caught in a vicious cycle, a positive feedback loop, a dizzying ride that she didn't know how to step off.

Oh, wait. I have a way to get to sleep. I have those pills from Dr. Moyer. Where did I put them?

She got out of bed and walked downstairs.

THERE WERE NO MEETINGS OR seminars today. None of the textbooks, periodicals, or mail in her office interested her. Dan didn't have anything ready for her to read. She had nothing new in her inbox. Lydia's daily email wouldn't come until after noon. She watched the movement outside her window. Cars zipped around the curves of Memorial Drive, and joggers ran along the curves of the river. The tops of pine trees swayed in the turbulent fall air.

She pulled all of the folders out of the bin marked HOWLAND REPRINTS from her file cabinet. She'd authored well over a hundred published papers. She held this stack of research articles, commentaries, and reviews, her truncated career's worth of thoughts and opinions, in her hands. It was heavy. Her thoughts and opinions carried weight. At least, they used to. She missed her research, thinking about it, talking about it, her own ideas and insights, the elegant art of her science.

She put the pile of folders down and selected her *From Molecules to Mind* textbook from the bookcase. It, too, was heavy. It was her proudest written achievement, her words and ideas blended with John's, creating something together that was unique in this universe, informing and influencing the words and ideas of others. She'd assumed they'd write another someday. She flipped through the pages without being lured in. She didn't feel like reading that either.

She checked her watch. She and John were supposed to go for a run at the end of the day. That was way too many hours away. She decided to run home.

Their house was only about a mile from her office, and she got there quickly and easily. Now what? She walked into the kitchen to make some tea. She filled the kettle with tap water, placed it back on the stove, and turned the burner knob to Hi. She went to get a tea bag. The tin container where she kept the tea bags wasn't anywhere on the counter. She opened the cabinet where she kept the coffee mugs. She stared instead at three shelves of plates. She opened the cabinet to the right of that, where she expected to see rows of glasses, but instead it housed bowls and mugs.

She took the bowls and mugs out of the cabinet and put them on the counter. Then, she removed the plates and placed them next to the bowls and mugs. She opened the next cabinet. Nothing right in there either. The counter was soon stacked high with plates, bowls, mugs, juice glasses, water glasses, wineglasses, pots, pans, Tupperware, pot holders, dish towels, and silverware. The entire kitchen was inside out. *Now, where did I have it all before?* The teakettle shrilled, and she couldn't think. She turned the burner knob to Off.

She heard the front door open. *Oh good, John's home early.*

"John, why did you do this to the kitchen?" she hollered.

"Alice, what are you doing?"

The woman's voice startled her.

"Oh, Lauren, you scared me."

It was her neighbor who lived across the street. Lauren didn't say anything.

"I'm sorry, would you like to sit down? I was about to make some tea."

"Alice, this isn't your kitchen."

What? She looked around the room—black granite countertops, birch cabinets, white tile floor, window over the sink, dishwasher to the right of the sink, double oven. Wait, she didn't have a double oven, did she? Then, for the first time, she noticed the refrigerator. The smoking gun. The collage of pictures stuck with magnets to its door were of Lauren and Lauren's husband and Lauren's cat and babies Alice didn't recognize.

"Oh, Lauren, look what I did to your kitchen. I'll help you put everything back."

"That's okay, Alice. Are you all right?"

"No, not really."

She wanted to run home to her own kitchen. Couldn't they just forget this happened? Did she really have to have the I-have-Alzheimer's-disease conversation right now? She hated the I-have-Alzheimer's-disease conversation.

Alice tried to read Lauren's face. She looked baffled and scared. Her face was thinking, *Alice might be crazy.* Alice closed her eyes and took a deep breath.

"I have Alzheimer's disease."

She opened her eyes. The look on Lauren's face didn't change.

Now, every time she entered the kitchen, she checked the refrigerator, just to be sure. No pictures of Lauren. She was in the right house. In case that didn't remove all doubt, John had written a note in big black letters and stuck it with a magnet to the refrigerator door.

ALICE,
DO NOT GO RUNNING WITHOUT ME.

MY CELL: 617-555-1122
ANNA: 617-555-1123
TOM: 617-555-1124

John had made her promise not to go running without him. She'd sworn she wouldn't and crossed her heart. Of course, she might forget.

Her ankle could probably use the time off anyway. She'd rolled it stepping off a curb last week. Her spatial perception was a bit off. Objects sometimes appeared closer or farther or generally somewhere other than where they actually were. She'd had her eyes checked. Her vision was fine. She had the eyes of a twenty-year-old. The problem wasn't with her corneas, lenses, or retinas. The glitch was somewhere in the processing of visual information, somewhere in her occipital cortex, said John. Apparently, she had the eyes of a college student and the occipital cortex of an octogenarian.

No running without John. She might get lost or hurt. But lately there was no running with John either. He'd been traveling a lot, and when he wasn't out of town, he left the house for Harvard early and worked late. By the time he got home, he was always too tired. She hated depending on him to go running, especially since he wasn't dependable.

She picked up the phone and dialed the number on the refrigerator.

"Hello?"

"Are we going for a run today?" she asked.

"I don't know, maybe, I'm in a meeting. I'll call you later," said John.

"I really need to go for a run."

"I'll call you later."

"When?"

"When I can."

"Fine."

She hung up the phone, looked out the window and then down at the running shoes on her feet. She peeled them off and threw them at the wall.

She tried to be understanding. He needed to work. But why didn't he understand that she needed to run? If something as simple as regular exercise really did counter the progression of this disease, then she should be running as often as she could. Each time he told her "Not today," she might be losing more neurons that she could have saved. Dying needlessly faster. John was killing her.

She picked up the phone again.

"Yes?" asked John, hushed and annoyed.

"I want you to promise that we'll run today."

"Excuse me for a minute," he said to someone else. "Please, Alice, let me call you after I get out of this meeting."

"I need to run today."

"I don't know yet when my day's going to end."

"So?"

"This is why I think we should get you a treadmill."

"Oh, fuck you," she said, hanging up.

She supposed that wasn't very understanding. She flashed to anger a lot lately. Whether this was a symptom of her disease advancing or a justified response, she couldn't say. She didn't want a treadmill. She wanted him. Maybe she shouldn't be so stubborn. Maybe she was killing herself, too.

She could always walk somewhere without him. Of course, this somewhere had to be somewhere "safe." She could walk to her office. But she didn't want to go to her office. She felt bored, ignored, and alienated in her office. She felt ridiculous there. She didn't belong there anymore. In all the expansive grandeur that was Harvard, there wasn't room there for a cognitive psychology professor with a broken cognitive psyche.

She sat in her living room armchair and tried to think of what to do. Nothing meaningful enough came to her. She tried to imagine tomorrow, next week, the coming winter. Nothing meaningful enough came to her. She felt bored, ignored, and alienated in her living room armchair. The late afternoon sun cast strange, Tim Burton shadows that slithered and undulated across the floor and up the walls. She watched the shadows dissolve and the room dim. She closed her eyes and fell asleep.

ALICE STOOD IN THEIR BEDROOM, naked but for a pair of ankle socks and her Safe Return bracelet, wrestling and growling at an article of clothing stretched around her head. Like a Martha Graham dance, her battle against the fabric shrouding her head looked like a physical and poetic expression of anguish. She let out a long scream.

"What's happening?" asked John, running in.

She looked at him with one panicked eye through a round hole in the twisted garment.

"I can't do this! I can't figure out how to put on this fucking sports bra. I can't remember how to put on a bra, John! I can't put on my own bra!"

He went to her and examined her head.

"That's not a bra, Ali, it's a pair of underwear."

She burst into laughter.

"It's not funny," said John.

She laughed harder.

"Stop it, it's not funny. Look, if you want to go running, you have to hurry up and get dressed. I don't have a lot of time."

He left the room, unable to watch her standing there, naked with her underwear on her head, laughing at her own absurd madness.

ALICE KNEW THAT THE YOUNG woman sitting across from her was her daughter, but she had a disturbing lack of confidence in this knowledge. She knew that she had a daughter named Lydia, but when she looked at the young woman sitting across from her, knowing that *she* was her daughter Lydia was more academic knowledge than implicit understanding, a fact she agreed to, information she'd been given and accepted as true.

She looked at Tom and Anna, also sitting at the table, and she could automatically connect them with the memories she had of her oldest child and her son. She could picture Anna in her wedding gown, in her law school, college, and high school graduation gowns, and in the Snow White nightgown she'd insisted on wearing every day when she was three. She could remember Tom in his cap and gown, in a cast when he broke his leg skiing, in braces, in his Little League uniform, and in her arms when he was an infant.

She could see Lydia's history as well, but somehow this woman sitting across from her wasn't inextricably connected to her memories of her youngest child. This made her uneasy and painfully aware that she was declining, her past becoming unhinged from her present. And how strange that she had no problem identifying the man next to Anna as Anna's husband, Charlie, who had entered their lives only a couple of years ago. She pictured her Alzheimer's as a demon in her head, tearing a reckless and illogical path of destruction, ripping apart the wiring from "Lydia now" to "Lydia then," leaving all the "Charlie" connections unscathed.

The restaurant was crowded and noisy. Voices from other tables competed for Alice's attention, and the music in the background moved in and out of the foreground. Anna's and Lydia's voices sounded the same to her. Everyone used too many pronouns. She struggled to locate who was talking at her table and to follow what was being said.

"Honey, you okay?" asked Charlie.

"The smells," said Anna.

"You want to go outside for a minute?" asked Charlie.

"I'll go with her," said Alice.

Alice's back tensed as soon as they left the cozy warmth of the restaurant. They'd both forgotten to bring their coats. Anna grabbed Alice's hand and led her away from a circle of young smokers hovering near the door.

"Ahh, fresh air," said Anna, taking a luxurious breath in and out through her nose.

"And quiet," said Alice.

"How are you feeling, Mom?"

"I'm okay," said Alice.

Anna rubbed the back of Alice's hand, the hand she was still holding.

"I've been better," she admitted.

"Same here," said Anna. "Were you sick like this when you were pregnant with me?"

"Uh-huh."

"How did you do it?"

"You just keep going. It'll stop soon."

"And before you know it, the babies will be here."

"I can't wait."

"Me, too," Anna said. But her voice didn't carry the same exuberance Alice's did. Her eyes suddenly filled with tears.

"Mom, I feel sick all the time, and I'm exhausted, and every time I forget something I think I'm becoming symptomatic."

"Oh, sweetie, you're not, you're just tired."

"I know, I know. It's just when I think about you not teaching anymore and everything you're losing—"

"Don't. This should be an exciting time for you. Please, just think about what we're gaining."

Alice squeezed the hand she held and placed her other one gently on Anna's stomach. Anna smiled, but the tears still spilled out of her overwhelmed eyes.

"I just don't know how I'm going to handle it all. My job and two babies and—"

"And Charlie. Don't forget about you and Charlie. Keep what you have with him. Keep everything in balance—you and Charlie, your career, your kids, everything you love. Don't take any of the things you love in your life for granted, and you'll do it all. Charlie will help you."

"He better," Anna threatened.

Alice laughed. Anna wiped her eyes several times with the heels of her hands and blew a long, Lamaze-like breath out through her mouth.

"Thanks, Mom. I feel better."

"Good."

Back inside the restaurant, they settled into their seats and ate dinner. The young woman across from Alice, her youngest child, Lydia, clanged her empty wineglass with her knife.

"Mom, we'd like to give you your big gift now."

Lydia presented her with a small, rectangular package wrapped in gold paper. It must have been big in significance. Alice untaped the paper. Inside were three DVDs—*The Howland Kids, Alice and John,* and *Alice Howland.*

"It's a video memoir for you. *The Howland Kids* is a collection of interviews of Anna, Tom, and me. I shot them this summer. It's our memories of you and our childhoods and growing up. The one with Dad is of his memories of meeting you and dating and your wedding and vacations and lots of other stuff. There are a couple of really great stories in that one that none of us kids knew about. The third one I haven't made yet. It's an interview of you, of your stories, if you want to do it."

"I absolutely want to do it. I love it. Thank you, I can't wait to watch them."

The waitress brought them coffee, tea, and chocolate cake with a candle in it. They all sang "Happy Birthday." Alice blew out the candle and made a wish.

NOVEMBER 2004

The movies that John had bought over the summer now fell into the same unfortunate category as the abandoned books they'd replaced. She could no longer follow the thread of the plot or remember the significance of the characters if they weren't in every scene. She could appreciate small moments but retained only a general sense of the film after the credits rolled. *That movie was funny.* If John or Anna watched with her, they would many times roar with laughter or jump with alarm or cringe with disgust, reacting in an obvious, visceral way to something that happened, and she wouldn't understand why. She would join in, faking it, trying to protect them from how lost she was. Watching movies made her keenly aware of how lost she was.

The DVDs Lydia had made came at just the right time. Each story told by John and the kids ran only a few minutes long, so she could absorb each one, and she didn't have to actively hold the information in any particular story to understand or enjoy the others. She watched them over and over. She didn't remember everything they talked about, but this felt completely normal, for each of her children and John didn't remember all of the details either. And when Lydia asked them all to recount the same event, each remembered it somewhat differently, omitting some parts, exaggerating others, emphasizing their own individual perspectives. Even biographies not saturated with disease were vulnerable to holes and distortions.

She could only stomach watching the *Alice Howland* video once. She used to be so eloquent, so comfortable talking in front of any audience. Now, she overused the word *thingy* and repeated herself an embarrassing number of times. But she felt grateful to have it, her memories, reflections, and advice recorded and pinned down, safe from the molecular mayhem of Alzheimer's disease. Her grandchildren would watch it someday and say, "That's Grandma when she could still talk and remember things."

She had just finished watching *Alice and John.* She remained on the couch with a blanket on her lap after the television screen faded to black and listened. The quiet pleased her. She breathed and thought of nothing for several minutes but the sound of the ticking clock on the fireplace mantel. Then, suddenly, the ticking took on meaning, and her eyes popped open.

She looked at the hands. Ten minutes until ten o'clock. *Oh my god, what am I still doing here?* She threw the blanket onto the floor, crammed her feet into her shoes, ran into the study, and clicked her laptop bag shut. *Where's my blue bag?* Not on the chair, not on the desk, not in the desk drawers, not in the laptop bag. She jogged up to her bedroom. Not on her bed, not on the night table, not on the dresser, not in the closet, not on the desk. She was standing in the hallway, retracing her whereabouts in her boggled mind, when she saw it, hanging on the bathroom doorknob.

She unzipped it. Cell phone, BlackBerry, no keys. She always put them in there. Well, that wasn't entirely true. She always meant to put them in there. Sometimes, she put them in her desk drawer, the silverware drawer, her underwear drawer, her jewelry box, the mailbox, and any number of pockets. Sometimes, she simply left them in the keyhole. She hated to think of how many minutes each day she spent looking for her own misplaced things.

She bolted back downstairs to the living room. No keys, but she found her coat on the wing chair. She put it on and shoved her hands in the pockets. Keys!

She raced to the front hallway, but then stopped before she could reach the door. It was the strangest thing. There was a large hole in the floor just in front of the door. It spanned the width of the hallway and was about eight or nine feet in length, with nothing but the dark basement below it. It was impassable. The front hall floorboards were warped and creaky, and she and John had talked recently about replacing them. Had John hired a contractor? Had someone been here today? She couldn't remember. Whatever the reason, there was no using the front door until the hole was fixed.

On her way to the back door, the phone rang.

“Hi, Mom. I’ll be over around seven, and I’ll bring dinner.”

“Okay,” said Alice, a slight rise in her tone.

“It’s Anna.”

“I know.”

“Dad’s in New York until tomorrow, remember? I’m sleeping over tonight. I can’t get out of work before six thirty, though, so wait for me to eat. Maybe you should write this down on the whiteboard on the fridge.”

She looked over at the whiteboard.

DO NOT GO RUNNING WITHOUT ME.

Provoked, she wanted to scream into the phone that she didn’t need a babysitter, and she could manage just fine alone in her own house. She breathed instead.

“Okay, see you later.”

She hung up the phone and congratulated herself on still having editorial control over her raw emotions. Someday soon, she wouldn’t. She would enjoy seeing Anna, and it would be good not to be alone.

She had her coat on and her laptop and baby blue bag slung over her shoulder. She looked out the kitchen window. Windy, damp, gray. Morning, maybe? She didn’t feel like going outside, and she didn’t feel like sitting in her office. She felt bored, ignored, and alienated in her office. She felt ridiculous there. She didn’t belong there anymore.

She removed her bags and coat and headed for the study, but a sudden thud and clink made her backtrack to the front hallway. The mail had just been delivered through the slot in the door, and it lay on top of the hole, somehow hovering there. It had to be balancing on an underlying beam or floorboard that she couldn’t see. *Floating mail. My brain is fried!* She retreated into the study and tried to forget about the gravity-defying hole in the front hallway. It was surprisingly difficult.

SHE SAT IN HER STUDY, hugging her knees, staring out the window at the darkened day, waiting for Anna to come over with dinner, waiting for John to return from New York so she could go for a run. She was sitting and waiting. She was sitting and waiting to get worse. She was sick of just sitting and waiting.

She was the only person she knew with early-onset Alzheimer's disease at Harvard. She was the only person she knew anywhere with early-onset Alzheimer's. Surely, she wasn't the only one anywhere. She needed to find her new colleagues. She needed to inhabit this new world she found herself in, this world of dementia.

She typed the words "early-onset Alzheimer's disease" into Google. It pulled up a lot of facts and statistics.

There are an estimated five hundred thousand people in the United States with early-onset Alzheimer's disease.

Early-onset is defined as Alzheimer's under the age of sixty-five.

Symptoms can develop in the thirties and forties.

It pulled up sites with lists of symptoms, genetic risk factors, causes, and treatments. It pulled up articles about research and drug discovery. She'd seen all this before.

She added the word "support" to her Google search and hit the return key.

She found forums, links, resources, message boards, and

chat rooms. For caregivers. Caregiver help topics included visiting the nursing facility, questions about medications, stress relief, dealing with delusions, dealing with night wandering, coping with denial and depression. Caregivers posted questions and answers, commiserating about and troubleshooting issues regarding their eighty-one-year-old mothers, their seventy-four-year-old husbands, and their eighty-five-year-old grandmothers with Alzheimer's disease.

What about support for the people with *Alzheimer's disease? Where are the other fifty-one-year-olds with dementia? Where are the other people who were in the middle of their careers when this diagnosis ripped their lives right out from under them?* She didn't deny that getting Alzheimer's was tragic at any age. She didn't deny that caregivers needed support. She didn't deny that they suffered. She knew that John suffered. *But what about me?*

She remembered the business card of the social worker at Mass General Hospital. She found it and dialed the number.

"Denise Daddario."

"Hi, Denise, this is Alice Howland. I'm a patient of Dr. Davis, and he gave me your card. I'm fifty-one, and I was diagnosed with early-onset Alzheimer's almost a year ago. I was wondering, does MGH run any sort of support group for people with Alzheimer's?"

"No, unfortunately we don't. We have a support group, but it's only for caregivers. Most of our patients with Alzheimer's wouldn't be capable of participating in that kind of forum."

"But some would."

"Yes, but I'm afraid we don't have the numbers to justify the resources it would take to get that kind of group up and running."

"What kinds of resources?"

"Well, with our caregivers' support group, about twelve to fifteen people meet every week for a couple of hours. We have a room reserved, coffee, pastries, a couple of people on staff who act as facilitators, and a guest speaker once a month."

"What about just an empty room where people with early-onset dementia can meet and talk about what we're experiencing?"

I can bring the coffee and jelly donuts, for god's sake.

"We'd need someone on staff at the hospital to oversee it, and we unfortunately don't have anyone available right now."

How about one of the two facilitators from your caregivers' support group?

"Can you give me the contact information for the patients you know of with early-onset dementia so I can try to organize something on my own?"

"I'm afraid I can't give out that information. Would you like to make an appointment to come in and talk with me? I have an opening at ten in the morning on Friday, December seventeenth."

"No thanks."

A NOISE AT THE FRONT door woke her from her nap on the couch. The house was cold and dark. The front door squeaked as it opened.

"Sorry I'm late!"

Alice rose and walked to the hallway. Anna stood there with a big brown paper bag in one hand and a jumbled pile of mail in the other. She was standing on the hole!

"Mom, all the lights are off in here. Were you sleeping?

You shouldn't be napping this late in the day, you'll never sleep tonight."

Alice walked over to her and crouched down. She put her hand on the hole. Only it wasn't empty space she felt. She ran her fingers over the looped wool of a black rug. Her black hallway rug. It'd been there for years. She smacked it with her open hand so hard the sound she made echoed.

"Mom, what are you doing?"

Her hand stung, she was too tired to endure the humiliating answer to Anna's question, and an overpowering peanut smell coming from the bag disgusted her.

"Leave me alone!"

"Mom, it's okay. Let's go in the kitchen and have dinner."

Anna put the mail down and reached for her mother's hand, the hand that stung. Alice flung it away from her and screamed.

"Leave me alone! Get out of my house! I hate you! I don't want you here!"

Her words hit Anna's face harder than if she'd slapped her. Through the tears that streamed down it, Anna's expression clenched into calm resolve.

"I brought dinner, I'm starving, and I'm staying. I'm going into the kitchen to eat, and then I'm going to bed."

Alice stood in the hallway alone, fury and fight raging madly through her veins. She opened the door and began pulling at the rug. She yanked with all her strength and was knocked down. She got up and pulled and twisted and wrestled it until it was entirely outside. Then, she kicked and screamed wildly at it until it limped down the front steps and lay lifeless on the sidewalk.

Alice, answer the following questions:

1. What month is it?
2. Where do you live?
3. Where is your office?
4. When is Anna's birthday?
5. How many children do you have?

If you have trouble answering any of these, go to the file named "Butterfly" on your computer and follow the instructions there immediately.

November
Cambridge
Harvard
September
Three

DECEMBER 2004

Dan's thesis numbered 142 pages, not including references. Alice hadn't read anything that long in a long time. She sat on the couch with Dan's words in her lap, a red pen balanced on her right ear, and a pink highlighter in her right hand. She used the red pen for editing and the pink highlighter for keeping track of what she'd already read. She highlighted anything that struck her as important, so when she needed to backtrack, she could limit her rereading to the colored words.

She became hopelessly stalled on page twenty-six, which was saturated in pink. Her brain felt overwhelmed and begged her for rest. She imagined the pink words on the page transforming into sticky pink cotton candy in her head. The more she read, the more she needed to highlight to understand and remember what she was reading. The more she highlighted, the more her head became packed with pink, woolly sugar, clogging and muffling the circuits in her brain that were needed to understand and remember what she was reading. By page twenty-six, she understood nothing.

Beep, beep.

She tossed Dan's thesis onto the coffee table and went to the computer in the study. She found one new email in her inbox, from Denise Daddario.

Dear Alice,

I've shared your idea for an early-stage dementia support group with the other early-onsetters here in our unit and with the folks at Brigham and Women's Hospital. I've heard back from three people who are local and very interested in this idea. They've given me permission to give you their names and contact information (see attachment).

You might also want to contact the Mass Alzheimer's Association. They may know of others who'd want to meet with you.

Keep me posted with how it goes, and let me know if I can provide you with any other information or advice. I'm sorry we couldn't formally do more for you here.

Good luck!

Denise Daddario

She opened the attachment.

Mary Johnson, age fifty-seven, Frontotemporal lobe dementia
Cathy Roberts, age forty-eight, Early-onset Alzheimer's disease
Dan Sullivan, age fifty-three, Early-onset Alzheimer's disease

There they were, her new colleagues. She read their names over and over. *Mary, Cathy, and Dan. Mary, Cathy, and Dan.* She began to feel the kind of wondrous excitement mixed with barely suppressed dread she'd experienced in the weeks before her first days of kindergarten, college, and graduate school. What did they look like? Were they still working? How long had they been living with their diagnoses? Were their symptoms the same, milder, or worse? Were they anything like her? *What if I'm much further along than they are?*

Dear Mary, Cathy, and Dan,

My name is Alice Howland. I am fifty-one years old and was diagnosed with early-onset Alzheimer's disease last year. I was a psychology professor at Harvard University for twenty-five years but essentially failed out of my position due to my symptoms this September.

Now I'm home and feeling really alone in this. I called Denise Daddario at MGH for information on an early-stage dementia support group. They only have one for caregivers, nothing for us. But she gave me your names.

I'd like to invite you all to my house for tea, coffee, and conversation this Sunday, December 5, at 2:00. Your caregivers are welcome to come and stay if you'd like. Attached are my address and directions.

I'm looking forward to meeting you,
Alice

Mary, Cathy, and Dan. Mary, Cathy, and Dan. Dan. Dan's thesis. He's waiting for my edits. She returned to the living room couch and opened Dan's thesis to page twenty-six. The pink rushed into her head. Her head ached. She wondered if anyone had replied yet. She abandoned Dan's thingy before she even finished the thought.

She clicked on her inbox. Nothing new.

Beep, beep.

She picked up the phone.

"Hello?"

Dial tone. She'd hoped it was Mary, Cathy, or Dan. *Dan. Dan's thesis.*

Back on the couch, she looked poised and active with the highlighter in her hand, but her eyes weren't focused on the letters on the page. Instead, she daydreamed.

Could Mary, Cathy, and Dan still read twenty-six pages and understand and remember all that they read? *What if I'm the only one who thinks the hallway rug could be a hole?* What if she was the only one declining? She could feel herself declining. She could feel herself slipping into that demented hole. Alone.

"I'm alone, I'm alone, I'm alone," she moaned, sinking further into the truth of her lonely hole each time she heard her own voice say the words.

Beep, beep.

The doorbell snapped her out of it. Were they here? Had she invited them over today?

"Just a minute!"

She rubbed her eyes with her sleeves, combed her fingers through her matted hair as she walked, took a deep breath, and opened the door. There was no one there.

Auditory and visual hallucinations were realities for about half of people with Alzheimer's disease, but so far she hadn't experienced any. Or maybe she had. When she was alone, there wasn't any clear way of knowing whether what she experienced was reality or her reality with Alzheimer's. It wasn't as if her disorientations, confabulations, delusions, and all other demented thingies were highlighted in fluorescent pink, unmistakably distinguishable from what was normal, actual, and correct. From her perspective, she simply couldn't tell the difference. The rug was a hole. That noise was the doorbell.

She checked her inbox again. One new email.

Hi Mom,

How are you? Did you go to the lunch seminar yesterday? Did you run? My class was great, as usual. I had another audition today for a bank commercial. We'll see. How's Dad doing? Is he home this week? I know last month was hard. Hang in there. I'll be home soon!

Love,

Lydia

Beep, beep.

She picked up the phone.

"Hello?"

Dial tone. She opened the top file cabinet drawer, dropped the phone inside, heard it hit the metal bottom beneath hundreds of hanging reprints, and slid the drawer shut. *Wait, maybe it's my cell phone.*

"Cell phone, cell phone, cell phone," she chanted aloud as she roamed the house, trying to keep the goal of her search present.

She checked everywhere but couldn't find it. Then she figured out that she needed to be looking for her baby blue bag. She changed the chant.

"Blue bag, blue bag, blue bag."

She found it on the kitchen counter, her cell phone inside, but off. Maybe the noise was someone's car alarm locking or unlocking outside. She resumed her position on the couch and opened Dan's thesis to page twenty-six.

"Hello?" asked a man's voice.

Alice looked up, eyes wide, and listened, as if she'd just been summoned by a ghost.

"Alice?" asked the disembodied voice.

"Yes?"

"Alice, are you ready to go?"

John appeared in the threshold of the living room looking expectant. She was relieved but needed more information.

"Let's go. We're meeting Bob and Sarah for dinner, and we're already a little late."

Dinner. She just realized she was starving. She didn't remember eating any food today. Maybe that was why she couldn't read Dan's thesis. Maybe she just needed some food. But the thought of dinner and conversation in a loud restaurant drained her further.

"I don't want to go to dinner. I'm having a hard day."

"I had a hard day, too. Let's go have a nice dinner together."

"You go. I just want to be home."

"Come on, it'll be fun. We didn't go to Eric's party. It'll be good for you to get out, and I know they'd like to see you."

No, they wouldn't. They'll be relieved that I'm not there. I'm a cotton candy pink elephant in the room. I make everyone uncomfortable. I turn dinner into a crazy circus act, everyone juggling their nervous pity and forced smiles with their cocktail glasses, forks, and knives.

"I don't want to go. Tell them I'm sorry, but I wasn't feeling up to it."

Beep, beep.

She saw John hear the noise, too, and she followed him into the kitchen. He popped open the microwave oven door and pulled out a mug.

"This is freezing cold. Do you want me to reheat it?"

She must've made tea that morning, and she'd forgotten to drink it. Then, she must've put it in the microwave to reheat it and left it there.

"No, thanks."

"All right, Bob and Sarah are probably already there waiting. Are you sure you don't want to come?"

"I'm sure."

"I won't stay long."

He kissed her and then left without her. She stood in the kitchen where he left her for a long time, holding the mug of cold tea in her hands.

SHE WAS ON HER WAY to bed, and John still hadn't returned from dinner. The blue computer light glowing in the study caught her attention before she turned to go upstairs. She went in and checked her inbox, more out of habit than out of sincere curiosity.

There they were.

Dear Alice,

My name is Mary Johnson. I'm 57 and was diagnosed with FTD five years ago. I live on the North Shore, so not

too far from you. This is such a wonderful idea. I'd love to come. My husband, Barry, will drive me. I'm not sure if he'll want to stay. We've both taken an early retirement and we're both home all the time. I think he'd like a break from me. See you soon,
Mary

Hi Alice,

I'm Dan Sullivan, 53 years old, diagnosed with EOAD 3 years ago. It runs in my family. My mother, two uncles, and one of my aunts had it, and 4 of my cousins do. So I saw this coming and have been living with it in the family since I was a kid. Funny, didn't make the diagnosis or living with it now any easier. My wife knows where you live. Not far from MGH. Near Harvard. My daughter went to Harvard. I pray every day that she doesn't get this.
Dan

Hi Alice,

Thank you for your email and invitation. I was diagnosed with EOAD a year ago, like you. It was almost a relief. I thought I was going crazy. I was getting lost in conversations, having trouble finishing my own sentences, forgetting my way home, couldn't understand the checkbook anymore, was making mistakes with the kids' schedules (I have a 15-year-old daughter and a 13-year-old son). I was only 46 when the symptoms started, so of course, no one ever thought it could be Alzheimer's.

I think the medications help a lot. I'm on Aricept and Namenda. I have good days and bad. On the good, people and even my family use it as an excuse to think that I'm

perfectly fine, even making this up! I'm not that desperate for attention! Then, a bad day hits, and I can't think of words or concentrate and I can't multitask at all. I feel lonely, too. I can't wait to meet you.
Cathy Roberts

P.S. Do you know about the Dementia Advocacy and Support Network International? Go to their website: www.dasninternational.org. It's a wonderful site for people like us in early stages and with early-onset to talk, vent, get support, and share information.

There they were. And they were coming.

MARY, CATHY, AND DAN REMOVED their coats and found seats in the living room. Their spouses kept their coats on, bid them a reluctant good-bye, and left with John for coffee at Jerri's.

Mary had chin-length blond hair and round, chocolate brown eyes behind a pair of dark-rimmed glasses. Cathy had a smart, pleasing face, and eyes that smiled before her mouth did. Alice liked her immediately. Dan had a thick mustache, a balding head, and a stocky build. They could've been professors visiting from out of town, members of a book club, or old friends.

"Would anyone like something to think?" asked Alice.

They stared at her and at one another, disinclined to answer. Were they all too shy or polite to be the first to speak up?

"Alice, did you mean 'drink'?" asked Cathy.

"Yes, what'd I say?"

"You said 'think.'"

Alice's face flushed. Word substitution wasn't the first impression she'd wanted to make.

"I'd actually like a cup of thinks. Mine's been close to empty for days, I could use a refill," said Dan.

They laughed, and it connected them instantly. She brought in the coffee and tea as Mary was telling her story.

"I was a real estate agent for twenty-two years. I suddenly started forgetting appointments, meetings, open houses. I showed up to houses with no keys. I got lost on my way to show a property in a neighborhood I'd known forever with the client in the car with me. I drove around for forty-five minutes when it should've taken less than ten. I can only imagine what she was thinking.

"I started getting angry easily and blowing up at the other agents in the office. I'd always been so easygoing and well liked, and suddenly, I was becoming known for my short fuse. I was ruining my reputation. My reputation was everything. My doctor put me on an antidepressant. And when that one didn't work, he put me on another, and another."

"For a long time, I just thought I was overtired and multitasking too much," said Cathy. "I was working part-time as a pharmacist, raising two kids, running the house, running around from one thing to the next like a chicken with my head cut off. I was only forty-six, so it never occurred to me that I might have dementia. Then, one day at work, I couldn't figure out the names of the drugs, and I didn't know how to measure out ten milliliters. Right then, I realized I was capable of giving someone the wrong amount of drug or even the wrong drug. Basically, I was capable of accidentally killing someone. So I took off my lab coat, went home early, and never went back. I was devastated. I thought I was going crazy."

"How about you, Dan? What were the first things you noticed?" asked Mary.

"I used to be really handy around the house. Then, one day, I couldn't figure out how to fix the things I'd always been able to fix. I always kept my workshop tidy, everything in its place. Now, it's a total mess. I accused my friends of borrowing my tools and messing up the place and not returning them when I couldn't find them. But it was always me. I was a firefighter. I started forgetting the names of the guys on the force. I couldn't finish my own sentences. I forgot how to make a cup of coffee. I'd seen the same things with my mom when I was a teenager. She had early-onset AD, too."

They shared stories of their earliest symptoms, their struggles to get a correct diagnosis, their strategies for coping and living with dementia. They nodded and laughed and cried over stories of lost keys, lost thoughts, and lost life dreams. Alice felt unedited and truly heard. She felt normal.

"Alice, is your husband still working?" asked Mary.

"Yes. He's been buried in his research and teaching this semester. He's been traveling a lot. It's been hard. But we both have a sabbatical year next year. So I just have to hold on and get to the end of next semester, and we'll be able to be home together for a whole year."

"You can make it, you're almost there," said Cathy.

Just a few more months.

ANNA SENT LYDIA INTO THE kitchen to make the white chocolate bread pudding. Noticeably pregnant now and no longer nauseated, Anna seemed to eat constantly, as if on a mission to make up for calories lost during the months of morning sickness.

"I have some news," said John. "I've been offered the position of chairman of the Cancer Biology and Genetics Program at Sloan-Kettering."

"Where's that?" asked Anna, through a mouthful of chocolate-covered cranberries.

"New York City."

No one said a word. Dean Martin belted out "A Marshmallow World" on the stereo.

"Well, you're not actually entertaining the idea of taking it, are you?" asked Anna.

"I am. I've been down there several times this fall, and it's a perfect position for me."

"But what about Mom?" asked Anna.

"She's not working anymore, and she rarely goes to campus at all."

"But she needs to be here," said Anna.

"No, she doesn't. She'll be with me."

"Oh, please! I come over at night so you can work late, and I sleep over whenever you're out of town, and Tom comes when he can on the weekends," said Anna. "We're not here all the time, but—"

"That's right, you're not here all the time. You don't see how bad it's getting. She pretends to know a lot more than she does. You think she's going to appreciate that we're in Cambridge a year from now? She doesn't recognize where she is now when we're three blocks away. We could very well be in New York City, and I could tell her it's Harvard Square, and she wouldn't know the difference."

"Yes, she would, Dad," said Tom. "Don't say that."

"Well, we wouldn't move before September. It's a long ways off."

"It doesn't matter when it is, she needs to stay here. She'll go downhill fast if you move away," said Anna.

"I agree," said Tom.

They talked about her as if she weren't sitting in the wing chair, a few feet away. They talked about her, in front of her, as if she were deaf. They talked about her, in front of her, without including her, as if she had Alzheimer's disease.

"This position is likely never to open up again in my lifetime, and they want me."

"I want her to be able to see the twins," said Anna.

"New York isn't that far. And there's no guarantee that you're all going to stay in Boston."

"I might be there," said Lydia.

Lydia stood in the doorway between the living room and kitchen. Alice hadn't seen her there before she spoke, and her sudden presence in the periphery startled her.

"I applied to NYU, Brandeis, Brown, and Yale. If I get into NYU and you and Mom are in New York, I could live with you and help out. And if you stay here, and I get into Brandeis or Brown, I can be around, too," said Lydia.

Alice wanted to tell Lydia that those were excellent schools. She wanted to ask her about the programs that most interested her. She wanted to tell her that she was proud of her. But her thoughts from idea to mouth moved too slowly today, as if they had to swim miles through black river sludge before surfacing to be heard, and most of them drowned somewhere along the way.

"That's great, Lydia," said Tom.

"So that's it. You're just going to continue about your life as if Mom doesn't have Alzheimer's, and we don't have anything to say about it?" asked Anna.

"I'm making plenty of sacrifices," said John.

He'd always loved her, but she'd made it easy for him. She'd been looking at their time left together as precious time. She didn't know how much longer she could hang on to herself, but she'd convinced herself that she could make it through their sabbatical year. One last sabbatical year together. She wouldn't trade that in for anything.

Apparently, he would. How could he? The question raged through the black river sludge in her head unanswered. How could he? The answer it found kicked her behind the eyes and choked her heart. One of them was going to have to sacrifice everything.

Alice, answer the following questions:

1. What month is it?
2. Where do you live?
3. Where is your office?
4. When is Anna's birthday?
5. How many children do you have?

If you have trouble answering any of these, go to the file named "Butterfly" on your computer and follow the instructions there immediately.

December
Harvard Square
Harvard
April
Three

JANUARY 2005

"Mom, wake up. How long has she been asleep?"

"About eighteen hours now."

"Has she done this before?"

"A couple of times."

"Dad, I'm worried. What if she took too many of her pills yesterday?"

"No, I checked her bottles and dispenser."

Alice could hear them talking, and she could understand what they were saying, but she was only mildly interested. It was like eavesdropping on a conversation between strangers about a woman she didn't know. She had no desire to wake up. She had no awareness that she was asleep.

"Ali? Can you hear me?"

"Mom, it's me, Lydia, can you wake up?"

The woman named Lydia talked about wanting to call a doctor. The man named Dad talked about letting the woman named Ali sleep some more. They talked about ordering Mexican and eating dinner at home. Maybe the smell of food in the house would wake up the woman named Ali. Then, the voices ceased. Everything was dark and quiet again.

SHE WALKED DOWN A SANDY path that led into dense woods. She ascended via a series of switchbacks out of the woods and onto a steep, exposed cliff. She walked to the edge and looked out. The ocean below her was frozen solid, its shore buried in high drifts of snow. The panorama before her appeared lifeless, colorless, impossibly still, and silent. She yelled for John, but her voice carried no sound. She turned to go back, but the path and the forest were gone. She looked down at her pale, bony ankles and bare feet. With no other choice, she readied to step off the cliff.

SHE SAT ON A BEACH chair and buried and unburied her feet in the warm, fine sand. She watched Christina, her best friend from kindergarten and still only five years old, flying a butterfly kite. The pink and yellow daisies on Christina's bathing suit, the blue and purple wings of the butterfly kite, the blues in the sky, the yellow sun, the red polish on her own toenails, indeed every color before her was more brilliant and striking than anything she'd ever seen. As she watched Christina, she was overwhelmed with joy and love, not so much for her childhood friend but for the bold and breathtaking colors of her bathing suit and kite.

Her sister, Anne, and Lydia, both about sixteen years old, lay next to each other on red, white, and blue striped beach towels. Their shiny, caramel bodies in matching bubble gum pink bikinis glistened in the sun. They, too, were glossy, cartoon-colored, and mesmerizing.

"Ready?" asked John.

"I'm a little scared."

"It's now or never."

She stood, and he strapped her torso into a harness attached to a tangerine orange parasail. He clicked and adjusted buckles until she felt snug and secure. He held on to her shoulders, pushing against the strong, invisible force willing her upward.

"Ready?" asked John.

"Yes."

He let go of her, and she soared with exhilarating speed into the palette of the sky. The winds she traveled on were dazzling swirls of robin's egg blue, periwinkle, lavender, and fuchsia. The ocean below was a rolling kaleidoscope of turquoise, aquamarine, and violet.

Christina's butterfly kite won its freedom and fluttered nearby. It was the most exquisite thing Alice had ever seen, and she wanted it more than anything she'd ever desired. She reached out to grab its string, but a sudden, strong shift in air current spun her around. She looked back, but it was obscured by the glowing sunset orange of her parasail. For the first time, she realized that she couldn't steer. She looked down at the earth, at the vibrant dots that were her family.

She wondered if the beautiful and spirited winds would ever bring her back to them.

LYDIA LAY CURLED ON HER side on top of the covers of Alice's bed. The shades were drawn, the room filled with soft, subdued daylight.

"Am I dreaming?" asked Alice.

"No, you're awake."

"How long have I been asleep?"

"A couple of days now."

"Oh no, I'm sorry."

"It's okay, Mom. It's good to hear your voice. Do you think you took too many pills?"

"I don't remember. I could've. I didn't mean to."

"I'm worried about you."

Alice looked at Lydia in pieces, close-up snapshots of her features. She recognized each one like people recognized the house they grew up in, a parent's voice, the creases of their own hands, instinctively, without effort or conscious consideration. But strangely, she had a hard time identifying Lydia as a whole.

"You're so beautiful," said Alice. "I'm so afraid of looking at you and not knowing who you are."

"I think that even if you don't know who I am someday, you'll still know that I love you."

"What if I see you, and I don't know that you're my daughter, and I don't know that you love me?"

"Then, I'll tell you that I do, and you'll believe me."

Alice liked that. *But will I always love her? Does my love for her reside in my head or my heart?* The scientist in her believed that emotion resulted from complex limbic brain circuitry, circuitry that was for her, at this very moment, trapped in the trenches of a battle in which there would be no survivors. The mother in her believed that the love she had for her daughter was safe from the mayhem in her mind, because it lived in her heart.

"How are you, Mom?"

"Not so good. This semester was hard, without my work, without Harvard, and this disease progressing, and your dad hardly ever home. It's been almost too hard."

"I'm so sorry. I wish I could be here more. Next fall, I'll be closer. I thought about moving back now, but I just got cast in this great play. It's a small part, but—"

"It's okay. I wish I could see you more, too, but I'd never let you stop living your life for me."

She thought about John.

"Your dad wants to move to New York. He got an offer at Sloan-Kettering."

"I know. I was there."

"I don't want to go."

"I couldn't imagine that you did."

"I can't leave here. The twins will be here in April."

"I can't wait to see those babies."

"Me, too."

Alice imagined holding them in her arms, their warm bodies, their tiny, curled fingers and chunky, unused feet, their puffy, round eyes. She wondered if they'd look like her or John. And the smell. She couldn't wait to smell her delicious grandchildren.

Most grandparents delighted in imagining their grandchildren's lives, the promise of attending recitals and birthday parties, graduations and weddings. She knew she wouldn't be here for recitals and birthday parties, graduations and weddings. But she would be here to hold them and smell them, and she'd be damned if she'd be sitting alone somewhere in New York instead.

"How's Malcolm?"

"Good. We just did the Memory Walk together in L.A."

"What's he like?"

Lydia's smile jumped ahead of her answer.

"He's very tall, outdoorsy, a little shy."

"What's he like with you?"

"He's very sweet. He loves how smart I am, he's so proud of my acting, he brags about me a lot, it's almost embarrassing. You'd like him."

"What are you like with him?"

Lydia considered this for several moments, as if she hadn't before.

"Myself."

"Good."

Alice smiled and squeezed Lydia's hand. She thought to ask Lydia what that meant to her, to describe herself, to remind her, but the thought evaporated too quickly to speak it.

"What were we just talking about?" asked Alice.

"Malcolm, Memory Walk? New York?" asked Lydia, offering prompts.

"I go for walks around here, and I feel safe. Even if I get a little turned around, I eventually see something that looks familiar, and enough people in the stores know me and point me in the right direction. The girl at Jerri's is always keeping track of my wallet and keys.

"And I have my support group friends here. I need them.

I couldn't learn New York now. I'd lose what little independence I still have. A new job. Your dad would be working all the time. I'd lose him, too."

"Mom, you need to tell all this to Dad."

She was right. But it was so much easier telling her.

"Lydia, I'm so proud of you."

"Thanks."

"In case I forget, know that I love you."

"I love you, too, Mom."

"I DON'T WANT TO MOVE to New York," said Alice.

"It's a long ways off, we don't have to make a decision on it now," said John.

"I *want* to make a decision on it now. I'm deciding now. I want to be clear about this while I still can be. I don't want to move to New York."

"What if Lydia's there?"

"What if she's not? You should've discussed this with me privately, before announcing it to the kids."

"I did."

"No, you didn't."

"Yes, I did, many times."

"Oh, so I don't remember? That's convenient."

She breathed, in through her nose, out through her mouth, allowing a calm moment to pull herself out of the elementary school argument they were spiraling into.

"John, I knew you were meeting with people at Sloan-Kettering, but I never understood that they were wooing you for a position for this upcoming year. I would've spoken up if I'd known this."

"I told you why I was going there."

"Fine. Would they be willing to let you take your sabbatical year and start a year from September?"

"No, they need someone now. It was difficult as it was negotiating them out that far, but I need the time to finish up some things in the lab here."

"Couldn't they hire someone temporary, you could take your sabbatical year with me, and then you could start?"

"No."

"Did you even ask?"

"Look, the field's so competitive right now, and everything's moving so rapidly. We're on the edge of some huge finds. I mean, we're knocking on the door to a cure for cancer. The drug companies are interested. And with all the classes and administrative crap at Harvard, it's just slowing me down. If I don't take this, I could ruin my one shot at discovering something that truly matters."

"This isn't your one shot. You're brilliant, and you don't have Alzheimer's. You're going to have plenty of shots."

He looked at her and said nothing.

"This next year is *my* one shot, John, not yours. This next year is my last chance at living my life and knowing what it means to me. I don't think I have much more time of really being me, and I want to spend that time with you, and I can't believe you don't want to spend it together."

"I do. We would be."

"That's bullshit, and you know it. Our life is here. Tom and Anna and the babies, Mary, Cathy, and Dan, and maybe Lydia. If you take this, you'll be working all the time, you know you will, and I'd be there all alone. This decision has nothing to do with wanting to be with me, and it takes everything I have left away. I'm not going."

"I won't be working all the time, I promise. And what if Lydia's living in New York? What if you get to stay with Anna and Charlie one week a month? There are ways we can work this out so you're not alone."

"What if Lydia's not in New York? What if she's at Brandeis?"

"That's why I think we should wait, make the decision later, when we have more information."

"I want you to take the sabbatical year."

"Alice, the choice for me isn't 'take the position at Sloan' or 'take a sabbatical year.' It's 'take the position at Sloan' or 'continue here at Harvard.' I just can't take the next year off."

He became blurry as her body trembled and her eyes burned with furious tears.

"I can't do this anymore! Please! I can't keep holding on without you! You can take the year off. If you wanted to, you could. I need you to."

"What if I turn this down, and I take the next year off, and you don't even know who I am?"

"What if I do, but after next year, I don't? How can you even consider spending the time we have left squirreled away in your fucking lab? I would never do this to you."

"I'd never ask you to."

"You wouldn't have to."

"I don't think I can do it, Alice. I'm sorry, I just don't think I can take being home for a whole year, just sitting and watching what this disease is stealing from you. I can't take watching you not knowing how to get dressed and not knowing how to work the television. If I'm in lab, I don't have to watch you sticking Post-it notes on all the cabinets and doors. I can't just stay home and watch you get worse. It kills me."

"No, John, it's killing *me,* not you. I'm getting worse,

whether you're home looking at me or hiding in your lab. You're losing me. I'm losing me. But if you don't take next year off with me, well, then, we lost you first. I have Alzheimer's. What's your fucking excuse?"

SHE PULLED OUT CANS AND boxes and bottles, glasses and dishes and bowls, pots and pans. She stacked everything on the kitchen table, and when she ran out of room there, she used the floor.

She took each coat out of the hall closet, unzipped and inverted all the pockets. She found money, ticket stubs, tissues, and nothing. After each strip search, she discarded the innocent coat to the floor.

She flipped the cushions off the couches and armchairs. She emptied her desk drawer and file cabinet. She dumped the contents of her book bag, her laptop bag, and her baby blue bag. She sifted through the piles, touching each object with her fingers to register its name in her head. Nothing.

Her search didn't require her to remember where she'd already looked. The heaps of unearthed stuff evidenced her previous excavation sites. From the looks of things, she'd covered the entire first floor. She was sweating, manic. She wasn't giving up. She raced upstairs.

She ransacked the laundry basket, the bedside tables, the dresser drawers, the bedroom closets, her jewelry box, the linen closet, the medicine cabinet. *The downstairs bathroom.* She ran back down the stairs, sweating, manic.

John stood in the hallway, ankle-deep in coats.

"What the hell happened in here?" he asked.

"I'm looking for something."

"What?"

She couldn't name it, but she trusted that somewhere in her head, she remembered and knew.

"I'll know when I find it."

"It's a complete disaster in here. It looks like we've been robbed."

She hadn't thought of that. It would explain why she couldn't find it.

"Oh my god, maybe someone stole it."

"We haven't been robbed. You've torn the house apart."

She spotted an untouched basket of magazines next to the couch in the living room. She left John and the theft theory in the hallway, lifted the heavy basket, poured the magazines onto the floor, fanned through them, and then walked away. John followed her.

"Stop it, Alice, you don't even know what you're looking for."

"Yes, I do."

"What then?"

"I can't say."

"What does it look like, what's it used for?"

"I don't know, I told you, I'll know when I find it. I have to find it, or I'll die."

She thought about what she'd just said.

"Where's my medication?"

They walked into the kitchen, kicking through boxes of cereal and cans of soup and tuna. John found her many prescription and vitamin bottles on the floor and the days-of-the-week dispenser in a bowl on the kitchen table.

"Here they are," he said.

The urge, the life-and-death need, didn't dissipate.

"No, that's not it."

"This is insane. You have to stop this. The house is trashed."

Trash.

She opened the compactor, pulled out the plastic bag, and dumped it.

"Alice!"

She ran her fingers through avocado skins, slimy chicken fat, balled tissues and napkins, empty cartons and wrappers, and other trash thingies. She saw the *Alice Howland* DVD. She held the wet case in her hands and studied it. *Huh, I didn't mean to throw this out.*

"There it is, that must be it," said John. "I'm glad you found it."

"No, this isn't it."

"All right, please, there's trash all over the floor. Just stop, go sit, and relax. You're frenzied. Maybe if you stop and relax, it'll come to you."

"Okay."

Maybe, if she sat still, she'd remember what it was and where she'd put it. Or maybe, she'd forget she was ever even looking for something.

THE SNOW THAT HAD BEGUN falling the day before and deposited about two feet over much of New England had just stopped. She might not have noticed but for the screeching sound of the wipers swinging back and forth across the newly dry windshield. John turned them off. The streets were plowed, but theirs was the only car on the road. Alice had always liked the serene quiet and stillness that followed a walloping snowstorm, but today it unnerved her.

John drove the car into the Mount Auburn Cemetery lot. A modest space for parking had been shoveled out, but the cemetery itself, the walking paths and gravestones, hadn't yet been uncovered.

"I was afraid it might still be like this. We'll have to come back another day," he said.

"No, wait. Let me just look at it for a minute."

The ancient black trees with their knuckled, varicose branches frosted in white ruled this winter wonderland. She could see a few of what were presumably the gray tops of the very tall, elaborate headstones that belonged to the once wealthy and prominent peaking above the surface of the snow, but that was it. Everything else was buried. Decomposed bodies in coffins buried under dirt and stone, dirt and stone buried under snow. Everything was black and white and frozen and dead.

"John?"

"What?"

She'd said his name too loudly, breaking the silence too suddenly, startling him.

"Nothing. We can go. I don't want to be here."

"WE CAN TRY GOING BACK later in the week if you want," said John.

"Back where?" asked Alice.

"To the cemetery."

"Oh."

She sat at the kitchen table. John poured red wine into two glasses and gave one to her. She swirled the goblet out of habit. She was regularly forgetting the name of her daughter, the actress one, but she could remember how to swirl her wineglass, and that she liked to. Crazy disease. She appreciated the wine's dizzying motion in the glass, its blood red color, its intense flavors of grape, oak, and earth, and the warmth she felt as it landed in her belly.

John stood in front of the opened refrigerator door and removed a block of cheese, a lemon, a spicy liquid thing, and a couple of red vegetables.

"How do chicken enchiladas sound?" he asked.

"Fine."

He opened the freezer and rummaged inside.

"Do we have any chicken?" he asked.

She didn't answer.

"Oh no, Alice."

He turned to show her something in his hands. It wasn't chicken.

"It's your BlackBerry, it was in the freezer."

He pressed its buttons, shook it, and rubbed it.

"It looks like it got water in it, we can see after it's thawed, but I think it's dead," he said.

She burst into ready, heartbroken tears.

"It's okay. If it's dead, we'll get you a new one."

How ridiculous, why am I this upset over a dead electronic organizer? Maybe she was really crying over the deaths of her mother, sister, and father. Maybe she was feeling emotion that she'd anticipated earlier but had been unable to express properly at the cemetery. That made more sense. But that wasn't it. Maybe the death of her organizer symbolized the death of her position at Harvard, and she was mourning the recent loss of her career. That also made sense. But what she felt was an inconsolable grief over the death of the BlackBerry itself.

FEBRUARY 2005

She slumped into the chair next to John, across from Dr. Davis, emotionally weary and intellectually tapped. She'd been taking various neuropsychological tests in that little room with that woman, the woman who administered the neuropsychological tests in the little room, for a torturously long time. The words, the information, the meaning in the woman's questions and in Alice's own answers were like soap bubbles, the kind children blew out of those little plastic wands, on a windy day. They drifted away from her quickly and in dizzying directions, requiring enormous strain and concentration to track. And even if she managed to actually hold a number of them in her sight for some promising duration, it was invariably too soon that *pop!* they were gone, burst without obvious cause into oblivion, as if they'd never existed. And now it was Dr. Davis's turn with the wand.

"Okay, Alice, can you spell the word *water* backwards for me?" he asked.

She would have found this question trivial and even insulting six months ago, but today, it was a serious question to be tackled with serious effort. She felt only marginally worried and humiliated by this, not nearly as worried and humiliated as she would've felt six months ago. More and more, she was experiencing a growing distance from her self-awareness. Her sense of Alice—what she knew and understood, what she liked and disliked, how she felt and perceived—was also like a soap bubble, ever higher in the sky and more difficult to identify, with nothing but the thinnest lipid membrane protecting it from popping into thinner air.

Alice spelled *water* forward first, to herself, extending the five fingers on her left hand, one for each letter, as she did.

"R." She folded down her pinkie. She spelled it forward to herself again, stopping at her ring finger, which she then folded down.

"E." She repeated the same process.

"T." She held her thumb and pointer finger like a gun. She whispered, "A, W," to herself.

"A, W."

She smiled, her left hand raised in a victorious fist, and looked at John. He spun his wedding ring and gave a dispirited smile.

"Good job," said Dr. Davis. He smiled widely and seemed impressed. Alice liked him.

"Now, I'd like you to point to the window after you touch your right cheek with your left hand."

She lifted her left hand to her face. *Pop!*

"I'm sorry, can you tell me the directions again?" asked Alice, her left hand still poised in front of her face.

"Sure," Dr. Davis obliged knowingly, like a parent who let a child get away with peeking at the top card in a game of cards or inching across the start line before yelling "go." "Point to the window after you touch your right cheek with your left hand."

Her left hand on her right cheek before he finished talking, she jerked her right arm at the window as fast as she could and let out a huge exhale.

"Good, Alice," said Dr. Davis, smiling again.

John offered no praise, no hint of pleasure or pride.

"Okay, now I'd like you to tell me the name and address I asked you to remember earlier."

The name and address. She had a loose sense of it, like the feeling of awakening from a night's sleep and knowing she'd had a dream, maybe even knowing it was about a particular thing, but no matter how hard she thought about it, the details of the dream eluded her. Gone forever.

"It's John Somebody. You know, you ask me this every time, and I've never been able to remember where that guy lives."

"Okay, let's take a guess. Was it John Black, John White, John Jones, or John Smith?"

She had no idea but didn't mind playing along.

"Smith."

"Does he live on East Street, West Street, North Street, or South Street?"

"South Street."

"Was the town Arlington, Cambridge, Brighton, or Brookline?"

"Brookline."

"Okay, Alice, last question, where's my twenty-dollar bill?"

"In your wallet?"

"No, earlier, I hid a twenty-dollar bill somewhere in the room, do you remember where I put it?"

"You did this while I was here?"

"Yes. Any ideas at all come to mind? I'll let you keep it if you find it."

"Well, if I'd known that, I would've been sure to figure out a way to remember it."

"I'm sure you would've. Any idea where it is?"

She saw the focus of his stare deviate to her right, just over her shoulder, for the briefest moment before settling back on her. She twisted around. Behind her, there was a whiteboard on the wall with three words scrawled on it in red marker: *Glutamate. LTP. Apoptosis.* The red marker lay on a tray at the bottom, right next to a folded twenty-dollar bill. Delighted, she stepped over to the whiteboard and claimed her prize.

Dr. Davis chuckled. "If all my patients were as smart as you, I'd go broke."

"Alice, you can't keep that, you saw him look at it," said John.

"I won it," said Alice.

"It's okay, she found it," said Dr. Davis.

"Should she be like this after only a year and being on medication?" asked John.

"Well, there are probably a few things going on here. Her illness probably started long before she was diagnosed last January. She and you and your family and her colleagues probably disregarded any number of symptoms as fluke, or normal, or chalked them up to stress, not enough sleep, too much to drink, and on and on. This could've gone on easily for a year or two or longer.

"And she's incredibly bright. If the average person has, say for simplicity, ten synapses that lead to a piece of information, Alice could easily have fifty. When the average person loses those ten synapses, that piece of information is inaccessible to them, forgotten. But Alice can lose those ten and still have forty other ways of getting to the target. So her anatomical losses aren't as profoundly and functionally noticeable at first."

"But by now, she's lost a lot more than ten," said John.

"Yes, I'm afraid she has. Her recent memory is now falling in the bottom three percent of those able to complete the tests, her language processing has degraded considerably, and she's losing self-awareness, all as we'd unfortunately expect to see.

"But she's also incredibly resourceful. She used a number of inventive strategies today to answer questions correctly that she couldn't actually remember correctly."

"But there were a lot of questions that she couldn't answer correctly, regardless," said John.

"Yes, that's true."

"It's just getting so much worse, so quickly. Can we up the dosage of either the Aricept or the Namenda?" asked John.

"No, she's at the maximum dosage already for both. Unfortunately, this is a progressive, degenerative disease with no cure. It gets worse, despite any medication we have right now."

"And it's clear she's either getting the placebo or this Amylix drug doesn't work," said John.

Dr. Davis paused as if considering whether to agree or disagree with this.

"I know you're discouraged. But I've often seen unexpected periods of plateau, where it seems to stall, and this can last for some time."

Alice closed her eyes and pictured herself standing solidly in the middle of a plateau. A beautiful mesa. She could see it, and it was worth hoping for. Could John see it? Could he still hope for her, or had he already given up? Or worse, did he actually hope for her rapid decline, so he could take her, vacant and complaisant, to New York in the fall? Would he choose to stand with her on the plateau or push her down the hill?

She folded her arms, unfolded her crossed legs, and planted her feet flat on the floor.

"Alice, are you still running?" asked Dr. Davis.

"No, I stopped a while ago. Between John's schedule and my lack of coordination—I can't seem to see curbs or bumps in the road, and I misjudge distances. I had some terrible falls. Even at home, I keep forgetting about the raised thingy in all the doorways, and I trip into every room I go in. I've got tons of bruises."

"Okay, John, I would either remove the doorway thingies or paint them a contrasting color, something bright, or cover them in brightly colored tape, so Alice can notice them. Otherwise, they just blend into the floor."

"All right."

"Alice, tell me about your support group," said Dr. Davis.

"There are four of us. We meet once a week for a few hours at each other's houses, and we email each other every day. It's wonderful, we talk about everything."

Dr. Davis and that woman in that little room had asked her a lot of probing questions today, questions designed to measure the precise level of destruction inside her head. But no one understood what was still alive inside her head better than Mary, Cathy, and Dan.

"I want to thank you for taking the initiative and filling the obvious gap we have in our support system here. If I get any new early stage or early-onset patients, can I tell them how to get in touch with you?"

"Yes, please do. You should also tell them about DASNI. It's the Dementia Advocacy and Support Network International. It's an online forum for people with dementia. I've met over a dozen people there, from all over the country and Canada and the UK and Australia. Well, I've never actually met them, it's all online, but I feel like I know them and they know me more intimately than many of the people I've known my whole life. We don't waste any time, we don't have enough of it. We talk about the stuff that matters."

John shifted in his seat and jiggled his leg.

"Thank you, Alice, I'll add that website to our standard packet of information. How about you, John? Have you yet talked with our social worker here or gone to any of the caregivers' support group meetings?"

"No, I haven't. I've had coffee a couple of times with the spouses of her support group people, but otherwise, no."

"You might want to consider getting some support yourself. You're not the one with the disease, but you're living with it, too, by living with Alice, and it's hard on the caregivers. I see the toll it takes every day with the family members who come in. There's Denise Daddario, the social worker, here and the MGH Caregivers' Support Group, and I know that the Massachusetts Alzheimer's Association has many local caregiver groups. The resources are there for you, so don't hesitate if you need them."

"All right."

"Speaking of the Alzheimer's Association, Alice, I just received their program for the annual Dementia Care Conference, and I see you're giving the opening plenary presentation," said Dr. Davis.

The Dementia Care Conference was a national meeting for professionals involved in the care of people with dementia and their families. Neurologists, general practice physicians, geriatric physicians, neuropsychologists, nurses, and social workers all gathered in one place to exchange information on approaches to diagnosis, treatment, and patient care. It sounded similar to Alice's support group and DASNI, but bigger and for those without dementia. This year's meeting was to be held next month in Boston.

"Yes," said Alice. "I meant to ask, will you be there?"

"I will, I'll be sure to be in the front row. You know, they've never asked me to give a plenary presentation," said Dr. Davis. "You're a brave and remarkable woman, Alice."

His compliment, genuine and not patronizing, was just the boost her ego needed after having been so ruthlessly pummeled by so many tests today. John spun his ring. He looked at her with tears in his eyes and a clenched smile that confused her.

MARCH 2005

Alice stood at the podium with her typed speech in her hand and looked out at the people seated in the hotel's grand ballroom. She used to be able to eyeball an audience and guess with an almost psychic accuracy the number of people in attendance. It was a skill she no longer possessed. There were a lot of people. The organizer, whatever her name was, had told her that over seven hundred people were registered for the conference. Alice had given many talks to audiences that size and larger. The people in her audiences past had included distinguished Ivy League faculty, Nobel Prize winners, and the world's thought leaders in psychology and language.

Today, John sat in the front row. He kept looking back

over his shoulder as he repeatedly wrung his program into a tight tube. She hadn't noticed until just now that he was wearing his lucky gray T-shirt. He usually reserved it for only his most critical lab result days. She smiled at his superstitious gesture.

Anna, Charlie, and Tom sat next to him, talking to one another. A few seats down sat Mary, Cathy, and Dan with their husbands and wife. Positioned front and center, Dr. Davis sat ready with his pen and notebook. Beyond them sat a sea of health professionals dedicated to the care of people with dementia. This might not be her biggest or most prestigious audience, but of all the talks she'd given in her life, she hoped this one would have the most powerful impact.

She ran her fingers back and forth across the smooth, gemmed wings of her butterfly necklace, which sat, as if perched, on the knobby tip of her sternum. She cleared her throat. She took a sip of water. She touched the butterfly wings one more time, for luck. *Today's a special occasion, Mom.*

"Good morning. My name is Dr. Alice Howland. I'm not a neurologist or general practice physician, however. My doctorate is in psychology. I was a professor at Harvard University for twenty-five years. I taught courses in cognitive psychology, I did research in the field of linguistics, and I lectured all over the world.

"I am not here today, however, to talk to you as an expert in psychology or language. I'm here today to talk to you as an expert in Alzheimer's disease. I don't treat patients, run clinical trials, study mutations in DNA, or counsel patients and their families. I am an expert in this subject because, just over a year ago, I was diagnosed with early-onset Alzheimer's disease.

"I'm honored to have this opportunity to talk with you

today, to hopefully lend some insight into what it's like to live with dementia. Soon, although I'll still know what it is like, I'll be unable to express it to you. And too soon after that, I'll no longer even know I have dementia. So what I have to say today is timely.

"We, in the early stages of Alzheimer's, are not yet utterly incompetent. We are not without language or opinions that matter or extended periods of lucidity. Yet we are not competent enough to be trusted with many of the demands and responsibilities of our former lives. We feel like we are neither here nor there, like some crazy Dr. Seuss character in a bizarre land. It's a very lonely and frustrating place to be.

"I no longer work at Harvard. I no longer read and write research articles or books. My reality is completely different from what it was not long ago. And it is distorted. The neural pathways I use to try to understand what you are saying, what I am thinking, and what is happening around me are gummed up with amyloid. I struggle to find the words I want to say and often hear myself saying the wrong ones. I can't confidently judge spatial distances, which means I drop things and fall down a lot and can get lost two blocks from my home. And my short-term memory is hanging on by a couple of frayed threads.

"I'm losing my yesterdays. If you ask me what I did yesterday, what happened, what I saw and felt and heard, I'd be hard-pressed to give you details. I might guess a few things correctly. I'm an excellent guesser. But I don't really know. I don't remember yesterday or the yesterday before that.

"And I have no control over which yesterdays I keep and which ones get deleted. This disease will not be bargained with. I can't offer it the names of the United States presidents in exchange for the names of my children. I can't give it the names of the state capitals and keep the memories of my husband.

"I often fear tomorrow. What if I wake up and don't know who my husband is? What if I don't know where I am or recognize myself in the mirror? When will I no longer be me? Is the part of my brain that's responsible for my unique 'meness' vulnerable to this disease? Or is my identity something that transcends neurons, proteins, and defective molecules of DNA? Is my soul and spirit immune to the ravages of Alzheimer's? I believe it is.

"Being diagnosed with Alzheimer's is like being branded with a scarlet *A*. This is now who I am, someone with dementia. This was how I would, for a time, define myself and how others continue to define me. But I am not what I say or what I do or what I remember. I am fundamentally more than that.

"I am a wife, mother, and friend, and soon to be grandmother. I still feel, understand, and am worthy of the love and joy in those relationships. I am still an active participant in society. My brain no longer works well, but I use my ears for unconditional listening, my shoulders for crying on, and my arms for hugging others with dementia. Through an early-stage support group, through the Dementia Advocacy and Support Network International, by talking to you today, I am helping others with dementia live better with dementia. I am not someone dying. I am someone living with Alzheimer's. I want to do that as well as I possibly can.

"I'd like to encourage earlier diagnosis, for physicians not to assume that people in their forties and fifties experiencing memory and cognition problems are depressed or stressed or menopausal. The earlier we are properly diagnosed, the earlier we can go on medication, with the hope of delaying progression and maintaining a footing on a plateau long enough to reap the benefits of a better treatment or cure soon. I still have hope for a cure, for me, for my friends with dementia, for my daughter who carries the same mutated gene. I may never be able to retrieve what I've already lost, but I can sustain what I have. I still have a lot.

"Please don't look at our scarlet *A*'s and write us off. Look us in the eye, talk directly to us. Don't panic or take it personally if we make mistakes, because we will. We will repeat ourselves, we will misplace things, and we will get lost. We will forget your name and what you said two minutes ago. We will also try our hardest to compensate for and overcome our cognitive losses.

"I encourage you to empower us, not limit us. If someone has a spinal cord injury, if someone has lost a limb or has a functional disability from a stroke, families and professionals work hard to rehabilitate that person, to find ways to cope and manage despite these losses. Work with us. Help us develop tools to function around our losses in memory, language, and cognition. Encourage involvement in support groups. We can help each other, both people with dementia and their caregivers, navigate through this Dr. Seuss land of neither here nor there.

"My yesterdays are disappearing, and my tomorrows are uncertain, so what do I live for? I live for each day. I live in the moment. Some tomorrow soon, I'll forget that I stood before you and gave this speech. But just because I'll forget it some tomorrow doesn't mean that I didn't live every second of it today. I will forget today, but that doesn't mean that today didn't matter.

"I'm no longer asked to lecture about language at universities and psychology conferences all over the world. But here I am before you today, giving what I hope is the most influential talk of my life. And I have Alzheimer's disease.

"Thank you."

She looked up from her speech for the first time since she began talking. She hadn't dared to break eye contact with the words on the pages until she finished, for fear of losing her place. To her genuine surprise, the entire ballroom was standing, clapping. It was more than she had hoped for. She'd hoped for two simple things—not to lose the ability to read during the talk and to get through it without making a fool of herself.

She looked at the familiar faces in the front row and knew without a doubt that she had far exceeded those modest expectations. Cathy, Dan, and Dr. Davis beamed. Mary was dabbing her eyes with a handful of pink tissues. Anna clapped and smiled without once stopping to wipe the tears that streamed down her face. Tom clapped and cheered and looked like he could barely keep himself from running up to hug and congratulate her. She couldn't wait to hug him, too.

John stood tall and unabashed in his lucky gray T-shirt, with an unmistakable love in his eyes and joy in his smile as he applauded her.

APRIL 2005

The energy required to write her speech, to deliver it well, and to shake hands and converse articulately with what seemed like hundreds of enthusiastic attendees at the Dementia Care Conference would have been enormous for someone without Alzheimer's disease. For someone with Alzheimer's, it was beyond enormous. She managed to function for some time afterward on the adrenaline high, the memory of the applause, and a renewed confidence in her inner status. She was Alice Howland, brave and remarkable hero.

But the high wasn't sustainable, and the memory faded. She lost a little of her confidence and status when she brushed her teeth with moisturizer. She lost a bit more when she tried all morning to call John with the television remote control. She lost the last of it when her own unpleasant body odor informed her that she hadn't bathed in days, but she couldn't muster up the courage or knowledge she needed to step into the tub. She was Alice Howland, Alzheimer's victim.

Her energy depleted with no reserve to draw upon, her euphoria waned, and the memory of her victory and confidence stolen, she suffered under an overwhelming, exhausting heaviness. She slept late and stayed in bed hours after waking. She sat on her couch and cried without specific reason. No amount of sleep or crying replenished her.

John woke her from a dead sleep and dressed her. She let him. He didn't tell her to brush her hair or teeth. She didn't care. He hurried her into the car. She leaned her forehead against the cold window. The world outside looked bluish gray. She didn't know where they were going. She felt too indifferent to ask.

John pulled into a parking garage. They got out and entered a building through a door in the garage. The white fluorescent lighting hurt her eyes. The wide hallways, the elevators, the signs on the walls: RADIOLOGY, SURGERY, OBSTETRICS, NEUROLOGY. *Neurology.*

They entered a room. Instead of the waiting room she expected to see, she saw a woman sleeping in a bed. She had swollen, closed eyes, and IV tubing taped to her hand.

"What's wrong with her?" whispered Alice.

"Nothing, she's just tired," said John.

"She looks terrible."

"Shh, you don't want her to hear that."

The room didn't look like a hospital room. It contained another bed, smaller and unmade, next to the one the woman was sleeping in, a large television in the corner, a lovely vase of yellow and pink flowers on a table, and hardwood floors. Maybe this wasn't a hospital. It could be a hotel. But then, why would the woman have that tube in her hand?

An attractive young man came in with a tray of coffee. *Maybe he's her doctor.* He wore a Red Sox hat, jeans, and a Yale T-shirt. *Maybe he's room service.*

"Congratulations," whispered John.

"Thanks. You just missed Tom. He'll be back this afternoon. Here, I got everyone coffee and a tea for Alice. I'll go get the babies."

The young man knew her name.

The young man returned rolling a cart carrying two clear plastic, rectangular tubs. Each tub contained a tiny baby, their bodies entirely swaddled in white blankets and the tops of their heads covered in white hats, so that only their faces showed.

"I'm going to wake her. She wouldn't want to sleep through you meeting them," said the young man. "Honey, wake up, we have visitors."

The woman woke up reluctantly, but when she saw Alice and John, an excitement entered her tired eyes and enlivened her. She smiled, and her face seemed to snap into place. *Oh my, that's Anna!*

"Congratulations, baby," said John. "They're beautiful," and he leaned down over her and kissed her forehead.

"Thanks, Dad."

"You look great. How are you feeling, okay?" asked John.

"Thanks, I'm okay, just exhausted. Ready, here they are. This is Allison Anne, and this little guy is Charles Thomas."

The young man handed one of the babies to John. He lifted the other baby, the one with a pink ribbon tied to its hat, and presented it to Alice.

"Would you like to hold her?" asked the young man.

Alice nodded.

She held the tiny, sleeping baby, her head in the crook of her elbow, her bum in her hand, her body up against her chest, her ear against her heart. The tiny, sleeping baby breathed tiny, shallow breaths through tiny, round nostrils. Alice instinctively kissed her blotchy pink, pudgy cheek.

"Anna, you had your babies," said Alice.

"Yes, Mom, you're holding your granddaughter, Allison Anne," said Anna.

"She's perfect. I love her."

My granddaughter. She looked at the baby with the blue ribbon in John's arms. *My grandson.*

"And they won't get Alzheimer's like I did?" asked Alice.

"No, Mom, they won't."

Alice inhaled deeply, breathing in the scrumptious smell of her beautiful granddaughter, filling herself with a sense of relief and peace she hadn't known in a long time.

"Mom, I got into NYU and Brandeis University."

"Oh, that's so exciting. I remember getting into school. What are you going to study?" asked Alice.

"Theater."

"That's wonderful. I used to go to Harvard. I loved it there. What school did you say you're going to?"

"I don't know yet. I got into NYU and Brandeis."

"Which one do you want to go to?"

"I'm not sure. I talked to Dad, and he really wants me to go to NYU."

"Do you want to go to NYU?"

"I don't know. It has the better reputation, but I like Brandeis better for me. I'd be near Anna and Charlie and the babies, and Tom, and you and Dad, if you stay."

"If I stay where?" asked Alice.

"Here, in Cambridge."

"Where else would I be?"

"New York."

"I'm not going to be in New York."

They sat next to each other on a couch folding baby clothes, separating the pinks from the blues. The television flashed images at them without the volume.

"It's just, if I accept at Brandeis, and you and Dad move to New York, then I'll feel like I'm in the wrong place, like I made the wrong decision."

Alice stopped folding and looked at the woman. She was young, skinny, pretty. She was also tired and conflicted.

"How old are you?" asked Alice.

"Twenty-four."

"Twenty-four. I loved being twenty-four. You have your whole life in front of you. Anything's possible. Are you married?"

The pretty, conflicted woman stopped folding and faced Alice squarely. She locked in on Alice's eyes. The pretty, conflicted woman had searching, honest, peanut butter brown eyes.

"No, I'm not married."

"Kids?"

"No."

"Then, you should do exactly what you want."

"But what if Dad decides to take the job in New York?"

"You can't make this kind of decision based on what other

people might or might not do. This is your decision, your education. You're a grown woman, you don't have to do what your father wants. Make it based on what's right for your life."

"Okay, I will. Thank you."

The pretty woman with the lovely peanut butter eyes let out an amused laugh and a sigh and resumed folding.

"We've come a long way, Mom."

Alice didn't understand what she meant. "You know," she said, "you remind me of my students. I used to be a student adviser. I was pretty good at it."

"Yes, you were. You still are."

"What's the name of the school you want to go to?"

"Brandeis."

"Where's that?"

"In Waltham, only a few minutes from here."

"And what are you going to study?"

"Acting."

"That's wonderful. Will you act in plays?"

"I will."

"Shakespeare?"

"Yes."

"I love Shakespeare, especially the tragedies."

"Me, too."

The pretty woman moved over and hugged Alice. She smelled fresh and clean, like soap. Her hug penetrated Alice much like her peanut butter eyes had. Alice felt happy and close to her.

"Mom, please don't move to New York."

"New York? Don't be silly. I live here. Why would I move to New York?"

"I DON'T KNOW HOW YOU do this," said the actress. "I was up with her most of the night, and I feel delirious. I made her scrambled eggs, toast, and tea at three a.m."

"I was up then. If we could get you to lactate, then you could help me feed one of these guys," said the mother of the babies.

The mother was sitting on the couch next to the actress, breast-feeding the baby in blue. Alice held the baby in pink. John walked in, showered and dressed, holding a coffee mug in one hand and a newspaper in the other. The women were wearing pajamas.

"Lyd, thanks for getting up last night. I really needed the sleep," said John.

"Dad, how on earth do you think you can go to New York and do this without our help?" asked the mother.

"I'm going to hire a home health aide. I'm looking to find someone starting now actually."

"I don't want strangers taking care of her. They're not going to hug her and love her like we do," said the actress.

"And a stranger isn't going to know her history and memories like we do. We can sometimes fill in her holes and read her body language, and that's because we know her," said the mother.

"I'm not saying that we won't still take care of her, I'm just being realistic and practical. We don't have to shoulder this entirely ourselves. You'll be going back to work in a couple of months and coming home every night to two babies you haven't seen all day.

"And you're starting school. You keep talking about how intense the program is. Tom's in surgery as we speak. You're all about to be busier than you've ever been, and your mother would be the last person to want you to compromise the quality of your own lives for her. She'd never want to be a burden to you."

"She's not a burden, she's our mother," said the mother.

They were talking too quickly and using too many pronouns. And the baby in pink had begun to fuss and cry, distracting her. Alice couldn't figure out what or who they were talking about. But she could tell by their facial expressions and tones that it was a serious argument. And the women in pajamas were on the same side.

"Maybe it makes more sense for me to take a longer maternity leave. I'm feeling a little rushed, and Charlie's okay with me taking more time, and it makes sense for being around for Mom."

"Dad, this is our last chance to spend time with her. You can't go to New York, you can't take that away."

"Look, if you'd accepted at NYU instead of Brandeis, you could've spent all the time you wanted with her. You made your choice, I'm making mine."

"Why doesn't Mom get a say in this choice?" asked the mother.

"She doesn't want to live in New York," said the actress.

"You don't know what she wants," said John.

"She's said she doesn't want to. Go ahead and ask her. Just because she has Alzheimer's doesn't mean she doesn't know what she does and doesn't want. At three in the morning, she wanted scrambled eggs and toast, and she didn't want cereal or bacon. And she definitely didn't want to go back to bed. You're choosing to dismiss what she wants because she has Alzheimer's," said the actress.

Oh, they're talking about me.

"I'm not dismissing what she wants. I'm doing the best I can to do what's right for both of us. If she got everything she unilaterally wanted, we wouldn't even be having this conversation."

"What the hell does that mean?" asked the mother.

"Nothing."

"It's like you don't get that she's not gone yet, like you think her time left isn't meaningful anymore. You're acting like a selfish child," said the mother.

The mother was crying now, but she seemed angry. She looked and sounded like Alice's sister, Anne. But she couldn't be Anne. That was impossible. Anne didn't have any children.

"How do you know she thinks this is meaningful? Look, it's not just me. The old her, before this, she wouldn't want me to give this up. She didn't want to be here like this," said John.

"What does that mean?" asked the crying woman who looked and sounded like Anne.

"Nothing. Look, I understand and appreciate everything you're saying. But I'm trying to make a decision that's rational and not emotional."

"Why? What's wrong with being emotional about this? Why is that a negative thing? Why isn't the emotional decision the right decision?" asked the woman who wasn't crying.

"I haven't come to a final decision yet, and the two of you aren't going to bully me into one. You don't know everything."

"So tell us, Dad, tell us what we don't know," said the crying woman, her voice shaking and threatening.

The threat silenced him for a moment.

"I don't have time for this now, I have a meeting."

He got up and abandoned the argument, leaving the

women and babies alone. He slammed the front door as he left the house, startling the baby in blue, which had just fallen asleep in the mother's arms. It wailed. As if it were contagious, the other woman began crying, too. Maybe she just felt left out. Now, everyone was crying—the pink baby, the blue baby, the mother, and the woman next to the mother. Everyone except Alice. She wasn't sad or angry or defeated or scared. She was hungry.

"What are we having for dinner?"

MAY 2005

They reached the counter after waiting a long time in a long line.

"All right, Alice, what do you want?" asked John.

"I'll have whatever you're having."

"I'm getting vanilla."

"That's fine, I'll have that."

"You don't want vanilla, you want something chocolate."

"Okay then, I'll have something chocolate."

It seemed simple and unproblematic enough to her, but he became visibly stressed by the exchange.

"I'll have a vanilla in a cone, and she'll have a chocolate fudge brownie in a cone, both large."

Away from the stores and crowded lines of people, they

sat on a graffiti-covered bench on the edge of a river and ate their ice creams. Several geese nibbled in the grass just a few feet away. The geese kept their heads down, consumed in the business of nibbling, completely unbothered by Alice and John's presence. Alice giggled, wondering if the geese thought the same thing about them.

"Alice, do you know what month it is?"

It had rained earlier, but the sky was clear now, and the heat from the sun and the dry bench warmed her bones. It felt so good to be warm. Many of the pink and white blossoms from the crab apple tree next to them were scattered across the ground like party confetti.

"It's spring."

"What month of spring?"

Alice licked her something chocolate ice cream and carefully considered his question. She couldn't remember the last time she'd looked at a calendar. It had been a long time it seemed since she needed to be at a certain place at a certain time. Or if she did need to be somewhere on a certain day at a certain time, John knew about it for her and made sure she got there when she was supposed to. She didn't use an appointment machine, and she no longer wore a wrist clock.

Well, let's see. The months of the year.

"I don't know, what is it?"

"May."

"Oh."

"Do you know when Anna's birthday is?"

"Is it in May?"

"No."

"Well, I think Anne's birthday is in the spring."

"No, not Anne, Anna."

A yellow truck groaned loudly over the bridge near

them and startled Alice. One of the geese spread its wings and honked at the truck, defending them. Alice wondered whether it was brave or a hothead, looking for a fight. She giggled, thinking about the feisty goose.

She licked her something chocolate ice cream and studied the architecture of the red-brick building across the river. It had many windows and a clock with old-fashioned numbers on a gold dome on its top. It looked important and familiar.

"What's that building over there?" asked Alice.

"That's the business school. It's part of Harvard."

"Oh. Did I teach in that building?"

"No, you taught in a different building on this side of the river."

"Oh."

"Alice, where's your office?"

"My office? It's at Harvard."

"Yes, but where at Harvard?"

"In a building on this side of the river."

"Which building?"

"It's in a hall, I think. You know, I don't go there anymore."

"I know."

"Then it really doesn't matter where it is, right? Why don't we focus on the things that really matter?"

"I'm trying."

He held her hand. His was warmer than hers. Her hand felt so good in his hand. Two of the geese waddled into the calm water. There were no people swimming in the river. It was probably too cold for people.

"Alice, do you still want to be here?"

His eyebrows bent into a serious shape, and the creases next to his eyes deepened. This question was important to him. She smiled, pleased with herself for finally having a confident answer for him.

"Yes. I like sitting here with you. And I'm not done yet."

She held up her something chocolate ice cream to show him. It had started to melt and drip down the sides of the cone onto her hand.

"Why, do we need to leave now?" she asked.

"No. Take your time."

JUNE 2005

Alice sat at her computer waiting for the screen to come to life. Cathy had just called, checking in, concerned. She said that Alice hadn't returned her emails in a while, that she hadn't been to the dementia chat room in weeks, and that she'd missed support group again yesterday. It wasn't until Cathy talked about support group that Alice knew who the concerned Cathy on the phone was. Cathy said that two new people had joined their support group, and that it had been recommended to them by people who'd attended the Dementia Care Conference and had heard Alice's speech. Alice told her that was wonderful news. She apologized to Cathy for worrying her and told her to let everyone know that she was okay.

But to tell the truth, she was very far from okay. She could still read and comprehend small amounts of text, but the computer keyboard had become an undecipherable jumble of letters. In truth, she'd lost the ability to compose words out of the alphabet letters on the keys. Her ability to use language, that thing that most separates humans from animals, was leaving her, and she was feeling less and less human as it departed. She'd said a tearful good-bye to okay some time ago.

She clicked on her mailbox. Seventy-three new emails. Overwhelmed and powerless to respond, she closed out of her email application without opening anything. She stared at the screen she'd spent much of her professional life in front of. Three folders sat on the desktop arranged in a vertical row: "Hard Drive," "Alice," "Butterfly." She clicked on the "Alice" folder.

Inside were more folders with different titles: "Abstracts," "Administrative," "Classes," "Conferences," "Figures," "Grant Proposals," "Home," "John," "Kids," "Lunch Seminars," "Molecules to Mind," "Papers," "Presentations," "Students." Her entire life organized into neat little icons. She couldn't bear to look inside, afraid she wouldn't remember or understand her entire life. She clicked on "Butterfly" instead.

Dear Alice,

You wrote this letter to yourself when you were of sound mind. If you are reading this, and you are unable to answer one or more of the following questions, then you are no longer of sound mind:

What month is it?
Where do you live?
Where is your office?

When is Anna's birthday?
How many children do you have?

You have Alzheimer's disease. You have lost too much of yourself, too much of what you love, and you are not living the life you want to live. There is no good outcome to this disease, but you have chosen an outcome that is the most dignified, fair, and respectful to you and your family. You can no longer trust your own judgment, but you can trust mine, your former self, you before Alzheimer's took too much of you away.

You lived an extraordinary and worthwhile life. You and your husband, John, have three healthy and amazing children, who are all loved and doing well in the world, and you had a remarkable career at Harvard filled with challenge, creativity, passion, and accomplishment.

This last part of your life, the part with Alzheimer's, and this end that you've carefully chosen, is tragic, but you did not live a tragic life. I love you, and I'm proud of you, of how you've lived and all that you've done while you could.

Now, go to your bedroom. Go to the black table next to the bed, the one with the blue lamp on it. Open the drawer to that table. In the back of the drawer is a bottle of pills. The bottle has a white label on it that says FOR ALICE *in black letters. There are a lot of pills in that bottle. Swallow all of them with a big glass of water. Make sure you swallow all of them. Then, get in the bed and go to sleep.*

Go now, before you forget. And do not tell anyone what you're doing. Please trust me.

Love,
Alice Howland

She read it again. She didn't remember writing it. She didn't know the answers to any of the questions but the one asking the number of children she had. But then, she probably knew that because she'd provided the answer in the letter. She couldn't be sure of their names. Anna and Charlie, maybe. She couldn't remember the other one.

She read it again, more slowly this time, if that was even possible. Reading on a computer screen was difficult, more difficult than reading on paper, where she could use a pen and highlighter. And paper she could take with her to her bedroom and read it there. She wanted to print it out but couldn't figure out how to make that happen. She wished her former self, she before Alzheimer's took too much of her away, had known to include instructions for printing it out.

She read it again. It was fascinating and surreal, like reading a diary that had been hers when she was a teenager, secret and heartfelt words written by a girl she only vaguely remembered. She wished she'd written more. Her words made her feel sad and proud, powerful and relieved. She took a deep breath, exhaled, and went upstairs.

She got to the top of the stairs and forgot what she had gone up there to do. It carried a sense of importance and urgency, but nothing else. She went back downstairs and looked for evidence of where she'd just been. She found the computer on with a letter to her displayed on the screen. She read it and went back upstairs.

She opened the drawer in a table next to the bed. She pulled out packets of tissues, pens, a stack of sticky paper, a bottle of lotion, a couple of cough candies, dental floss, and some coins. She spread everything out on the bed and touched each item, one at a time. Tissues, pen, pen, pen, sticky paper, coins, candy, candy, floss, lotion.

"Alice?"

"What?"

She spun around. John stood in the doorway.

"What are you doing up here?" he asked.

She looked at the items on the bed.

"Looking for something."

"I have to run back to the office to pick up a paper I forgot. I'm going to drive, so I'll only be gone for a few minutes."

"Okay."

"Here, it's time, take these before I forget."

He handed her a glass of water and a handful of pills. She swallowed each one.

"Thank you," she said.

"You're welcome. I'll be right back."

He took the empty glass from her and left the room. She lay down on the bed next to the former contents of the drawer and closed her eyes, feeling sad and proud, powerful and relieved as she waited.

"ALICE, PLEASE, PUT YOUR ROBE, hood, and cap on, we need to leave."

"Where are we going?" asked Alice.

"Harvard Commencement."

She inspected the costume again. She still didn't get it.

"What does *commencement* mean?"

"It's Harvard graduation day. *Commencement* means beginning."

Commencement. Graduation from Harvard. A beginning. She turned the word over in her mind. Graduation from Harvard marked a beginning, the beginning of adulthood, the beginning of professional life, the beginning of life after

Harvard. *Commencement.* She liked the word and wanted to remember it.

They walked along a busy sidewalk wearing their dark pink costumes and plush black hats. She felt conspicuously ridiculous and entirely untrusting of John's wardrobe decision for the first several minutes of their walk. Then, suddenly, they were everywhere. Masses of people in similar costumes and hats but in a variety of colors funneled from every direction onto the sidewalk with them, and soon they were all walking in a rainbow costume parade.

They entered a grassy yard shaded by big, old trees and surrounded by big, old buildings to the slow, ceremonial sounds of bagpipes. Alice shivered with goose bumps. *I've done this before.* The procession led them to a row of chairs where they sat down.

"This is Harvard graduation," said Alice.

"Yes," said John.

"Commencement."

"Yes."

After some time, the speakers began. Harvard graduations past had featured many famous and powerful people, mostly political leaders.

"The king of Spain spoke here one year," said Alice.

"Yes," said John. He laughed a little, amused.

"Who is this man?" asked Alice, referring to the man at the podium.

"He's an actor," said John.

Now, Alice laughed, amused.

"I guess they couldn't get a king this year," said Alice.

"You know, your daughter is an actress. She could be up there someday," said John.

Alice listened to the actor. He was an easy and dynamic speaker. He kept talking about a picaresque.

"What's a picaresque?" asked Alice.

"It's a long adventure that teaches the hero lessons."

The actor talked about his life's adventure. He told them he was here today to pass on to them, the graduating classes, the people about to begin their own picaresques, the lessons he'd learned along his way. He gave them five: Be creative, be useful, be practical, be generous, and finish big.

I've been all those things, I think. Except, I haven't finished yet. I haven't finished big.

"That's good advice," said Alice.

"Yes, it is," said John.

They sat and listened and clapped and listened and clapped for longer than Alice cared to. Then, everyone stood and walked slowly in a less orderly parade. Alice and John and some of the others entered a nearby building. The magnificent entryway, with its staggeringly high, dark wooden ceiling and towering wall of sunlit stained glass, awed Alice. Huge, old, and heavy-looking chandeliers loomed over them.

"What is this?" asked Alice.

"This is Memorial Hall, it's part of Harvard."

To her disappointment, they spent no time in the magnificent entryway and moved immediately into a smaller, relatively unimpressive theater room, where they sat down.

"What's happening now?" asked Alice.

"The Graduate School of Arts and Sciences students are getting their Ph.D.s. We're here to see Dan graduate. He's your student."

She looked around the room at the faces of the people in the dark pink costumes. She didn't know which one was

Dan. She didn't, in fact, recognize any of the faces, but she did recognize the emotion and the energy in the room. They were happy and hopeful, proud and relieved. They were ready and eager for new challenges, to discover and create and teach, to be the heroes in their own adventures.

What she saw in them, she recognized in herself. This was something she knew, this place, this excitement and readiness, this beginning. This had been the beginning of her adventure, too, and although she couldn't remember the details, she had an implicit knowing that it had been rich and worthwhile.

"There he is, on the stage," said John.

"Who?"

"Dan, your student."

"Which one?"

"The blond."

"Daniel Maloney," someone announced.

Dan stepped forward and shook hands with the man on the stage in exchange for a red folder. Dan then raised the red folder high over his head and smiled in glorious victory. For his joy, for all that he had surely achieved to be here, for the adventure that he would embark upon, Alice applauded him, this student of hers whom she had no memory of.

ALICE AND JOHN STOOD OUTSIDE under a big white tent among the students in dark pink costumes and the people who were happy for them and waited. A young, blond man approached Alice, grinning broadly. Unhesitating, he hugged her and kissed her on the cheek.

"I'm Dan Maloney, your student."

"Congratulations, Dan, I'm so happy for you," said Alice.

"Thank you so much. I'm so glad you were able to come and see me graduate. I feel so lucky to have been your student. I want you to know, you were the reason I chose linguistics as my field of study. Your passion for understanding how language works, your rigorous and collaborative approach to research, your love of teaching, you've inspired me in so many ways. Thank you for all your guidance and wisdom, for setting the bar so much higher than I thought I could reach, and for giving me plenty of room to run with my own ideas. You've been the best teacher I've ever had. If I achieve in my life a fraction of what you've accomplished in yours, I'll consider my life a success."

"You're welcome. Thank you for saying that. You know, I don't remember so well these days. I'm glad to know that you'll remember these things about me."

He handed her a white envelope.

"Here, I wrote it all down for you, everything I just said, so you can read it whenever you want and know what you gave to me even if you can't remember."

"Thank you."

They each held their envelopes, hers white and his red, with deep pride and reverence.

An older, heavier version of Dan and two women, one much older than the other, came over to them. The older, heavier version of Dan carried a tray of bubbly white wine in skinny glasses. The young woman handed a glass to each of them.

"To Dan," said the older, heavier version of Dan, holding up his glass.

"To Dan," said everyone, clinking the skinny glasses and taking sips.

"To auspicious beginnings," added Alice, "and finishing big."

THEY BEGAN WALKING AWAY FROM the tents and the old, brick buildings and the people in costumes and hats to where it was less populated and noisy. Someone in a black costume yelled and ran over to John. John stopped and let go of Alice's hand to shake hands with the person who'd yelled. Caught in her own forward momentum, Alice kept walking.

For a stretched-out second, Alice paused and made eye contact with a woman. She was sure she didn't know the woman, but there was meaning in the exchange. The woman had blond hair, a phone by her ear, and glasses over her big, blue, startled eyes. The woman was driving in a car.

Then, Alice's hood pulled suddenly tight around her throat, and she was jerked backward. She landed hard and unsuspecting on her back and banged her head on the ground. Her costume and plush hat offered little protection against the pavement.

"I'm sorry, Ali, are you okay?" asked a man in a dark pink robe, kneeling beside her.

"No," she said, sitting up and rubbing the back of her head. She expected to see blood on her hand but didn't.

"I'm sorry, you walked right into the street. That car almost hit you."

"Is she okay?"

It was the woman from the car, her eyes still big and startled.

"I think so," said the man.

"Oh my god, I could've killed her. If you didn't pull her out of the way, I might've killed her."

"It's okay, you didn't kill her, I think she's okay."

The man helped Alice stand. He felt and looked at her head.

"I think you're all right. You're probably going to be really sore. Can you walk?" he asked.

"Yes."

"Can I give you a ride somewhere?" asked the woman.

"No, no, that's all right, we're fine," said the man.

He put his arm around Alice's waist and his hand under her elbow, and she walked home with the kind stranger who had saved her life.

SUMMER 2005

Alice sat in a big, comfortable, white chair and puzzled over the clock on the wall. It was the kind with hands and numbers, which was much harder to read than the kind with just numbers. *Five maybe?*

"What time is it?" she asked the man sitting in the other big, white chair.

He looked at his wrist.

"Almost three thirty."

"I think it's time for me to go home."

"You are home. This is your home on the Cape."

She looked around the room—the white furniture, the

pictures of lighthouses and beaches on the walls, the giant windows, the spindly little trees outside the windows.

"No, this isn't my house. I don't live here. I want to go home now."

"We're going back to Cambridge in a couple of weeks. We're here on vacation. You like it here."

The man in the chair continued reading his book and drinking his drink. The book was thick and the drink was yellowish brown, like the color of her eyes, with ice in it. He was enjoying and absorbed in both, the book and the drink.

The white furniture, the pictures of lighthouses and beaches on the walls, the giant windows, and the spindly little trees outside the windows didn't look at all familiar to her. The sounds here weren't familiar to her either. She heard birds, the kinds that live at the ocean, the sound of the ice swirling and clinking in the glass when the man in the chair drank his drink, the sound of the man breathing through his nose as he read his book, and the ticking of the clock.

"I think I've been here long enough. I'd like to go home now."

"You are home. This is your vacation home. This is where we come to relax and unwind."

This place didn't look like her home or sound like her home, and she didn't feel relaxed. The man reading and drinking in the big, white chair didn't know what he was talking about. Maybe he was drunk.

The man breathed and read and drank, and the clock ticked. Alice sat in the big, white chair and listened to the time go by, wishing someone would take her home.

SHE SAT IN ONE OF the white, wooden chairs on a deck drinking iced tea and listening to the shrill cross talk of unseen frogs and twilight bugs.

"Hey, Alice, I found your butterfly necklace," said the man who owned the house.

He dangled a jeweled butterfly by a silver chain in front of her.

"That's not my necklace, that's my mother's. And it's special, so you'd better put it back, we're not supposed to play with it."

"I talked to your mom, and she said that you could have it. She's giving it to you."

She studied his eyes and mouth and body language, looking for some sign that would give away his motive. But before she could get a proper read on his sincerity, the beauty of the sparkling blue butterfly seduced her, overriding her rule-abiding concerns.

"She said I could have it?"

"Uh-huh."

He leaned over her from behind and fastened it around her neck. She ran her fingers over the blue gems on the wings, the silver body, and the diamond-studded antennae. She felt a smug thrill rush through her. *Anne's going to be so jealous.*

SHE SAT ON THE FLOOR in front of the full-length mirror in the bedroom she slept in and examined her reflection. The girl in the mirror had sunken, darkened circles under her eyes. Her skin looked loose and spotty all over and wrinkled at the corners of her eyes and along her forehead. Her thick, scraggly eyebrows needed to be tweezed. Her curly hair was mostly black, but it was also noticeably gray. The girl in the mirror looked ugly and old.

She ran her fingers over her cheeks and forehead, feeling her face on her fingers and her fingers on her face. *That can't be me. What's wrong with my face?* The girl in the mirror sickened her.

She found the bathroom and flicked on the light. She met the same image in the mirror over the sink. There were her golden brown eyes, her serious nose, her heart-shaped lips, but everything else, the composition around her features, was grotesquely wrong. She ran her fingers over the smooth, cool glass. *What's wrong with these mirrors?*

The bathroom didn't smell right either. Two shiny, white step stools, a brush, and a bucket sat on sheets of newspaper on the floor behind her. She squatted down and breathed in through her serious nose. She pried the lid off the bucket, dipped the brush in, and watched creamy white paint dribble down.

She started with the ones she knew were defective, the one in the bathroom and the one in the bedroom she slept in. She found four more before she was finished and painted them all white.

SHE SAT IN A BIG, white chair, and the man who owned the house sat in the other one. The man who owned the house was reading a book and drinking a drink. The book was thick and the drink was yellowish brown with ice in it.

She picked up an even thicker book than the one the man was reading from the coffee table and thumbed through it. Her eyes paused on diagrams of words and letters connected to other words and letters by arrows, dashes, and little lollipops. She landed on individual words as she browsed through the pages—disinhibition, phosphorylation, genes, acetylcholine, priming, transience, demons, morphemes, phonological.

"I think I've read this book before," said Alice.

The man looked over at the book she held and then at her.

"You've done more than that. You wrote it. You and I wrote that book together."

Hesitant to take him at his word, she closed the book and read the shiny blue cover. *From Molecules to Mind* by John Howland, Ph.D. and Alice Howland, Ph.D. She looked up at the man in the chair. *He's John.* She flipped to the front pages. "Table of Contents. Mood and Emotion, Motivation, Arousal and Attention, Memory, Language." *Language.*

She opened the book to somewhere near the end. "An infinite possibility of expression, learned yet instinctive, semanticity, syntax, case grammar, irregular verbs, effortless and automatic, universal." The words she read seemed to push past the choking weeds and sludge in her mind to a place that was pristine and still intact, hanging on.

"John," she said.

"Yes."

He put his book down and sat up straight at the edge of his big, white chair.

"I wrote this book with you," she said.

"Yes."

"I remember. I remember you. I remember I used to be very smart."

"Yes, you were, you were the smartest person I've ever known."

This thick book with the shiny blue cover represented so

much of what she used to be. *I used to know how the mind handled language, and I could communicate what I knew. I used to be someone who knew a lot. No one asks for my opinion or advice anymore. I miss that. I used to be curious and independent and confident. I miss being sure of things. There's no peace in being unsure of everything all the time. I miss doing everything easily. I miss being a part of what's happening. I miss feeling wanted. I miss my life and my family. I loved my life and family.*

She wanted to tell him everything she remembered and thought, but she couldn't send all those memories and thoughts, composed of so many words, phrases, and sentences, past the choking weeds and sludge into audible sound. She boiled it down and put all her effort into what was most essential. The rest would have to remain in the pristine place, hanging on.

"I miss myself."

"I miss you, too, Ali, so much."

"I never planned to get like this."

"I know."

SEPTEMBER 2005

John sat at the end of a long table and took a large sip from his black coffee. It tasted extremely strong and bitter, but he didn't care. He didn't drink it for its taste. He'd drink it faster if he could, but it was scalding hot. He'd need two or three more large cups before he'd become fully alert and functional.

Most of the people who came in bought their caffeine to go and hurried on their way. John didn't have lab meeting for another hour, and he felt no compelling pressure to get to his office early today. He was content to take his time, eat his cinnamon scone, drink his coffee, and read the *New York Times.*

He opened to the "Health" section first, as he'd done with every newspaper he'd read for over a year now, a habit that had long ago replaced most of the hope that originally inspired the behavior. He read the first article on the page and cried openly as his coffee cooled.

AMYLIX FAILS TRIAL

According to the results of Synapson's Phase III study, patients with mild to moderate Alzheimer's disease who took Amylix during the fifteen-month trial failed to show a significant stabilization of dementia symptoms compared with placebo.

Amylix is a selective amyloid-beta–lowering agent. By binding soluble Abeta 42, this experimental drug's aim is to stop progression of the disease, and it is unlike the drugs currently available to patients with Alzheimer's, which can at best only delay the disease's ultimate course.

The drug was well tolerated and sailed through Phases I and II with much clinical promise and Wall Street expectation. But after a little over a year on the medication, the cognitive functioning of the patients receiving even the highest dose of Amylix failed to show improvement or stabilization as measured by the Alzheimer's Disease Assessment Scale and scores on Activities of Daily Living, and they declined at a rate that was significant and expected.

EPILOGUE

Alice sat on a bench with the woman and watched the children walking by them. Not really children. They weren't the kind of small children who lived at home with their mothers. What were they? Medium children.

She studied the faces of the medium children as they walked. Serious, busy. Heavy-headed. Headed on their way somewhere. There were other benches nearby, but none of the medium children stopped to sit. Everyone walked, busy on their way to where they must go.

She didn't need to go anywhere. She felt lucky about this. She and the woman she sat with listened to the girl with very long hair play her music and sing. The girl had a lovely voice and big, happy teeth and a lot of skirt with flowers all over it that Alice admired.

Alice hummed along to the music. She liked the sound of her hum blended with the voice of the singing girl.

"Okay, Alice, Lydia will be home any minute. You want to pay Sonya before we go?" asked the woman.

The woman was standing, smiling, and holding money. Alice felt invited to join her. She got up, and the woman handed her the money. Alice dropped it in the black hat on the brick ground by the singing girl's feet. The singing girl kept playing her music but stopped singing for a moment to talk to them.

"Thanks, Alice, thanks, Carole, see you soon!"

As Alice walked with the woman among the medium children, the music became quieter behind them. Alice didn't really want to leave, but the woman was going, and Alice knew she should stay with her. The woman was cheerful and kind and always knew what to do, which Alice appreciated because she often didn't.

After walking for some time, Alice spotted the red clown car and the big nail polish car parked in the driveway.

"They're both here," said the woman, seeing the same cars.

Alice felt excited and hurried into the house. The mother was in the hallway.

"My meeting ended quicker than I thought it would so I came back. Thanks for filling in," said the mother.

"No problem. I stripped her bed but didn't have a chance to remake it. Everything's still in the dryer," said the woman.

"Okay, thanks, I'll get it."

"She had another good day."

"No wandering?"

"Nope. She's my trusty shadow now. My partner in crime. Right, Alice?"

The woman smiled, nodding enthusiastically. Alice smiled and nodded back. She had no idea what she was agreeing to, but it was probably fine with her if the woman thought so.

The woman began collecting books and bags by the front door.

"Is John coming up tomorrow?" asked the woman.

A baby they couldn't see started crying, and the mother disappeared into another room.

"No, but we've got it covered," said the mother's voice.

The mother came back carrying a baby dressed in blue, kissing him repeatedly on the neck. The baby still cried, but his heart really wasn't in it anymore. The mother's fast kisses were working. The mother plugged a sucking thing into the baby's mouth.

"You're okay, little goose. Thanks, Carole, so much. You're a godsend. Have a great weekend, see you Monday."

"See you Monday. Bye, Lydia!" the woman yelled.

"Bye, thanks, Carole!" a voice yelled from somewhere in the house.

The baby's big, round eyes met Alice's, and he smiled in recognition behind his sucking thing. Alice smiled back, and the baby responded with a wide-mouthed laugh. The sucking thing fell to the floor. The mother squatted down and picked it up.

"Mom, you want to hold him for me?"

The mother passed the baby to Alice, and he slid comfortably into her arms and on her hip. He began pawing at her face with one of his wet hands. He liked doing this, and Alice liked letting him. He grabbed her bottom lip. She pretended to bite it and eat it while making wild animal noises.

He laughed and moved on to her nose. She sniffed and sniffed and pretended to sneeze. He moved up to her eyes. She squinted so she wouldn't get poked and blinked to try to tickle his hand with her eyelashes. He moved his hand up her forehead to her hair, tightened his little fist, and pulled. She gently unclenched his hand and replaced her hair with her index finger. He found her necklace.

"See the pretty butterfly?"

"Don't let him put that in his mouth!" called the mother, who was in another room but within eyeshot.

Alice wasn't about to let the baby mouth her necklace, and she felt wrongly accused. She walked into the room where the mother was. It was crowded with all kinds of birthday party–colored baby-seat things that beeped and buzzed and talked when the babies banged on them. Alice had forgotten that this was the room with all the loud seats. She wanted to leave before the mother suggested she put the baby in one of them. But the actress was in here, too, and Alice wanted to be in their company.

"Is Dad coming this weekend?" asked the actress.

"No, he can't, he said next week. Can I leave them with you and Mom for a little while? I need to go to the store. Allison should sleep another hour."

"Sure."

"I'll be quick. Need anything?" the mother asked as she walked out of the room.

"More ice cream, something chocolate!" yelled the actress.

Alice found a soft toy with no noisy buttons and sat down while the baby explored it in her lap. She smelled the top of his almost-bald head and watched the actress read. The actress looked up at her.

"Hey, Mom, will you listen to me do this monologue I'm working on for class and tell me what you think it's about? Not the story, it's kind of long. You don't have to remember the words, just tell me what you think it's about emotionally. When I'm done, tell me how I made you feel, okay?"

Alice nodded, and the actress began. Alice watched and listened and focused beyond the words the actress spoke. She saw her eyes become desperate, searching, pleading for truth. She saw them land softly and gratefully on it. Her voice felt at first tentative and scared. Slowly, and without getting louder, it grew more confident and then joyful, playing sometimes like a song. Her eyebrows and shoulders and hands softened and opened, asking for acceptance and offering forgiveness. Her voice and body created an energy that filled Alice and moved her to tears. She squeezed the beautiful baby in her lap and kissed his sweet-smelling head.

The actress stopped and came back into herself. She looked at Alice and waited.

"Okay, what do you feel?"

"I feel love. It's about love."

The actress squealed, rushed over to Alice, kissed her on the cheek, and smiled, every crease of her face delighted.

"Did I get it right?" asked Alice.

"You did, Mom. You got it exactly right."

POSTSCRIPT

The clinical trial drug Amylix, described in this book, is fictional. It is, however, similar to real compounds in clinical development that aim to selectively lower levels of amyloid-beta 42. Unlike the currently available drugs, which can only delay the disease's ultimate progression, it is hoped that these drugs will stop the progression of Alzheimer's. All other drugs mentioned are real, and the depiction of their use and efficacy in the treatment of Alzheimer's disease is accurate as of the writing of this story.

For more information about Alzheimer's disease and clinical trials, go to http://www.alz.org/alzheimers_disease_clinical_studies.asp.

Readers Club Guide for

Still Alice

by Lisa Genova

Discussion Questions

1. When Alice becomes disoriented in Harvard Square, a place she's visited daily for twenty-five years, why doesn't she tell John? Is she too afraid to face a possible illness, worried about his possible reaction, or some other reason?

2. After Alice first learns she has Alzheimer's disease, "The sound of her name penetrated her every cell and seemed to scatter her molecules beyond the boundaries of her own skin. She watched herself from the far corner of the room" (p. 71). What do you think of Alice's reaction to the diagnosis? Why does she disassociate herself to the extent that she feels she's having an out-of-body experience?

3. Do you find irony in the fact that Alice, a Harvard professor and researcher, suffers from a disease that causes her brain to atrophy? Why do you think the author, Lisa Genova, chose this profession? How does her past academic success affect Alice's ability, and that of her family, to cope with Alzheimer's?

4. "He refused to watch her take her medications. He could be midsentence, midconversation, but if she got out her plastic days-of-the-week pill dispenser, he left the room" (p. 90). Is John's reaction understandable? What might be the significance of his frequently fiddling with his wedding ring when Alice's health is discussed?

5. When Alice's three children, Anna, Tom, and Lydia, find out they can be tested for the genetic mutation that causes Alzheimer's, only Lydia decides she doesn't want to know. Why does she decline? Would you want to know if you had the gene?

6. Why is her mother's butterfly necklace so important to Alice? Is it only because she misses her mother? Does Alice feel a connection to butterflies beyond the necklace?

7. Alice decides she wants to spend her remaining time with her family and her books. Considering her devotion and passion for her work, why doesn't her research make the list of priorities? Does Alice most identify herself as a mother, wife, or scholar?

8. Were you surprised at Alice's plan to overdose on sleeping pills once her disease progressed to an advanced stage? Is this decision in character? Why does she make this difficult choice? If they found out, would her family approve?

9. As the symptoms worsen, Alice begins to feel as if she's living in one of Lydia's plays: "(Interior of Doctor's Office. The neurologist left the room. The husband spun his ring. The woman hoped for a cure.)" (p. 142). Is this thought process a sign of the disease, or does pretending it's not happening to her make it easier for Alice to deal with reality?

10. Do Alice's relationships with her children differ? Why does she read Lydia's diary? And does Lydia decide to attend college only to honor her mother?

11. Alice's mother and sister died when she was only a freshman in college, and yet Alice has to keep reminding herself they're not

about to walk through the door. As the symptoms worsen, why does Alice think more about her mother and sister? Is it because her older memories are more accessible, she's thinking of happier times, or she's worried about her own mortality?

12. Alice and the members of her support group, Mary, Cathy, and Dan, all discuss how their reputations suffered prior to their diagnoses because people thought they were being difficult or possibly had substance abuse problems. Is preserving their legacies one of the biggest obstacles to people suffering from Alzheimer's disease? What examples are there of people still respecting Alice's wishes, and at what times is she ignored?

13. "One last sabbatical year together. She wouldn't trade that in for anything. Apparently, he would" (p. 226). Why does John decide to keep working? Is it fair for him to seek the job in New York considering Alice probably won't know her whereabouts by the time they move? Is he correct when he tells the children she would not want him to sacrifice his work?

14. Why does Lisa Genova choose to end the novel with John reading that Amylix, the medicine that Alice was taking, failed to stabilize Alzheimer's patients? Why does this news cause John to cry?

15. Alice's doctor tells her, ". . . you may not be the most reliable source of what's been going on" (p. 55). Yet, Lisa Genova chose to tell the story from Alice's point of view. As Alice's disease worsens, her perceptions indeed get less reliable. Why would the author choose to stay in Alice's perspective? What do we gain, and what do we lose?

Enhance Your Book Club

1. If you'd like to learn more about Alzheimer's or help those suffering from the disease, please visit www.alzheimers.org.uk or www.alzheimers.org.au

2. The Harvard University setting plays an important role in

Still Alice. You can take a virtual tour of the university at www.hno.harvard.edu/tour/guide.html.

3. In order to help her mother, Lydia makes a documentary of the Howlands' lives. Make one of your own family and then share the videos with the group.

4. To learn more about *Still Alice* or to get in touch with Lisa Genova, visit www.StillAlice.com.

A Conversation with Lisa Genova

What is *Still Alice* about?

Still Alice is about a young woman's descent into dementia through early-onset Alzheimer's disease. Alice is a fifty-year-old psychology professor at Harvard when she starts experiencing moments of forgetting and confusion. But, like most busy, professional people her age would, she at first attributes these signs to normal aging, too much stress, not enough sleep, and so on. But as things get worse, as things do with this disease, she eventually sees a neurologist and learns that she has early-onset Alzheimer's.

As Alice loses her ability to rely on her own thoughts and memories, as she loses her cerebral life at Harvard, where she'd placed all her worth and identity, she is forced to search for answers to questions like "Who am I now?" and "How do I matter?" As the disease worsens and continues to steal pieces of what she'd always thought of as her *self,* we see her discover that she is more than what she can remember.

What inspired you to write *Still Alice*?

There were a few things, but the main one was my grandmother had Alzheimer's in her eighties. Looking back, I'm sure she'd had it for years before our family finally opened our eyes to it. There's a level of forgetting that's considered normal for aging grandparents, so you let a lot go by. By the time we were caring for her, she was pretty far along into the disease. And it hit us hard. She'd always been an intelligent, independent, vibrant, and active woman. And we watched this disease systematically disassemble her. She didn't know her kids' names, that she'd even had them (she had nine), where she lived, to go to the bathroom when she needed to, she didn't recognize her own face in the mirror. I used to watch her fuss over these plastic baby dolls as if they were real babies. It was heartbreaking. And yet, I also found it oddly fascinating. I was in graduate school at the time, getting my Ph.D. in neuroscience at Harvard. And so the neuroscientist in me wondered what was going on in her brain. We could see the results of the destruction on the outside. I wondered about the chains of events that were causing the destruction on the inside. And I wondered what it must be like when those parts of the brain that are responsible for your own awareness and identity are no longer accessible. I kept wondering: What is having Alzheimer's disease like from the point of view of the person with Alzheimer's? My grandmother was too far along to communicate an answer to this question, but someone with early-onset, in the early stages, would be able to. This was the seed for *Still Alice*.

Did your professional background help in the writing of *Still Alice*?

Yes, it did. I think the most important way it helped was, over and over again, it gave me access to the right people to talk to. The Ph.D. in neuroscience from Harvard was like a golden, all-access pass. From the clinical side—the chief of neurology at Brigham and Women's Hospital in Boston, neuropsychological testing at Mass General, genetic counselors, caregiver support group leaders, and the world's thought leaders in Alzheimer's research, to the patient side—people living with disease and their caregivers, my professional background and credentials gave people the assurance they needed to feel comfortable letting me in and revealing what they know.

And, in my conversations with physicians and scientists, having an understanding of the molecular biology of this disease certainly gave me the knowledge and the vocabulary to ask the right kinds of questions and the ability to understand the implications of their answers.

How did you get involved with the National Alzheimer's Association?

Before *Still Alice* was even published, it seemed to me that I'd created a story that, although fictional, was in fact a truthful and respectful depiction of life with Alzheimer's. And it was unique in that it presented this depiction from the point of view of the person with Alzheimer's, rather than the caregiver. The lion's share of information written about Alzheimer's is from the point of view of the caregiver.

So I thought the Alzheimer's Association might be interested in the book in some way, perhaps endorsing it or providing a link to it from their website. I contacted their marketing department and gave them the link to the book's website, which I'd also created before the book was published. They responded by saying that they don't normally consider "partnering" with books, but they asked for a copy of the manuscript. Soon after that, their marketing rep contacted me, saying they loved the book. They wanted to give it their stamp of approval and asked if I would write the blog for the nationwide Voice Open Move campaign they were launching at the end of that month.

That really forced me to make a decision about the book. *Still Alice* wasn't published yet. It could take years for it to find a publishing house and become available to readers. Realizing that I'd created something that the Alzheimer's Association thought was valuable, that could help educate and reassure the millions of people trying to navigate a world with Alzheimer's, I felt an urgent responsibility to get the book out immediately. So I said yes to the blog and yes to the affiliation. I then self-published *Still Alice.* It was an opportunity I couldn't pass up.

How did you decide what information was crucial to include in *Still Alice*?

I knew I'd never be able to capture *everyone's* experience with Alzheimer's. But I knew I could capture the essence of it. And I checked in regularly with people who have early-onset Alzheimer's to make sure it all rang true. They were my litmus test. The earliest symptoms were important to portray, to show how they are deflected and denied. I felt a duty to show what the diagnosis process should look like. For so many people with early-onset, the road to a diagnosis of Alzheimer's is long and incredibly arduous, the symptoms often mistaken for other potential culprits, like depression, for years. This is probably the only place in the book I deviated from representing the truth as it plays out for most people. I gave Alice a straight-and-narrow shot to diagnosis, both in the interest of providing an example of what should happen and of creating a story that wasn't five hundred pages long. I also felt it was important for Alice to consider suicide. I thought long and hard about the decision to include this. As with the death penalty or abortion, people have very strong opinions about the right to end your own life when faced with a terminal illness, and I didn't want to alienate any readers. But I found that everyone I knew diagnosed with Alzheimer's under the age of sixty-five had considered suicide. That's extraordinary. The average fifty-year-old doesn't think about killing himself, but every fifty-year-old with Alzheimer's does. This is where this disease forces you to go. So I felt Alice had to go there as well.

Are you working on any current writing projects?

I've begun writing my next novel, *Left Neglected.* This is a story about a woman in her midthirties who is like so many women I know today—multitasking all day long, trying to be everything to everyone at work and at home, spread extremely thin. One typical morning, late for work, racing in her car after dropping her kids off at school and day care, she tries to phone in to a meeting she should already be at when she takes her eyes off the road for one second too long. And in that blink of an eye, all the rapidly moving parts of her overscheduled life come to a screeching halt. She suffers a traumatic head injury. Her memory and intellect are intact. She can still talk and count. But she has lost all interest in and the ability to perceive information coming from the left side of space.

The left side of the world is gone. She has Unilateral Neglect.

She finds herself living in a bizarre hemi-existence, where she eats food only on the right side of her plate, reads only the right half of a page, and can easily forget that her left arm and hand even belong to her. Through rehabilitation, she struggles not only to recover the very idea of left, but also to recover her life, the one she had always meant to live.

While working with the Dementia Advocacy and Support Network, you spoke daily with people suffering from Alzheimer's. What was that experience like for you? What were the most common struggles that these people faced?

It's been an amazing experience. These people aren't there to be superficial or beat around the bush. They don't have the time to waste. We support each other and talk about the stuff that matters, so our conversations are often filled with vulnerability and bravery, love and humor, frustration and excitement. And when you share yourself like that, it leads to deep and intimate friendship. I truly love and admire the friends I've made through this group. Many I still know only through email. I've come to meet some in person at Alzheimer's conferences, and it's a great experience. We're colleagues in our Advocacy pursuits.

People with Alzheimer's stand on ground that is constantly shifting beneath their feet. Familiar symptoms get worse (more frequent or intensified) or new symptoms emerge, so just when people think they've adapted to it all, made all the adjustments and accommodations needed, there's more work to do. This can be frustrating, exhausting, demoralizing. I see all that.

I think the most common struggle I see people face, though, is the alienation and loneliness. Because this disease takes people out of their formerly fast-paced, personally fulfilling careers; because everyone else stays busy in their busy lives and people with this disease have to slow down; and because of the enormous stigma placed on having Alzheimer's, people with early-stage Alzheimer's find themselves extremely alone. That's why these online groups are so invaluable. They bring these people from all parts of the country together to share their common experience and break the isolation.

Do you believe we need to be more educated on Alzheimer's?

I do, especially about early-onset and the early stages of Alzheimer's. There are over a half million people in the United States alone under the age of sixty-five diagnosed with dementia, and they're not included in what gets talked about when people talk about Alzheimer's. The general public knows what the eighty-five-year-old grandparent in end stages of the disease looks and sounds like, but they have little idea what the fifty-year-old parent with Alzheimer's looks and sounds like. It's high time this group had a face and a voice.

A greater awareness of the early symptoms and experiences matters because people need to recognize the symptoms so they can get diagnosed and on proper medication sooner. It matters because people with early-onset need resources (like access to support groups) that are now primarily given to caregivers. It matters because drug companies need to start to recognize this as a sizable group worthy of inclusion in their clinical trials. Right now, many people with early-onset Alzheimer's cannot enroll in clinical trials because they are too young. It matters because families deserve to plan properly for the future, both financially and emotionally. It matters because awareness will reduce the stigma placed on people still living their lives with this disease.

Which writers inspire you?

Oliver Sacks is my biggest inspiration. In fact, *The Man Who Mistook His Wife for a Hat* was really the spark that ignited my interest in neuroscience to begin with. There's this quote from him:

> *"In examining disease, we gain wisdom about anatomy and physiology and biology. In examining the person with disease, we gain wisdom about life."*

That's everything right there. That's what I hope to do with my writing, both fiction and nonfiction.

What are you currently reading?

Oddly enough, I'm reading *A New Earth* by Eckhart Tolle, but not because Oprah told me to. It was recommended to me last August by a friend of mine with Alzheimer's. I was interviewing him for my next book, and he was excitedly telling me about all the incredible new discoveries he'd made, from meditation to diet and exercise to self-awareness. He told me I absolutely had to read *A New Earth* and that it would change my life. He was right.

I'm also reading *The Lace Reader* by Brunonia Barry. Amazing!

Do you have any advice for aspiring writers?

I know so many aspiring writers who are sitting in a holding pattern, with a work completed, waiting to find a literary agent. They're stuck, unable to give themselves permission to write the next book because they're waiting to find out if their work is "good enough," waiting to find out if they're a "real writer." This state of waiting, of not writing and self-doubt, is the worst state any writer can be in. My advice is this: If you don't find a literary agent falling into your lap quickly enough, if you feel like your work is done and is ready to be shared with the world, self-publish. Give your work to the world. Let it go. And keep writing. Freedom! I was recently in my car listening to Diablo Cody, who wrote the screenplay for *Juno,* on NPR and when asked what advice she had for aspiring screenwriters, she said, "Self-publish." I yelled alone in my car, "Woohoo! See?! Diablo Cody agrees with me, and she's just been nominated for an Academy Award!"

Explain your writing schedule.

I have a newborn baby boy, so these days it's catch as you can. But for *Still Alice,* I wrote in Starbucks every day while my then six-year-old daughter was in school. I found writing from home too difficult. There were too many distractions—phone calls to return, food to eat in the fridge, laundry to do, bills to pay. You know you're procrastinating when you're paying bills instead of writing the next scene! At Starbucks, there were no excuses. Nothing else to do but write. You can't even daydream there for long without looking crazy. So you just put your head down and do it. And I found I always had to stop short to go pick up my daughter from school. I'd be right in the middle of a great scene, right in the zone, and it would be time to get my daughter. And that would be it for the day. I wouldn't get back to it until the next morning. I stuck to that. My time to write was my time to write, and my time with my daughter belonged to us. I think having a limited number of hours each day to write kept me hungry to get back to it. I never dreaded it or experienced writer's block. Every day, I couldn't wait to get back to Starbucks, drink chai tea lattes, and write.

What advancements do you see being made in the fight against Alzheimer's?

Awareness leading to earlier diagnosis is important. Although the current drugs available for treating Alzheimer's do not change the ultimate course of this disease, they can stave off its progression for a significant amount of time, allowing the person with Alzheimer's to live on a sort of plateau, to enjoy the capabilities they still have for a longer time. And the sooner someone is diagnosed and put on medication that keeps them on that plateau, the more likely they'll be able to reap the benefits of a better treatment when one becomes available.

The other advancement I see is that the next generation of drugs for Alzheimer's will be disease altering—they will stop the progression of the disease. It used to be the standard thought that amyloid plaques and/or neurofibrillary tangles got deposited in the brain, and these things "gunked" up the neurons and caused them to die. And this neuronal death caused Alzheimer's.

Here's the new thinking.

The cognitive deficits—the symptoms of dementia—occur *before* the plaques form, before the neurons die. In the brain of someone with Alzheimer's, there is too much of a soluble protein called amyloid-beta 42. Either too much is made or not enough is cleared away. When too much is present, these individual little peptides stick together and form small oligomers. These gluey oligomers of amyloid-beta 42 lodge in synapses—the spaces between neurons—and interfere with synaptic transmission, the ability of neuron number one to "talk" to neuron number two. And when this happens, new information isn't learned. Or old information can't be accessed. Synaptic plasticity suffers. Over time, because this synapse isn't working properly and because of inflammation and other problems, that nerve axon terminal will retract. Eventually, unable to function, the neuron will die, leaving behind empty space (the atrophy seen on an MRI) and possibly a heap of amyloid-beta 42 in an amyloid plaque.

So it all starts as an attack on the synapses. The degree of dementia correlates only with synapse dysfunction, not with neuronal loss, not with number of plaques, not with atrophy on an MRI.

The cure for dementia, then, the kind of treatments that will be disease altering, will

- impede production of amyloid-beta 42,
- increase clearance of already produced amyloid-beta 42,
- prevent amyloid-beta 42 from sticking to itself so it can't form oligomers, or
- rip these already formed oligomers apart.

The beauty and the hope in all of these treatments is that people suffering from symptoms of dementia can be treated *before* they've experienced any neuron death. If the synapses are fixed, neurotransmission can work again. Function can be restored!

In choosing to tell a story about a woman with Alzheimer's disease, why did you make Alice a fifty-year-old Harvard professor rather than an eighty-year-old retired grandmother?

Well, one is that the fifty-year-old will notice and be alarmed by this disease in its earliest moments. Because we as a culture expect eighty-five-year-olds to be forgetful, because retired grandparents are no longer accountable to corporate bosses, because they don't have to produce a certain number and quality of widgets each day, because they might be widowed and living alone with no one to regularly witness the full extent of what is happening, because it is far easier to deny what is happening well after we suspect it or even trip over it, we don't usually see Alzheimer's in its beginning. In someone who is fifty, who is at the peak of her career, whose status in life and identity depends on a highly functioning brain, you'll see the beginning. And when the rug is pulled out, it's a long and terrifying fall.

There is a line in the book where Alice's doctor tells her, ". . . you may not be the most reliable source of what's been going on." Yet you chose to tell the story from Alice's point of view. Doesn't that get difficult to do as Alice's disease worsens and her perceptions indeed get less reliable?

It sure does, but I thought it was the most powerful choice. In telling the story through Alice's lens, I sit the reader right up against her Alzheimer's. It should feel uncomfortably close at times. You should feel her confusions and frustrations and terror right along with her. And yes, this choice forces us to lose what's going on inside the thoughts of her husband and the other characters, but we get an insider's perspective into the mind of someone slipping further and further into Alzheimer's. Most people without Alzheimer's never get to sit in that seat.

What is your favorite scene in the book?

There are probably two. One is a small scene with Alice and her three children. The kids are all arguing over whether their mother should be trying to remember something or not. Alice asks what time they'll be going to a play the next day. Her son tells her not to worry about it, she doesn't need to try to remember something she doesn't have to because they're not going to go without her. Her oldest daughter thinks she should be exercising her memory whenever possible, the sort of "use it or lose it" philosophy. The youngest thinks they should just let their mom know the information, and she can do with it what she wants. This is pretty common in families where someone has Alzheimer's. There's disagreement and people dig in their heels and take things personally. It's rife with conflict. In this scene, they argue and hurt one another's feelings and never agree, all in front of Alice. People talk about people with Alzheimer's all the time right in front of them, as if they're not there.

The other is the first paragraph. I just love everything about it. It still gives me the chills, and I've probably read it a hundred times.

What has the response been to *Still Alice* from the Alzheimer's community? How about from the non-Alzheimer's community, from people who have no connection to this disease?

Overwhelmingly positive. I can't tell you how much this means to me. For someone with Alzheimer's, or a caregiver of a loved one with this, to tell me that I got it right, that it's uncanny how true it all was, that they saw themselves all over the book, well, that's the highest compliment I can get. That I told the truth about this disease. This really became an important goal of mine while I was doing the research for the book and I came to know more and more people living with Alzheimer's. And it became a careful line to walk, to not overdramatize or romanticize this disease, yet not minimize it either.

And the National Alzheimer's Association has endorsed it. Of all the books out there on the topic of Alzheimer's, mine is the only one, to my knowledge, to have this stamp from them.

There are people who've read the book who have no personal connection to Alzheimer's and who've given me feedback. It's a moving story, and I think it works because it's about so much more than Alzheimer's. It doesn't lecture or preach or get too clinical. It's about identity and living a life that matters and about what a crisis does to relationships. And it's been incredibly rewarding to know that the book has given these readers a new awareness and sensitivity to the realities of living with Alzheimer's.

A Note on the Author

Lisa Genova, a first-time novelist, holds a Ph.D. in neuroscience from Harvard University and is an online columnist for the National Alzheimer's Association. She lives with her family in Massachusetts.